THE CARE AND FEEDING OF AN ALPHA *Male*

Titles by Jessica Clare

THE GIRL'S GUIDE TO (MAN)HUNTING

THE CARE AND FEEDING OF AN ALPHA MALE

eSpecial

THE BILLIONAIRE OF BLUEBONNET

THE CARE AND FEEDING OF AN ALPHA *Male*

JESSICA CLARE

HEAT
New York

THE BERKLEY PUBLISHING GROUP
Published by the Penguin Group
Penguin Group (USA) Inc.
375 Hudson Street, New York, New York 10014, USA

Penguin Group (Canada), 90 Eglinton Avenue East, Suite 700, Toronto, Ontario M4P 2Y3, Canada (a division of Pearson Penguin Canada Inc.) • Penguin Books Ltd., 80 Strand, London WC2R 0RL, England • Penguin Group Ireland, 25 St. Stephen's Green, Dublin 2, Ireland (a division of Penguin Books Ltd.) • Penguin Group (Australia), 250 Camberwell Road, Camberwell, Victoria 3124, Australia (a division of Pearson Australia Group Pty. Ltd.) • Penguin Books India Pvt. Ltd., 11 Community Centre, Panchsheel Park, New Delhi—110 017, India • Penguin Group (NZ), 67 Apollo Drive, Rosedale, Auckland 0632, New Zealand (a division of Pearson New Zealand Ltd.) • Penguin Books (South Africa) (Pty.) Ltd., 24 Sturdee Avenue, Rosebank, Johannesburg 2196, South Africa

Penguin Books Ltd., Registered Offices: 80 Strand, London WC2R 0RL, England

This book is an original publication of The Berkley Publishing Group.

Cover art by Collage Photographer / Veer.
Cover design by Lesley Worrell.
Text design by Tiffany Estreicher.

PUBLISHING HISTORY
Heat trade paperback edition / October 2012

Library of Congress Cataloging-in-Publication Data

Clare, Jessica.
The care and feeding of an alpha male / Jessica Clare.—Heat trade paperback ed.
p. cm.
ISBN 978-0-425-25316-8 (pbk.)
I. Title.
PS3603.L353C37 2012
813'.6—dc23
2012007753

PRINTED IN THE UNITED STATES OF AMERICA

10 9 8 7 6 5 4 3 2 1

For my parents, who pass out bookmarks at bingo, wear T-shirts of my book covers, and tell everyone quite proudly that their daughter is a romance novelist. I love you guys.

ONE

So when are you going to marry that nice young man of yours?"

The elderly woman smiled, the sequins on her green evening gown blinding as she bent over and signed her name to the silent auction paperwork that Beth Ann held out to her. "I think you've kept him waiting long enough, young lady."

"Oh, I think he'll have to wait a bit longer," Beth Ann said lamely. She wished the woman would just go away. God, this party was a mistake. Beth Ann should have guessed that everyone here would still consider her and Allan as a couple. It didn't matter that they'd been history for the last year now. No one at this party was more than a casual acquaintance, or a business partner of a family member, and they wouldn't know that Beth Ann and Allan had broken up again, this time for good. And a cocktail party? Not the place to discuss the status (or lack of one) of her previous relationship.

Beth Ann shoved the envelope into Mrs. Douglas's hand. "Thank you for your donation. The Bluebonnet Historical Society appreciates your participation."

Mrs. Douglas took the envelope she'd won and reached out and patted her on the hand. "I'm just saying, my dear, that you shouldn't keep a man like that dangling too long, or you might lose him."

That's my hope, Beth Ann thought to herself. She exchanged a few more pleasantries with the elderly woman, and then made a hasty getaway to the refreshment table, trying to keep the smile pinned to her face despite her simmering thoughts.

She was starting to hate parties like this. Or rather, she'd hated them ever since she'd dumped Allan once and for all. He was a nice guy. Great with kids. Ambitious. Her high school sweetheart. She knew him better than anyone else.

And he couldn't keep his dick in his pants.

The first time he'd confessed to cheating on her, she'd blamed herself. Their sex life had gotten cold, so it must have been her fault that he had strayed. She'd gone to counseling to work through her anger and at home, tried to be more adventuresome in bed. She'd gone out of her way to make the relationship work. Forgave him when he groveled. Things had gone back to normal, and she'd prided herself on loving her relationship—and her man—enough to work on it. The second time he'd cheated, she was baffled. And hurt. Hadn't they worked through this? She'd broken up with him, but Allan had been devastated at losing her. He'd worked so hard to get back into her good graces, prove that he loved and cared for her, that she thought that this time, it'd be different. This time, he'd learned his lesson. And so she'd taken him back again.

The third and fourth times he'd cheated on her, well, she didn't know what the hell she'd been thinking.

Number five had been the last straw. For the last year, she'd told Allan that she'd been volunteering at the historical society, when in truth, she'd been going to beauty school. She thought he would be upset that she was spending so much time out of the house, but he'd been thrilled by her commitment to the city. Of course, she found out why later. The same day she became licensed, she'd found out that he'd been cheating with his secretary. In their house. In their bed. The sex in their relationship had fallen off again, so she should have guessed. And that time, when she'd caught him cheating, he'd skipped straight from the apologies right to buying her gifts. As if her hurt feelings were just irritating emotions that he couldn't be bothered with. She realized that he might love her, but he didn't respect her. Or, it seemed, want her. Which was fine with Beth Ann. She'd long ceased to be interested in their physical relationship, and the rest of it was a joke, too.

And she'd finally had enough.

She'd broken it off with Allan on New Year's. For good. She was her own person now, not "Allan's sweet little fiancée." Or worse, Allan's "long suffering" woman. She'd finally, finally had enough and had dumped him. And while being single for the first time in nine years was lonely and odd . . . she liked it. And she liked who she was now.

She was no longer "sweet, suffering in silence for love of

Allan" Beth Ann. She was her own person. Beth Ann, salon owner and businesswoman. And she liked that new Beth Ann.

Now if she could just get everyone else on the same page as her. Mrs. Douglas's ignorance was forgivable—she only saw the elderly woman at fund-raisers, and those only happened a few times a year. But that didn't excuse the old friends, the bridge club buddies, the society friends, the business acquaintances, and all the others who'd come up to her over the course of the evening with the same types of comments.

So where's your other half?

When are you and Allan going to kiss and make up?

I don't see Allan with you.

Hey, can you give Allan a message for me?

She'd gritted her teeth and endured politely, deflecting questions. No, Allan wasn't with her. They weren't together anymore. No, *really*. No, they weren't getting back together. No, she hadn't moved on to someone else. No, that didn't mean she was holding a torch for Allan.

People would smile and give her faintly puzzled looks, as if they couldn't understand why a perfectly nice woman like herself wouldn't marry her high school sweetheart after being engaged for so long.

That part was her fault. Allan's business ran on customers and referrals. Gossip would destroy him, and the truth of their relationship? Would definitely be a career destroyer for him—as well as terribly embarrassing for her. She still loved Allan even if she didn't want to be with him. And so she'd kept her mouth shut about the affairs. He'd been discreet enough—all his mistresses had been out of town, and he'd been careful to cover his tracks.

No one in Bluebonnet suspected the truth as to why she'd gone back and forth so many times with Allan before finally breaking it off with him. If people asked why they'd gone their separate ways, she simply told them the relationship had run its course. Which, of course, made everyone think that she was crazy. Allan Sunquist was a wonderful guy—nice, funny, wealthy, and devoted to her. Or so they all thought. Allan didn't help things, either. He seemed to think that it was just a matter of time before Beth Ann took him back, and that he simply had to say the right thing or give her enough sad, puppy-dog eyes to melt her heart and she'd forgive him all the hurt.

It was good that he wasn't here tonight. She'd been able to concentrate on the fund-raiser.

A hand grabbed her arm. "There you are. Can I see you for a minute?"

Her mother. Surprised, Beth Ann allowed Jeanette Williamson to drag her toward the ladies' room. "What's going on, Mom?"

" 'Jeanette' out in public, dear," her mother said with a frown. Her free hand held an empty champagne glass and she handed it to a passing waiter, then took a fresh one off of his tray. "We need to talk, Beth Ann. I need a favor."

Beth Ann stifled a groan. A favor? Now? "We're kind of busy, *Jeanette*," she said, stressing her mother's name. "There's still two rounds of the silent auction to be awarded—"

Her mother sipped from her champagne glass and waved her hand. "I can handle that. I need you to do something else. Now go into the bathroom. I don't want anyone to hear us."

Rolling her eyes, Beth Ann obeyed. The party—a fund-raiser for several local historical societies—was one of her family's favorite events. And while she wasn't big on history, she recognized a lot of the familiar faces from society parties. Even though the Williamsons lived in quiet Bluebonnet, her father had friends in high places, and as a result, they went to a lot of benefits and fund-raisers. Beth Ann volunteered at her fair share because it was expected of her as Allan's fiancée and her father's daughter. This party was no exception, and the beautiful room was filled elbow to elbow with people in cocktail dresses, wineglasses in hand as they strolled past the silent auction placards she'd carefully placed on the tables earlier that day.

Luckily, the women's restroom was empty. She moved into it and locked the door behind them, then did a quick scan under the stalls. No one. Good. She turned around and observed her mother swigging her champagne through the massive gilt mirror. "What is it?"

Jeanette waved, trying to swallow her drink, and Beth Ann leaned against the marble countertop of the sink while she waited. If she was with Miranda at a party, she'd have sat up on the countertop and swung her legs, but her mother wouldn't have approved of that. So she settled for checking her updo for out-of-place strands of hair and examining her figure in her short, swingy cocktail dress. It was glittery and had spaghetti straps and revealed a lot of skin. Allan would have hated it.

Beth Ann had picked it for that exact reason.

"Your sister," Jeanette said, and tilted her glass to get the last sip of champagne.

Beth Ann frowned. "What's Lucy done this time?"

"I knew that when she begged to stay home it was a mistake. I just knew it." Jeanette put the champagne glass down on the counter and threw her hands up in the air. "I called home and she's not there. She's off with those DwarfQuester people—"

"QuestMasters," Beth Ann corrected.

"All I know is that they dress up in costumes and pretend to be elves and dragons. And your sister is hanging out with them again."

"She's seventeen, Mom. It's a harmless group." Maybe a little on the geeky side, but pretty benign as far as friends went. "Besides, how do you know Lucy is with them? I thought she had a headache?"

"She *said* she had a headache," her mother accused. "But she told me a week ago that they were having a big campout and all of the DwarfQuesters in the area—"

"QuestMasters."

"That's what I said. She said they were all going to a big campout where they could all dress up and frolic all weekend with the fairies."

Er, okay. That sounded a little strange. "So it's like a big slumber party?"

"Yes, and I forbid her to go. There will be boys there. I don't want her getting into a compromising situation. The last thing your father needs for his reelection next year is an unwed teenage daughter with a baby on her hip. You saw what it did to Sarah Palin."

Beth Ann rolled her eyes. "Mom, she's hanging out with friends. She's not getting pregnant."

"I don't want her with them. You saw her new boyfriend, didn't you?"

She'd seen him. He was short, scrawny, and had a goatee

that was so long that he'd braided it and tied it back with a red rubber band. "I think so."

Her mother leaned in. "She calls him 'Colossus.' Now what do you think that is for?"

Oh gawd. She did not want to have this conversation with her mother, who was currently tipsy in a fund-raiser bathroom. "I'm sure she's fine—"

"Not if she is with Colossus. She asked me last week if I could get her birth control." Her brows went up. "What do you think of that?"

Beth Ann winced. "At least she's asking?"

Jeanette gave her a scathing look.

"Okay, okay." She threw her hands up. "What do you want me to do?"

"I want you to find that campground and bring your sister home."

"But I can't leave right now. The auction isn't done and—"

Someone knocked at the bathroom door.

Jeanette dusted off her clothing with precise fingers and examined her conservative dress in the mirror. "Your father doesn't know anything about this, of course. He's meeting with Senator Brown to discuss how he launched himself." She gave Beth Ann a pointed look. "You know that's his dream."

Beth Ann wisely did not point out that her father would need to do a bit more than be mayor for a town with a population of two thousand people before he would have a senatorial seat handed to him. "Fine."

They slipped out of the bathroom with a smile and a nod at the woman waiting.

"You're going to go now?" her mother insisted, smiling cheerfully at one of her friends nearby.

"Do I have any choice? It's either that or let Lucy get impregnated by the Colossus, right?" Her mother gave her a scathing look, warning her to keep her tone down. "Just let me grab my purse—"

Jeanette grabbed Beth Ann's arm and steered her toward the kitchen. "I'll get your purse. I suggest you go out that way."

Puzzled, Beth Ann looked at the kitchen, and then back at her mother. "Why?"

"Because I just saw Allan enter."

Ugh. This evening had just gone from bad to worse. She leaned in and gave her mother a quick peck on the cheek. "I'm heading out as we speak."

Her mother grabbed another champagne glass from a waiter. "It's probably best that you go anyhow. I can't drive—I've been drinking."

Like a fish, Beth Ann thought to herself. She headed for the coordinator and made her excuses—of course they didn't mind if she left early, they just hoped everything was okay. Beth Ann smiled and cited a migraine, even rubbing her temples to add conviction to her lie. How awful was it that her mother was going to send Beth Ann out to hunt down Lucy while she swigged cocktails and mingled with her father? Pretty awful, but not surprising in the slightest.

She was starting to think Lucy had the right idea.

Beth Ann had almost made it to the kitchen door when a hand grabbed one of the spaghetti straps of her dress, halting her in place.

"Bethy-babe," Allan cooed. He was dressed in a sharp tux, his hair a little longer than it should have been, but he was still handsome. He gave her a warm smile that seemed a little too broad to be sincere. "Been looking everywhere for you, babe."

She pried his fingers from her dress strap. "Hey, Allan. I have to go—"

"Don't I get a kiss? I'm wearing your favorite cologne." He leaned in so she could smell him.

Beth Ann side-stepped him carefully. "I'm sure it's lovely, Allan. But I really do have to go—"

He frowned back at her, as if realizing just now that she wasn't thrilled to see him. "You're not staying? We haven't had a chance to talk about the Halloween Festival yet."

"What about it?" Every year, Bluebonnet put on a big Halloween Festival that brought in tourists from several counties over. It was tradition, complete with hay rides, costumes, and everything else you could imagine. It was also still at least six weeks away.

He straightened his tie and proudly informed her, "I signed you up to be on the committee. With me."

Beth Ann gritted her teeth. "You're joking."

"Why would I joke? You love committees!"

"That was before I started running my own business, Allan," she said in exasperation. "Back when I had nothing to do except be social and wait on you. I have a job now, and it takes up a lot of my free time."

He nodded sympathetically, and for a moment, she thought she'd finally gotten through to him and he understood. He touched her shoulder, scowled at her dress, and then said in a gentle voice, "We'll discuss this later."

She should have known better. Allan didn't change. He just thought up more schemes to place them both in the same room again, in the hopes that she'd weaken and fall back into his arms. She flicked his hand off her shoulder. "There is no 'later.' I'm leaving."

"But I just got here. I thought we'd do the rounds together."

So everyone could continue to think they were a couple? Not a chance. She gestured at the kitchen. "Really, *really* have to go. Was nice seeing you, though—"

He grabbed her wrist when she turned. "Bethy-babe, I want you to know something."

She sighed. Turned. Waited.

He leaned in close as if sharing a secret. "I didn't bring a date to this party. Because I knew you would be here."

That irritated her. He clearly thought that her presence still equaled fiancée. "You should have brought a date, Allan. We're *not* together. You *can* do things like that. I could have brought a date, too."

"But you didn't," he said smugly, and hope lit his handsome features. "Is it because you still care for me?"

She sighed and made a concerted effort not to pinch the bridge of her nose in irritation. "I will always love you as a friend, Allan," she said, stressing the word *friend* so he wouldn't get his hopes up. "But you and me are done. There is no 'us.' There is no doing the rounds together, because we aren't together. Okay?"

He gave her a wounded look of pain. "I . . . see."

Great. Now she was the bad guy. Allan had this way of turning everything around to where it seemed like she was the unreasonable one. In the past, she hadn't realized this. When he'd been upset, she'd apologize all over herself, desperate to make him happy. Now, though, she just felt annoyed. He was clearly trying to manipulate her emotions. She hated that. So she pasted a bright smile on her face and patted his cheek. "Gotta go. Was nice seeing you!"

Then, she turned and swiftly headed for the swinging kitchen doors.

"Wait, Bethy-babe! Please. I just want to talk . . ."

She did not turn around.

She got into her car and drove out of the city and pulled onto the highway. Her parents had OnStar in their car but Beth Ann's cute little Volkswagen Beetle didn't have anything close to that. She didn't even have GPS, and she couldn't manage that on her phone while driving. So she did the next best thing—called her friend Miranda.

"Hey, girl. Where are you? It's late." Miranda sounded sleepy, and she could hear the sound of a movie being turned down in the background.

"Sorry. Did I interrupt something?"

"Nah. Dane and I are just watching a movie. Spending a little quality time together before he leaves me for the weekend for a bunch of businessmen." She gave a mock sniff. "Stupid overnight campouts."

She heard Dane mumble something in the background, and then heard Miranda's squeal erupt into a giggle.

Beth Ann resisted the urge to toss the phone on the floor in a mixture of jealousy and annoyance. "I need you to do me a favor, Mir. If you have a sec. I'm driving back from the big fund-raiser in Houston and need you to Google something for me."

Fat raindrops began to splash on her windshield as Miranda typed into the computer on the other side of the phone. "Okay, what am I looking for?"

"QuestMasters. It's some costume group. They're having a big campout this weekend and Lucy ran off to go to it. My mother had a fit."

"Aren't you a little too old to be Lucy's watchdog?" Miranda said with amusement.

"Apparently not," Beth Ann replied dryly. "As long as I live at home, I live to serve." After she'd left Allan, she hadn't been able to afford a place of her own *and* a salon. She'd chosen, and on nights like tonight, well, Jeanette made her regret her choice.

"Think you'll move out soon?"

"Lord, I hope so." She didn't think she'd be able to stand another few months living under her parents' roof. "Any luck with the search?"

She heard Miranda clicking around on the other side of the computer, and then a stifled giggle. "Does it involve guys that dress up like hobbits?"

"That's probably it," Beth Ann said with a sigh. The rain didn't appear to be letting up. Just her luck. "Does it say anything about camping?"

"Ooo, there's a Tournament of Knights this weekend in Arcane Forest."

"Arcane Forest?"

"Apparently it's some privately owned property not far from the Daughtry Ranch."

Masculine murmuring rumbled in the background. Miranda laughed again. "Dane says to tell you that he's run into them before on the ranch property. They get pissy if you don't address them properly when they are in costume." She paused, then chuckled. "He just told me he was berated by a man in a fur loincloth while scouting a trail."

"A fur loincloth?" Man, she hoped his name was not Colossus. She steered toward the next exit. "Never mind about the loincloth, honey. I don't think I want to know. What exit do I need to take?"

Miranda walked her through the directions until Beth Ann had them memorized. "Thanks for your help, Mir."

"Call me back if you meet a handsome, dashing wizard."

"Very funny."

"Do you need help?"

"No, I've got this covered." Surely it wouldn't be too hard to find Lucy. She'd just look for the most normal girl there.

"It's no trouble. Dane says we can send maybe Colt or Grant your way—"

Beth Ann groaned. Miranda frequently mentioned Grant in Beth Ann's presence, and she was starting to wonder if it was because Grant was wealthy, good-looking, and single. It smelled of a hookup. And Colt? Miranda knew better. Colt was a jerk. "Do not even think about sending anyone my way. You are not setting me up with one of Dane's friends."

"It's not a hookup! I promise. But it sounds like you could use a hero—"

"I don't, I promise. Now, I've got to go. Talk to you later." She clicked off the phone just as the rain began to pour down in torrents. She made a left at a colorful wooden sign stuck in the side of the road—almost missed it, actually—and started to go down a dirt road that was quickly turning to mud. Yuck. Not that she had a choice.

The woods were dark and, around these parts, there were no lights to see by. It was made all the more dark and creepy by the fact that she was driving down some deserted road late at night, and she had no clue where she was going.

Definitely time to move back out again, she thought to herself. Ever since she'd been forced to move back in, she'd been pulled between her headstrong mother and equally headstrong younger sister. An apartment next month, she decided. Didn't matter how small it was. As it was, when things at home got a little hairy, she retreated to her salon. She had an air mattress on the floor in the back room, next to where she kept the tanning bed. It served as a getaway well enough, though it was time for something more permanent.

A line of cars appeared in the distance, and her little Volkswagen skidded in the mud as she turned into an equally sludgy dirt parking lot. Stumps lined the edges of the parking lot, and a veritable fleet of vehicles of all makes and shapes were parked haphazardly. She noticed a row of Porta-Potties off to one side, and a small, lit cloth pavilion across from it. Well. This must be the place.

Beth Ann parked her car between two pickups that looked as if they'd seen better days. She searched vainly for an umbrella in the backseat. Finding none, she sighed and tucked her keys in her purse, then got out of the car.

Rain pounded on her head, immediately turning her elegant updo into a flat mess. The splatters hit her bare arms and she looked down at her sequined, strappy heels and winced. They were already starting to stick in the mud of the parking lot. Ugh. She picked her way carefully across the sea of cars, heading toward the tent. She could hear people laughing, and someone was playing a flute of some kind. Her shoe skidded in the mud once, and she nearly fell facefirst.

Lucy was getting an earful when she found her, Beth Ann decided. She approached the tent and two men in bright, colorful baggy pants appeared. One wore a fur hat that was getting soaked in the rain, and the other's head was shaved bald.

They both looked to be much, much older than Lucy or her boyfriend. Surprised, Beth Ann crossed her arms, hugging her already-soaked formal dress to her body. "I'm sorry, is this the big QuestMaster shindig?"

The shaved man made a flourish with his hand and bowed to her. "Good eve, milady."

Okay. "I'm guessing yes? I'm looking for Lucy. Lucy Williamson. She's here tonight."

The man in the fur hat peered at her through the rain and then drank a large gulp from the enormous beer mug in his hand. "Sounds like a mundane name to me."

"Mundane? I'm not sure I follow—"

"Mundane, fair wench," Baldy said with a leer at her wet form, "Is what you be, lass."

A man laughed uproariously inside the tent.

Well, wasn't this fun. "Look. I just want to find Lucy. Can you call her?"

"There be no mundane technology allowed on the Quest grounds for the duration of the Tourney, milady."

"Super. I'll just call her phone myself." She dug through her purse and tugged out her phone.

The furred-hat one immediately put his hand over her own. "Ye'll not be needing that, wench."

All right, now. It was raining, and muddy, and she was starting to get a little irritated at this "wench" business. "That's nice and all, but my sister is grounded, and I need to bring her home before she gets into even more trouble." She jerked her hand away from his with a polite smile and held the phone up. No service.

Fiddlesticks.

She gestured at the path leading into the woods. A rickety wooden gate covered it and she could see a few cook fires and lights in the distance, and heard the sound of laughter. "Is that where all the campers are? I'll just head over and look for her—"

The bald one stepped in front of the gate. "Milady, you must first pay the entry fee if you wish to join the Tourney."

"I don't want to join the Tourney. I'm just going to check for my sister—"

"I'm afraid we canna let ye do that, lass," Fur-head said, now mimicking a bad Scottish accent. "Only those that pay the toll may enter the QuestMaster grounds for the weekend."

These guys were going to drive her insane. "Fine. Whatever. How much is the toll?" She had a few bucks on her.

"Fifty dollars," Baldy said proudly.

"Fifty . . . what? Fifty dollars? You're kidding me."

"Everyone must pay the toll," he repeated stubbornly. "If ye don't wish to pay, we shall have to escort ye from the king's lands, milady."

King's lands, her patoot. "I don't have that much cash on me."

Baldy inclined his head ever so slightly. "We take checks, milady."

"Naturally. Fine. I'll write you a check." She headed into the tent to write it. Even under the tent, the air was muggy and gross. Her hair was dripping into her eyes and she was pretty sure her makeup was running down her face. Lovely. Maybe she could be one of the hideous monsters they were hunting this weekend. Long live the swamp hag.

Beth Ann began to write out the check, and then began to shiver. She glanced up. "I don't suppose you have a flashlight for sale while I'm at it? Or a jacket?"

"Such things are forbidden in QuestMasters," Fur hat said in a stiff voice, as if outraged by the thought.

Okay, she'd go stomping around in the dark to find Lucy. Whatever. She eyed his cloak—it looked a lot warmer than her thin sequined dress that was even now sticking to her body. "Don't suppose I could buy that cloak off of you?"

"Tis not for sale—"

"Fifty dollars," she offered.

He took it off with a flourish. "All yours."

She pulled out a new check, wrote it, and handed it over.

He smiled and handed her a clipboard. "Sign in, milady, with your QuestMaster name."

"Oh, um, I don't have one. How about I come back when I think of one, and then I'll sign in, okay?" At his nod, she took the cloak he handed her and pitched it over her shoulders. To her surprise, they then handed her a grocery bag. "What's this?"

"Party favors," Baldy said with a wink. "Shall I escort you throughout the Tourney grounds in search of our fair maiden?"

She dug through the bag. To her surprise, she pulled out a box of condoms. There was also a roll of toilet paper in the bag, and a bottle of cheap rum.

This was the big party her sister had gone to? Where they passed out boxes of condoms as soon as you paid to get in? Beth Ann clutched the bag to her chest and smiled tightly. "Actually, I think I'll go find her on my own, thanks."

The fur-headed one stepped out in the rain with her to open the gate. "Luck to thee, fair lady. May ye steer clear of the dragons in the forest."

"I'll keep that in mind," she said dryly, and headed down the path.

The rain pelted her, the ground underneath her feet slushy and sucking at her strappy Louboutin sandals. She was pretty sure they were ruined, but she hadn't brought a spare pair of shoes. That was fine—she hated these shoes anyhow, and they were far too pricey for a beautician to own, anyhow. They'd been a gift—an apology from Allan when he'd cheated on her. She didn't regret ruining them. She wouldn't have worn them if she'd have thought she'd be spending her Friday night in a muddy forest looking for Lucy, after all.

The two men didn't follow her down the path, just went back into the tent at the front. She clutched the bag and stumbled down the dark, overgrown path, heading for the first campfire in the distance.

"Wait, milady," called a voice behind her.

She turned, hopeful. Maybe she wouldn't have to go searching in the woods after all. "My sister?"

But the man—Baldy—jogged out to her, and presented her with an apple.

Beth Ann stared at it for a moment, then back at him, confused. "I'm not sure I follow."

"By QuestMaster rules, if a gentleman wishes to show a lady his favor, he presents her with an apple."

How terribly awkward. "Oh, well, listen, honey. That's nice, but—"

He leaned in. "It is all in how you receive the gift, milady. An apple from a potential lover can be a teasing token." He leaned in as if sniffing the apple, and turned a hot gaze on her.

Beth Ann took a step backward. "That's nice of you, but I'm not sure—"

As she watched, he turned over the apple and began to tongue the base. Over and over, stabbing it with the tip of his tongue and continuing to give her the same heated glance. As if he were making love to the thing.

Oh, mercy. This was rather horrifying.

He held the poor, violated apple out to her, then bowed.

She raised a hand in the air. "I really must pass."

Baldy frowned. "That's not how the game is played. You must accept it and then demonstrate your decline of my favor by using the apple."

She was doing no such thing. Beth Ann pulled out her phone and checked the time. "It's getting late and I really have to go. Sorry. I'll have to learn the rules next time." She gave him a tight smile, and then disappeared down the path as quickly as she could.

Lord, to think that an apple could be used in such a graphic manner.

To her relief, he didn't follow her. She did, however, run into three more girls a bit farther down the path. They were about Lucy's age and dressed like wenches. Very loose wenches. They smiled as they sauntered past, ignoring the rain, and she noticed each one carried a beer mug and an apple. She continued on to the nearby campsite, and smiled at the people gathered there as she approached. More teenage girls were here, and she scanned the faces, looking for Lucy. No luck. These girls were scantily dressed and sat on the laps of men in tunics and capes. All were oblivious of the rain pouring down. One couple in the back of the group was making out as if they didn't realize they were in public. Or in a rainstorm.

"Excuse me," Beth Ann said, stepping forward and giving them a little wave.

"A fairy," one of the girls said with a drunken giggle, raising a mug. "Behold her sparkle."

"Yep, that's me," Beth Ann said cheerfully, determined to put a pleasant face on things. "Sparkly. Isn't that nice of you. Listen, honey, I'm looking for Lucy Williamson. Have any of you seen her?"

One of the men stood and gave her a puzzled look. "I know not of a Lucy."

"Sounds like a mundane name," another wench piped up, then belched.

"There are no mundanes here this eve, milady," said another.

This was going to be a long, long night.

TWO

Two hours later, she was no closer to finding Lucy. If her sister had been hiding at one of the campsites, her friends and fellow QuestMasters had done an excellent job of concealing her. Everyone she asked had never heard of a Lucy, and she didn't know her sister's QuestMaster name. Everyone, it seemed, had one. She'd met a Sparkle Blossom, a Megan the Fair, a Ragnar the Great (who didn't seem so great), and three different Aragorns.

She'd also met a lot of drunks and had run across a lot of people making out. She'd been propositioned more tonight than she'd ever been in her life. Apparently the QuestMasters geared up for the big tourney tomorrow by drinking heavily and sleeping with anything that said yes. And here she'd thought they camped out in the woods because they were into nature. Turned out they were just into underage, unsupervised drinking. She'd seen more teenagers carrying bottles than she'd seen adults to supervise them.

The rain didn't seem to be slowing down the QuestMasters any. They wandered from campsite to campsite, laughing and drinking despite the rain and now inches-deep mud. Most of the campfires had gone out in the torrential downpour and her newly purchased cloak was little more than a sodden blanket around her shoulders. She'd taken off her shoes when they'd started to sink in the mud instead of slide. Now she carried them in the bag along with the condoms and alcohol.

And despite all her searching, still no sign of Lucy. But every time she passed another couple making out in the open, or another teenage girl swinging past with a drinking horn, she was even more determined to find her sister. Seventeen was a little too young for this sort of thing, and some of the men here were older than Beth Ann.

It was getting harder to tell the trail from the rest of the ground, since it was all turning into a sludge. She tripped over a root and pitched forward, but caught herself on a nearby bush. Ahead, she could see someone moving and heard the clinking of a costume. "Hello?"

A girl approached and in the low light of a nearby torch, it looked as if she wore a belly dancer costume that was soaked in rain and mud to the point that it was indecent. Her other arm carried multiple bottles of booze, from what Beth Ann could tell. She glanced at Beth Ann's dress, then back at her. "You with the cops?"

"Do I look like a cop?"

The girl squinted at Beth Ann in the darkness. "No?" she said hopefully.

She crossed her arms over her chest, wishing for the hundredth time that she had a flashlight, or that it'd stop raining for five minutes. "I'm not one." When the girl sagged with relief, she pressed on. "Are there cops here? At the Tourney?"

The girl shifted her burden in her arms uneasily. "Maybe."

"My goodness, why would cops be here?" Beth Ann smiled, as if totally oblivious to the minor in front of her carrying alcohol. "That's just silly."

"I know," the girl blurted, relaxing a little. "But that's what I heard back at the Templar camp."

"Templar camp?"

The girl gestured behind her. "Back there. It's quite a ways into the woods but they have the best alcohol."

Maybe that's where Lucy had headed. "That sounds like where I want to go. Can you show me the way?"

The girl shook her head. "I need to vacate the premises if the cops are here. Someone at the Templar camp told me they were making people leave."

Well, good for the cops. They were going to have a field day with this place. She raised her voice to speak over the downpour. "I'm looking for Lucy Williamson."

The girl fidgeted in place, her wet hair plastered to her skull. "I don't know her."

"I know," she bit out, then forced the pleasant smile back to her face. "I don't know her QuestMaster name. But she's tall and skinny with blond hair and bright green nails." She'd painted them for her sister just yesterday.

The other girl brightened. "I think I saw her earlier. She hang out with Lord Colossus?"

"Yes!" Finally, she was getting somewhere. "Have you seen her tonight? Where?"

Again, the girl gestured into the thick woods. "Back at the Templar camp."

Beth Ann gave her a thumbs-up as the rain picked up once more. "Thank you."

All right, she'd find this damn Templar camp once and for all.

What a way to spend a Friday night, Colt thought to himself. His mouth curved in a cynical twist as the man in front of him seemed determined to try and back his car out of the parking lot that had turned into a bowl of mud. The tires spun uselessly as Colt crossed his arms over his rain slicker.

The man finally turned and looked back at Colt. "It's stuck."

"I know." He gestured at the parking lot full of cars. "They all are. Entire road's washed out."

"Even the dirt road?" The man seemed clearly skeptical. "We can't walk out to the highway?"

"You can," Colt said lazily. "Mud's two feet deep along the way."

"What do we do?" said the half-naked woman at the knight's side.

Colt gritted his teeth. He kept getting the same damn questions from all these people. He knew it was because they were all drunk—or high—but it was getting tiresome. "I'm with the local fire department. We're here to evacuate the campground and take you somewhere dry until the situation with your cars can be assessed."

"The fire department?" the woman exclaimed in surprise. She gave him an appreciative look that made him uncomfortable. "Really?"

Damn it. He was tired of babysitting a bunch of drunks. When they'd called him to help out this evening, this was not what he'd had in mind. He'd volunteered, of course, since he'd thought there were people in danger. Not really—turned out that there were just a bunch of idiot teenagers that needed to be fished out of the mud. "Leave your vehicle and head out to the end of the main road. An all-terrain vehicle will be swinging by shortly to pick up more people."

They'd already taken several loads of the group—drunk and obnoxious to a nearby motel under renovation. The owner had generously volunteered his rooms for the group at no charge, and Colt wasn't entirely sure the man knew what he'd gotten into. He pulled a label off a sheet and handed it to the guy. "Put this on your windshield. Leave your keys with me, and your name. We're making arrangements to have your vehicles removed once the road is safe again."

The fire department wasn't used to dealing with this sort of thing. Getting a cat out of a tree? Fine. Hauling a car out of the mud, sure. Hauling a hundred drunk teenagers out of the mud? Not so much. After watching the fire chief scratch his head for a few minutes, Colt had suggested that they get the keys from the teenagers, tag the cars, and organize a list of who needed to be towed. They could deliver the cars once they were freed from the mud. Problem solved.

The fire chief had liked that idea. In fact, he'd liked it so much that he'd given Colt the job. And Colt? Well, someday he was going to learn to shut up so he wouldn't have to deal with idiots like the one standing before him, protectively clutching his keys.

The man—who was dressed as a barbarian, if the Conan hat was any indication—slapped the sticker on the inside of his windshield and gave Colt a suspicious look. "How can I trust that you won't steal my car?"

Colt eyed the 1992 Pontiac the man had been determined to move. The tires were bald, the paint peeling, and he was pretty sure there was a foot of trash on the floorboards of the vehicle. "Not interested, I assure you."

The man gave him another skeptical look until another volunteer showed up. Mike. He looked at the barbarian, and then at Colt. "How's the evacuation coming, Waggoner?"

"Just about done rounding up keys," he told Mike. "Then I'll do one last sweep of the woods to make sure we have everyone."

Mike nodded, adjusting in his rain slicker. He glanced over at the kids, then back to Colt. "The rain's not letting up. Entire campsite's just about washed out. I was told that a hundred fifty people signed in at the gate, and we're rounding up the last few right now."

Colt nodded, staring into the deep woods, wet and dark with rain. The trees were barely discernible with no moon out and a steady downpour. "Sweep shouldn't take long, then."

Mike nodded. "We're almost done here. Then you boys can head back home."

The barbarian handed his keys to Colt suddenly, and Mike paused, waiting while Colt tagged the keys with the man's information, and then added them to the pile in the bucket he was carrying. As the two walked away to the main area where the teens were being evacuated, Mike snorted and looked over at Colt. "Isn't this the most ridiculous thing you've ever seen?"

"It's pretty up there."

"My one night alone with my wife and I get to spend it pulling Frodo and his buddies out of the mud." He nodded at the helmet of the man walking away. "What's he supposed to be?"

"Don't know. I'm afraid to ask." Colt double-checked the tags on the keys and slapped a sticker on the inside window of the car, away from the rain. The sticker marked that the vehicle had been noted and the keys collected for eventual towing. That vehicle taken care of, he moved farther down the swampy parking lot, his rain boots sucking in the mud with every step. He checked the cars for more of the emergency stickers, making sure that each one had been taken care of. The last thing he wanted was to miss a car and have to hunt down the owner at a later date. This needed to be a one-and-done scenario.

There was a small car he'd missed, sunk into the mud between two trucks. The sides of the vehicle were heavily splattered, as if it had arrived after the rain had begun and had to plow through the mud. The two trucks next to it were sunk deep, the owners having tried to move their vehicles when they realized the rain was coming down so heavily. Tried, and failed, succeeding only at swamping the car next to it with even more mud. Even through the coating of filth, he recognized the light lime green of the car, and the make. A Volkswagen. Curious, Colt ran a hand over the back windshield, wiping away the splatters of mud.

The window read CALIFORNIA DREAMIN' and the salon phone number. Underneath the logo, it read HAIR NAILS WAXES TANNING.

Well, he'd be damned. Snobbish, prim Beth Ann Williamson was here in this drunken mudfest? That didn't seem right. He scratched his chin, scowling at the sight of the car. No way she'd be here with this crowd. She thought she was too good for this sort of thing. If a leather-kilted barbarian—or whatever he was supposed to be—approached someone as proper and high-maintenance as Beth Ann, she'd probably call the cops. He peered into the back of the car.

"What are you doing?" A girl's voice called at him, accusing.

Colt turned with a scowl, staring down at the bedraggled blond head of what looked like Beth Ann Williamson's younger sister. Patty, he thought for a moment. No, Lucy. A local girl. He knew the Williamsons—everyone that had grown up in Bluebonnet did—even if they didn't know him. Or want to know him.

He gestured at the car. "That your sister's ride?"

Lucy crossed her arms over a damp velvet dress. It was ridiculous-looking, the heavy skirts two feet deep with mud, and the entire thing was so weighty it looked like it was going to drag her down with it. "Might be hers. Why are *you* wanting to know?"

Ah yes. She was definitely a Williamson. Unwilling to let the teenager rile him, Colt ignored her nasty tone and gestured at the car. "I need her keys so we can arrange a tow when the tractors get here. Go tell her."

Lucy looked uncomfortable. She didn't move.

"What?"

She didn't move.

"What?" he repeated irritably. These damn idiots were getting on his nerves. They all acted like they were being carted off to jail rather than rescued from a washout. "Talk."

Lucy fidgeted, and that annoyed Colt. He knew Beth Ann wasn't a fan of his—the opposite, really. Had she said something to her sister to make her want to avoid him? Be wary of him? Lucy was too young to remember him well, since he'd left for the marines right after high school. He'd been gone for nine long years, way too long for a kid to remember . . . , but she might know his younger brothers. Impatience flashed through him. Was this just another Williamson being a snob to a Waggoner? If so, he didn't have time for this shit.

"Do I need to remind you that this is an emergency situation?" He gestured at the Bluebonnet Emergency Services logo on the sleeve of his jacket. "If your sister isn't willing to comply with the rescue—"

"That's not it," Lucy said quickly. "I haven't seen her."

"You haven't seen her?" He arched an eyebrow.

The girl fidgeted. "I thought she was here to take me home, so I had people cover for me. She probably thinks I'm off at the Templar camp." Lucy shrugged again, wiping her wet hair away from her face with bright green fingernails.

A wave of sheer irritation flashed through him. This girl had deliberately led her sister astray and risked her safety. And in the process, she'd created more work for him.

He turned, hands on his hips, and surveyed the parking lot.

This entire evening was a mess. In the distance, he saw volunteers laughing and joking around with men in costumes. He thought he might have even seen one take a swig of an offered drink as they waited for a ride. Disgraceful. The military would have never run an evacuation like this.

He knew the others weren't military—they were just volunteers from the city that had abandoned their Friday night plans to fish out a bunch of drunk kids—and adults—from a mudslide of a campground. It didn't mean it didn't irritate him. No one had their act together, and here he was, taking keys from a bunch of drunk ingrates when he could have been somewhere else. Anywhere else.

And now this. The fact that prissy, prim Beth Ann, unofficial Queen of Bluebonnet, was lost wandering in the woods? It got on his last nerve, because he knew he was going to have to be the one to rescue her ass. And wasn't that going to be fun. It was bad enough when he ran across her in town and she glared daggers at him. Now he was going to spend his Friday night tracking her down in the woods, where she would no doubt glare daggers at him again, as if the rain and mud were his fault.

She thought everything was his fault anyhow. He was pretty sure she still blamed him for being Dane's friend, and Dane had hurt her best friend Miranda in the past. It didn't matter that Dane and Miranda were engaged. She might tolerate Dane now, but that toleration didn't extend to his friends. Colt knew she still disliked him. The feeling was mutual.

Colt looked back at the sniffling, drenched girl. "Where's this Templar camp?" he growled.

Lucy hastily stammered directions, and he was able to guess.

It sounded like these "Templar" idiots liked to camp right on the edge of the Daughtry land. They were probably the ones Dane had run into before. If so, he knew where that was. "You," he said in a low voice, and pointed to the waiting ATV. "Go with them."

"But my sister?"

"I'll find her and send her on her way."

"But—"

Colt gave the girl a menacing look.

"Uh, tell Beth Ann I said hi and that I'm sorry," Lucy said in a rush, and then dashed for the waiting group, her boots squelching in the thick mud with every step.

That was better. He headed toward Rob, the head of the volunteer outfit, and handed him the bucket of keys. "All tagged."

"You've been a huge help, Colt. I can't thank you enough, man," Rob said. "We're just about done here. We have a full headcount, so we just need to clear everyone out and get them set up at the Johnson Motel."

Full headcount? Then Beth Ann had come through while he'd been talking to her sister? He noticed the clipboard Rob was holding. "Can I see that?"

Rob handed it over, and Colt scanned the scribbles of handwriting. Lord Colossus. Aragorn. Tasha the Wind Dancer. What the hell was this crap? He skimmed the list of strange names, looking for Beth Ann's. It wasn't there. Either she truly wasn't out here, or she hadn't signed in. Or she was going by a name like Pixy Rainbow-Child, which he doubted. Still, if she wasn't here, then why was her car stuck in the mud with all the others? He handed it back to Rob and squinted at the woods.

"There a problem?" Rob asked.

"I'm going to do a final sweep of the campgrounds," Colt told him. "Make sure there's no one else lingering out there."

"Mike already did a sweep," Rob informed him, then clapped him on the back. "You can go home, take a load off. We appreciate you helping out on such short notice."

He'd be willing to bet that Mike hadn't found this so-called Templar camp. "Happy to help out. Just the same," Colt drawled. "I'll swing through. Ease my mind a little." He nodded at Rob. "If I find someone, I'll bring 'em back to the motel in my Jeep." It was safely parked on the side of the highway a mile and a half away, clear of any mud or flooding.

"If I don't hear from you, I'll assume you're just fine, then," Rob said cheerfully.

"I'll check in," Colt said.

"Oh, that's not necessary—" At Colt's look, he realized he'd said something wrong, and added, "But, uh, check in anyhow."

"I'll check in," Colt repeated, his words a little flat. The military would never leave a man out in the field and not have him check in. That was just bullshit.

"Good call," Mike said, slapping Colt on the back.

"Can't be too careful." He patted the plastic-covered satellite phone at his belt. "I'll call you later and let you know when I've left."

"Gotcha," Rob said, and stuck out a hand. "Thanks again, man."

"You bet," Colt said. He made a mental note to discuss additional training for the volunteer group when he got back. They were pretty sad as far as volunteer groups went. And while he didn't expect them to follow military tenets, common sense was still necessary.

Colt grabbed a flashlight, tipped his sodden baseball cap at Rob, and headed off into the woods and the downpour. He ignored the twinge in his bad knee. It'd just have to wait.

He checked every campsite. They all seemed to go in a half circle through the woods and were pretty easy to find. He was disgusted at the sight of them, too. Fire pits too close to tents—luckily for them, the water had washed away any embers—cans and empty bottles everywhere. Some of it was the rain but some of it, he knew, was carelessness, and he hated that. Damn idiots. He hated to see the land being ruined by a bunch of fools. They could stand a few lessons on wilderness survival themselves, he thought. Of course, Grant would see this as a business opportunity.

But Grant wasn't out here in the middle of the night, in the rain and the mud. Colt was, and he found their lack of care annoying as shit.

The Templar camp wasn't anywhere in the neat half circle of campsites, and he knew it wouldn't be. When Lucy had mentioned it, she'd made it sound like quite a hike away, and had noted a stream with a fallen log that he was familiar with. He finished his sweep of all of the other campsites first, just to be sure. He found each one full of debris, camping gear, and discarded foam weapons. The rain hadn't let up, and the ground was turning into a muddy sludge. Whoever had purchased this land hadn't bothered to do anything but clear away the trees for the parking lot. No wonder all the cars were stuck in the morass of mud.

When he'd finished checking all the campsites, he doubled back and headed deeper into the woods, looking for the Templar campsite—or Beth Ann.

The trail was mostly washed out at this point, but Colt didn't need it. Even in the downpour, he knew which direction he was headed; an advantage, he suspected, that Beth Ann probably did not have. But he took his time, searching the area to make sure that there were no other stragglers, and watching his steps. It was dark, and wet, and cold, and those three things would be an unpleasant combination for anyone not used to the elements.

He went farther into the woods, past the circle of campsites. He found the stream Lucy had mentioned, now swollen and overflowing, and crossed the log that served as a bridge to the other side. He'd been making his way slowly through the woods for some time, noticing that the ground sloped up ever so gently, when he heard a loud crash in the brush ahead.

Colt clicked off his flashlight, listening. Despite the steady patter of raindrops, he could hear something moving in the dense trees ahead, so he stopped to listen. While there were a few wildcats in the area—not many—they wouldn't be out in the storm. Wild boar might, though, or a coyote.

He paused, waiting.

Another crash. Then, a softly muttered, "Fiddlesticks."

He didn't know whether to laugh or roll his eyes in annoyance. Of course she was out here. His suspicions were confirmed when a low call of "Lucy? Lucy, are you out here?" echoed through the woods.

He stepped forward out of the brush, toward her.

It took him a moment or two to find her—he was mostly

following the thrashes—when he turned on his flashlight again, and the light caught on something glittering.

"Who's there?" she called at the same time, a bit of hope in her voice. "Lucy?"

He stepped out toward her and caught his first good look at Beth Ann Williamson.

She was soaked. Her long blonde hair was plastered to her skull, her bangs like daggers over her pale forehead. She wore some sort of blanket over her shoulders, and a peach-colored sparkly dress clung to her wet body like a second skin. Her breasts were outlined by the damp, clinging fabric, and the shadow of her nipples could be seen through the pale material. Not that he needed that to see them—her nipples were hard as rocks and standing at attention. Her dress was so thin he could even see the vee of her hips under the fabric, and his cock automatically hardened at the sight. Her legs were slick and damp and pale with cold. Below the knee, her calves and feet were covered in mud. She'd clearly been wearing a lot of makeup before coming out—it was smeared over her high cheekbones and dribbled down her face in black streams. She clutched a bag in her hand.

She looked like an utter wreck.

At the sight of him, Beth Ann stopped short. A look of surprise crossed her face, and then her eyes narrowed. "What are *you* doing here?"

He was kind of used to that sort of response from her. They'd formed a momentary truce when Miranda and Dane had gotten engaged, but it had quickly fizzled back into intense dislike on both sides. "I'm here saving your ass."

She huffed, an action that made her wet breasts heave and his cock jerk in response at the sight. "I don't need saving, Colt. I need to find my sister."

She was so outraged at the sight of him. It was damn funny to watch. And, okay, a little arousing. "You look like something out of a horror movie," he drawled, unable to quit looking at those magnificent, heaving wet breasts. She was something out of a horror movie all right. The hot, sexy starlet that took her top off and got fucked by someone for five minutes on screen. Damn. He shifted in the mud. Why the hell was he so turned on by the sight of her all wet and helpless? She had a fine body, but it came attached to that yapping mouth of hers.

A mouth that had just dropped open in shock. "A horror movie?" Beth Ann repeated, stunned. "How *dare* you!"

"That's not what I meant," he began, and then scowled when she glared at him and turned her back. She was determined to find insult in whatever he said, it'd seem. Prickly woman. Madder than hell and still trying to be a lady about things. "You're misunderstanding me. I'm here to rescue you."

"Rescue me? Oh, *really*." Beth Ann turned as if the word made her furious. She put her hands on her hips, the wet bag bouncing against her side as she did. "Here to be the big hero?"

Well, he didn't like to think of it that way. "I guess."

"Is this some sort of macho joke?"

He raised an eyebrow. Why would he joke about a rescue?

She laughed, the sound bitter and harsh. "Oh, this is unreal. You really do think you're here to rescue me, don't you? How cute. I'm sure that's what everyone told you—that poor little Beth Ann Williamson is desperate for a man to sweep her off her feet and rescue her from her situation. That I'm just waiting for

Prince Charming to swoop in and save the day." Her mouth pursed into a polite little smile, made all the more ridiculous by the makeup running down her face. "Look, Colt, I don't know why you feel this need to show up here and try to play the hero, but the last thing I want is another man deciding that I can't take care of myself and trying to take over my life. So you can just go away now. I don't need saving, and I don't need your help. Oh, and tell Miranda that I said nice try."

He didn't see what Miranda had to do with anything. "You're turning down a rescue?"

She laughed and flicked her hand, as if shooing a fly. "Oh, I am turning down the entire kit and caboodle. The rescue *and* the person it came attached to."

All right, now he was getting annoyed. He leaned back, studied her. "Oh *really*?"

"Yes, really," she said viciously. "I don't know if you were aware, but not every woman in the vicinity needs saving."

"I don't know," he drawled, knowing any response he made would irritate her. "You look pretty helpless to me."

That did it. Her entire body stiffened and she jerked upright. Her mouth clenched into a firm line. Beth Ann Williamson definitely had a stick up her ass tonight. "I am not *helpless*," she seethed. "Just because I am female does not mean I need you to swoop in and be a hero. Sometimes we can save ourselves, you know." She gestured at him with incensed, quick little motions. "I realize that's difficult to get through that pile of meat on top of your shoulders that men like to call a brain, but it's true. Not all women are helpless. Not this woman, for sure. And I certainly don't need you stomping in and making my life miserable like you always do, so why don't you just go *away*?"

Go away? He was here, standing in the rain and waiting to save her ass, the ungrateful woman. But that wasn't what she wanted. She wanted to rescue herself. As if the thought of a man helping her out of the woods was somehow insulting to her. Fine. "You expect me to just leave you flailing in this mud all night? In the dark?"

"Yes," she said firmly. "I don't need your help and I sure don't need you here right now, following me around. Go bother someone else."

He was beyond annoyance now. The woman was irrational. "And so you want me to leave?"

She turned and looked off into the woods, as if in exasperation. As if he were keeping her from finding her sister. "Did I stutter?"

Ah yes. This was the Beth Ann he knew. Colt put his hands up. "Fine then. I will leave you alone. Out here. Just like you want."

"Good," she bit out, then glanced down at his pants. He thought she was going to comment on the wood he was sporting despite her nasty attitude. But she pointed at his pocket, where he'd tucked his flashlight, with a finger that was wrinkled and shaking with cold. "Can I buy that flashlight from you?"

"I reckon not," he said with a drawl.

She scowled at him. "God, I hate you. Go find someone else to harass."

And with that, she stomped off into the woods again.

Fuck you, too, he thought to himself. Here he was, trying to help her out and she bit his head off, treated him as if he were garbage for even daring to think she might need help. His spine stiffened anew as he watched her crash through the underbrush, and then her form disappeared back into the shadows. "Lucy?"

Guess he should have told her that the camp was evacuated. Nah. Let her stew in her own juices for a bit. Teach her a lesson.

He rubbed the front of his wet trousers, willing his damn dick to stop standing at attention. She might have had a mighty fine pair of breasts—slick, heaving breasts with tight, hard nipples—but unless he had a piece of masking tape for her mouth, the reality of Beth Ann was going to ruin the fantasy every time.

He crouched on his haunches and clicked his flashlight off, enjoying the sound of her stumbling through the woods. She'd call Lucy's name, and then every so often, she'd break off and he'd hear her swear. Not "fuck" or "shit" or "damn," but expressions like "fudge" or "fiddlesticks" or "drat." It was ridiculous.

It was also ridiculous that every muttered "fiddlesticks" made his cock stir again. Such a clean, pretty mouth. He wondered if she ever let herself go, even in bed. And then he imagined her clean, pretty mouth saying dirty things to him.

Damn. He needed to get laid if he was having sexual fantasies about Beth Ann. She'd probably frown with genteel distaste if he even touched her. He rubbed his hand along the front of his jeans again, and then pulled out his sat phone, and dialed Rob.

"Glad to hear from ya, Colt. Find anyone else?"

He thought for a moment, and heard another polite utterance

in the distance. "Nah," he lied. "Nobody. I'm heading out myself."

"Good on ya," Rob said. "See you 'round. Thanks again for volunteering, man."

"Anytime," Colt said, and terminated the call.

He wasn't leaving. He was going to teach Miss Beth Ann Williamson some manners, though, and it'd start with a nice weekend out in the wild. Maybe she'd learn to be a lot nicer that way. Maybe she'd learn that being unpleasant to a Waggoner wasn't the smartest idea. And maybe she'd learn that the next time he showed up to rescue her, she could be civil, at least.

She could sure use a lesson in humility, and he had the time to do it. Even more than that, it'd give him an intense amount of pleasure to see her spend the weekend muddy and struggling.

Dane would tell him he needed a hobby. But Dane was a good guy; everyone in town liked him. And Colt was a Waggoner. The family in town that was most reviled. Beth Ann was the daughter of the mayor, and had grown up pampered and privileged.

The way he saw it, this was like a gift, and there was nothing he'd like more than to watch Beth Ann Williamson get a little dirty.

After listening to her thrash her way through the bushes and the thick, clinging mud for another hour or so, Colt decided to take pity on her. Beth Ann was determined, he'd give her that.

She was also going in the wrong direction. If she were looking for a specific camp, she was heading away from them and actually toward the parking lot. Of course, judging by her stumbling and continued calling, she didn't know that.

So he stepped out of the woods and clicked the flashlight back on. "Miss Beth Ann," he drawled in way of greeting.

She looked exhausted, a new swipe of mud over her cheek. She'd pulled that stupid blanket thing tight around her body and her blue lips trembled from cold. The night had gotten cool and crisp, and though the rain had let up for now, it hadn't made it any warmer. Judging from the thick cloud cover overhead, he suspected there would be more rain.

She gave him a weary look when he reappeared. "Not you again."

"Me again," he drawled.

"Look," she said in a tight voice, "this has been a night from hell and I really don't need you stalking me."

Stalking her? What the hell.

"Now, unless you want to tell me where the Trojan camp is—"

"Templar," he corrected.

Her head tilted and she cut off midstream. "Templar. That's right. You know where it is?"

He gave her a brief nod, enjoying the way she bared her teeth in frustration at his affirmation.

"Why didn't you say something?"

"I tried."

"No, you came here and told me I looked like a hideous beast and then said you were here to rescue me—"

"That's not what I said—"

"So you'll forgive me if I don't take too kindly to being told

I'm not only ugly, but I'm helpless and stupid because I'm female," she bit out. "Now are you going to help me or not?"

Not, he wanted to say, but he noticed her full lower lip was quivering with cold.

"You want the Templar camp?" he asked, voice short.

"Yes, I do."

"Follow me," he said, and turned around, walking past her back to the direction of the camp. He'd actually found it a half hour ago—she'd more or less wandered right past it—but he hadn't felt the need to point it out to her. If she'd have looked up, she'd probably have seen the crude tree houses that made up the camp.

But she hadn't looked up. And she hadn't had a flashlight, either. She'd been wandering the woods, cold and alone and not terrified in the slightest. Instead, she was determined to find her sister.

He had to admire that, even if he didn't like her much.

Colt led the way through the brush. He hadn't heard one complaint out of her mouth just yet, something he had respect for. People that got out in the wild and complained that it was wet and muddy were idiots in his book.

After about ten minutes of pushing through the trees and mud, Colt spotted one of the shacklike tree houses above. He turned back to Beth Ann, who was close on his heels. "We're here."

"Here?" She frowned and pushed past him, staring up at the trees and the tree houses, and then the scatter of discarded camping equipment at the base of the trunks. Folding camping chairs circled around the long-dead firepit, which was now nothing more than a dirty puddle on the ground. "It's deserted."

"Yeah."

"Where is everyone?"

"Evacuated."

Her confused expression focused back on him. "Evacuated? From the camp? By who?"

"Volunteer Emergency Services." He pointed at the patch on his sleeve. "Like me."

She stared at him, astonished. Her mascara-rimmed eyes were wide. "They're not here," she repeated. "Is anyone here?"

He pointed at her, then pointed at himself, enjoying her astonished expression a little too much, though he kept his poker face on.

She thought for a minute, then stared back at the deserted, washed-out campsite. "And Lucy went with them? Where'd they go?"

"Nearby motel," Colt said. "It's under construction but the owner's letting them all stay the night until the cars can be towed."

One delicately arched eyebrow went up. "How long have you known that they're gone?"

He kept his face smooth. "'Bout two hours."

THREE

He waited for the explosion. The show of nasty temper. For her to snap and berate him. Call him a piece of shit for keeping her out here.

Instead, she stared thoughtfully at the campground, then back at him. "I suppose you were going to leave me out here until I stopped raging about how I could save myself?"

"The thought occurred to me," he said dryly.

She stared at the trees, then back at him. "Only two hours? My tirade didn't make you madder than that?"

He didn't know what to think of her humor. "Are you aware of how pitiful you look?"

Beth Ann's hands flew to her face and she wiped at her cheek, smearing mud across it self-consciously. She stared into the woods, then back at him. "You're really here to rescue me, aren't you?"

"I am."

"And I was pretty nasty to you, wasn't I?"

"You were." Though he *had* said the thing about the horror movie. He just hadn't meant it in the way she'd taken it.

"Miranda and Dane didn't send you?"

"Nope."

She grimaced. "Fiddlesticks." She glanced back over at him, wiped another wet lock of hair off of her brow. And sighed. "I've had a bad night. I thought you were . . . never mind." Beth Ann sighed and tilted her face back, letting the rain splatter on her cheeks. After a long moment, she said, "My life seems to be full of men trying to save me from myself, and I took it out on you. Sorry about that."

An apology from Beth Ann Williamson was not exactly what he expected. "No worries."

"I guess I deserved this." She gestured at the wet, sludgy forest. And she laughed. "Beth Ann Williamson, this really takes the cake."

That . . . had not been the reaction he'd been anticipating. He'd expected more anger. Now she was laughing at herself. She wasn't furious, or crying. She was . . . amused. Chagrined at how she'd acted. And damn if that reaction hadn't done things to his fantasies of her. At first he'd been daydreaming about angry sex with her—her furious lips mashing against his own as he fucked her against a tree. Now he was picturing those wet, slick breasts under his hands as she laughed and sweetly gave in to him.

Fuck. He clicked the flashlight off so she wouldn't see how hard he was.

"Sorry if I ranted at you earlier," she said, rubbing her arms under the blanket thing. "I was having a bad night, and the last thing I wanted was some man telling me he was going to come and rescue me, and I took it out on you. I apologize."

"No harm," he said slowly, watching her.

She rubbed her arms again, then turned to face him. "I appreciate you coming after me."

He nodded, his eyes intent on her face. Even covered in mud and running makeup, she had the prettiest face he'd ever seen. He wanted to do rough, raw, dirty things to that sweet face. To see those lips curve around his cock as he fed it into her hungry mouth.

She tilted her head. "You ok?"

He coughed into his hand, distracted. "Fine."

"Well," she said, dropping her hands to her side in an expression of defeat. "Guess we'd better call it a night."

"A night?" he echoed, still distracted by the thought of him and Beth Ann, fucking. The visual was driving him crazy. Why was he suddenly obsessed with the thought of fucking Beth Ann? Was it because he needed to get laid? Because she was beautiful? Because she was gleaming and wet and wearing a dress that left nothing to the imagination?

Or because when she'd realized that she'd taken everything the wrong way, she'd laughed at herself? That she hadn't complained about her fate? That underneath the blond hair and glittery dress, the town's delicate beautician had a sweet mouth and a core of steel?

He liked that steel. He liked the sweet mouth even more.

"A night?" she repeated. "They're still evacuating, right?"

He started, then shook his head. "Nah. They're done. You weren't on the roster so they left."

She looked at him in shock. "They left? B-but-but you're still here."

"They left without me, too," he said, lying. "I planned on hiking back to the Daughtry Ranch . . . before."

Her voice gave a wobble. "Be . . . fore?"

He nodded. "Before the river washed that part out. I'm stranded, too."

Dane and Grant would have told him he was full of shit. Punched him in the arm for making up stories and trying to pull one over them. They would have hiked to the river to take a look at it anyhow. Hell, you didn't even have to cross the Trinity River to cut across the ranch's property. You could just skirt it wide.

Of course, Beth Ann didn't know that.

And he didn't know why he lied to her, but he found himself adding, "We're stuck here until at least tomorrow. Sorry."

"Tomorrow?" Her jaw dropped. "We—we can't leave?" She stared into the trees as if seeing them in a new light.

He was surely going to hell for lying. "Might even be Sunday before we can get out of here. Depends on the weather."

Again, she gave a little self-deprecating laugh. "Well, I suppose if I'm going to be stuck in the mud, at least it's with you, right?"

Damned if his cock didn't turn into a bar of iron right about then. "Oh?"

"You're the survivalist. This is your gig. The sort of thing you do for funsies."

Ah. He nodded again.

This whole revenge thing would work a lot better if she'd go back to screaming at him, or pouting. If she would just throw a nice Southern belle fit and make him realize this was a big dumbass move led by his dick, and how she really was spoiled and silly, he'd change his mind and drive her home.

But instead, she sighed and tilted her head back, letting the rain dump on her face. It spattered constantly, a reminder that she wasn't going anywhere anytime soon.

"Well," she said after a moment. "Guess we should find someplace dry to sleep."

And again, he was surprised by Beth Ann Williamson. And he wanted her.

"Guess so," he drawled.

She was stuck out here. Stuck out in this muddy hell with none other than Colt Waggoner, the surliest, most arrogant man she knew.

And, she admitted privately, the most attractive.

No, this evening was not exactly a banner for her. She was tired, cold, exhausted, and hungry. But at least Lucy was safe and hopefully not shacking up with Colossus. The Johnson Motel was small and if everyone here had been evacuated, she doubted anyone had privacy.

Good. Someone else's Friday night had been ruined, too. She felt a vicious bolt of pleasure at that.

Rain splattered on her head again, and Beth Ann looked up just as it began to pour once more.

"Shelter?" she said, turning to Colt.

He pointed at the trees, his eyes mere slits in the darkness. "We can try those."

She followed his gesture and noticed a plank ladder nailed to the tree. Her gaze went up to the wooden floor about fifteen feet above her head, nestled in the trees. How had she missed a tree house? "Think it's safe?"

He headed over to the ladder, and she noticed that he favored his right leg.

"Are you okay?" Beth Ann asked, crossing her arms over her chest.

He turned and gave her a blank look. "What?"

"Your leg? Did you hurt it?" She hoped not. She was feeling guilty enough that he was stranded out here looking for her.

"No," he said in that flat voice.

"But—"

"Knee injury from a while back. Flares up in the weather." And he gave her a pointed look. "You gonna stand out here and let it rain on you all night?"

"Well, no—"

"Then climb up this ladder," he said in that flat voice that never let her know what he was thinking. That was one of the things she disliked about Colt—between those narrow, hard eyes and that almost too-firm jaw, the man didn't look like he was ever amused by anything. She wondered if his face would break if he smiled.

Probably.

Okay, fine, she'd climb that darn ladder. Beth Ann wrapped the loops of the stupid bag that held her Louboutins around her wrist and approached it. The rungs didn't look all that sturdy, but at a glance over at his surly expression, she decided to chance it anyhow. She put her hands on the first step and began to climb. The planks were slippery and her feet were slick with mud, so she took it slow. Once, her foot slipped, and Colt was there to put his hands on her ass, supporting her. His hand was warm and she felt that touch all the way to her toes. Her body flushed with reaction . . . and desire. Oh *lord*.

"Careful," he warned in that hard voice, making the bolt of lust wither and die.

Why was she attracted to such a hard, unpleasant man? It must have been desperation. She hadn't had sex in well over a year and a half, long before she'd broken up with Allan, and she was turned on by a handsome man touching her. That was all. And she was cold. His hot hand on her body had seemed like a bolt of heat and she'd responded to the warmth. Nothing more.

The tree house interior was small—a long room that seemed too small for human habitation. It was barely wide enough for both her and Colt to stand shoulder to shoulder, and the roof was short enough that Colt had to duck. But it was dry—mostly. Rain and wind leaked in from the far corner, and that was where a sodden pile of blankets lay.

Lovely. Not that she would have touched those blankets anyhow, but it would have been nice to have options.

The other side of the room had a mini cooler and a stack of bottles—more rum. She leaned over and flipped open the cooler. "Apples," she said in disgust.

"Apples?"

She straightened. "Yeah. They do a game with apples apparently. If someone offers you an apple and you take a bite out of it, it means you want to sleep with them." She shuddered in memory of the evening. "I was offered a lot of apples tonight."

His laugh was a short, dry bark. "I'll bet."

For some reason, that made her feel a little better about the situation. That, and the fact that the rain wasn't pounding on her head. She swung off her sodden cloak and moved to the edge of the tree house where the building was open to the night air, and wrung it out. Water streamed down. It had been a nice idea, but it was made of velour and the fabric didn't really repel water. "Gonna be a cold night."

Colt said nothing. Probably thinking how stupid she was for coming out here in a pair of dress shoes and a sparkling, skimpy mini dress. But heck, she hadn't planned on being out here, either. It was just luck. Really bad luck.

She'd had a string of that lately.

Beth Ann turned and bumped into dry skin. Dry, warm skin. She gasped and stepped backward, toward the ledge.

His hand shot out and grabbed her. "Careful."

"Sorry," she muttered, stepping back toward him and to the side. It was dark in the tree house and he'd clicked his flashlight off—maybe to save the battery? "You, um, you took your shirt off. Want me to wring it for you?"

"It's dry," he said, and she felt him press it into her hand. "For you."

"Oh." Oh, that heavenly man. "Think we can hang up my dress and the cloak and see if they're dry by morning?"

He paused for a minute. Then, "Fine," he rasped. She heard his boots clomp on the floorboards. "I'll wait outside—"

"It's raining," she said before he could leave. "You can just, you know, turn around. I'd hate for you to get all wet again."

"Fine," he said in that same gruff voice. "I'm turned."

His voice sounded a little farther away, as if he had turned his back to her. She hesitated for a moment, then slipped out of the cold dress. It had been so pretty on the rack. She hated it now. Useless, pathetic scrap that didn't offer her a bit of warmth. She didn't even have a bra on—the stupid dress had a built-in shelf. All she had underneath was a nude thong. Quickly, she shimmied out of the dress and slipped the new shirt on, nearly sighing with how warm her body immediately felt.

She heard him shift. "Better?"

"Much better," Beth Ann said, feeling blissfully warmer already. "Oh God, thank you."

"'Course," he said in that short, clipped voice. "Gimme your dress."

She handed the sodden heap to him, and the cloak, and through the darkness, she could make out him hanging them.

"Hooks," he said. "Nearly busted my head on one of them."

She laughed at that.

"I see my pain makes you smile," he said in that hard voice, but it had an edge of teasing to it.

"I have to admit, the thought of grim and scary Colt Waggoner being laid low by a clothing hook did make me smile," she said.

"Grim and scary, eh?"

Oh, now she'd gone and offended him again. "Something like that," she said lightly. Now that Colt's warmth had left the shirt, she was beginning to shiver again. It was much better than before, but still not enough.

"I'm going to take my pants off so they can dry, too," he said.

"Oh, of course," she said, hating the blush creeping over her cheeks. Totally a practical move. Not that she could see anything in the dark at all.

She heard his clothing rustling and the sound of his boots being unlaced. The rain had picked up outside and she listened to it rather than the sounds of him undressing.

"Think it'll let up by morning?" she asked him with a sigh.

"Hope so," he said in a flat voice. "Don't wanna stay here all weekend."

"Me, either," she said, and rubbed her arms again. "Too cold and everything's all wet."

"Still cold?" Suddenly he was behind her, and she felt the warmth radiating off his body. Okay, he was standing like, inches away from her. Was he wearing boxers? Briefs? What did he look like almost naked? Her nipples tightened all over again. *Stop it,* she told herself. Not the appropriate time for rescuer fantasies. She didn't even like the man.

"Maybe it'll just take me a bit to heat up," she said hopefully, just as a raindrop splattered on her head from the ceiling. She stumbled to the side and felt her arm brush his body. God, it was unfair that he was so warm and it was so cold.

He said nothing for a long moment, then, "I have an idea, but it's not ideal."

"Nothing about this is ideal," she said. "Lay it on me."

"I have a rain slicker," he said. "Our only waterproof blanket, of a sort. We're both down to nothing and you're still cold."

"Are you suggesting we share body heat?"

"Something like that," he said, the words seemingly stiff.

"I am all for that right about now," she said, trying not to sound too eager. Oh, hello, delicious torment. She'd been about to suggest it herself but didn't want to seem like an eager tramp. *Hi, can I rub my body all up against your hard one? I swear it's just because I'm cold. The thought of your rippling abs and my eighteen months without sex has nothing to do with it in the slightest.*

"Here," he said, handing her the slicker. "Let's move over to that corner. It's the driest."

His hand lightly brushed her shoulder and nudged her forward, and Beth Ann followed. She felt the boards creak as he shifted down to the ground, and then she heard him pat his leg. "Come on."

Oh boy. Heart fluttering with anxiety and a mixture of things she didn't want to define, she slid down to the floor next to him, and curled up, hugging her legs close. His warm arm was suddenly touching her legs and he pulled her body against his, and she tilted and leaned back against him.

"Don't be shy," he said in that same almost-mocking voice. "Shy means cold."

She realized she'd sat down right between his legs. He'd spread them wide to accommodate her body, and her legs eased over one of his thighs, until her feet dangled off to the side and she curled halfway, sitting in his lap.

He reached around her and pulled the slicker over the two of them like a blanket. Then she felt his arms slide around her waist. "Relax," he said. "Not gonna touch you. Platonic."

No, she suspected he wouldn't, but she was all too acutely

aware of where she was sitting, and what she was laying against. For example, right now her cheek lay against a metal chain that she was pretty sure were his dog tags. Imagining those on his naked chest was rather . . . delicious.

Not that she should be thinking about that sort of thing. Especially right now. His cock jutted like iron, and she'd definitely noticed how hard it was. "I'm feeling something decidedly unplatonic against my side," she pointed out.

"Involuntary," he said. "I'm alive and you're female and almost naked."

All good points, and he was definitely warm and hard under her. "I see. Well, you sure know how to make a girl feel special."

He chuckled. "Didn't realize that was what you wanted tonight. You want to feel special, you got to ask."

Charming. "Platonic," she repeated.

"Platonic," he agreed. "Not dead."

He was going to be in a world of hurt in the morning, Colt decided. Beth Ann—pretty, unattainable Beth Ann Williamson—had fallen asleep in his arms, wearing nothing but a scrap of panties, his T-shirt, and a rain slicker that covered them both. He was pretty sure she wasn't wearing a bra. She'd turned a little after she'd fallen asleep and mashed her full breasts against his chest, and it had taken every ounce of his strength not to groan aloud. His dick was as hard as steel, and his knee throbbed, and he didn't care.

She snuggled up against him and slept, oblivious to their cold, wet surroundings. And he kept his hands carefully on her back, because he was afraid to put them anywhere else. Her thighs were too exposed, her front too tempting.

What the fuck was he doing? Why had he lied to her about the two of them being stranded? Had he wanted to teach her a lesson so badly that he'd felt like traipsing through the mud with her at his side all weekend? Was he that much of a masochist to enjoy a woman's weeping and exhaustion? This was his own damn fault. He'd forced her to stay out here in the wild because he'd lied to her about being stranded.

Worse than that, she wasn't crying or complaining about fatigue. She wasn't being tortured by this. She was snuggling up against him. Even worse than *that*, he was attracted to her. Really, really attracted—could stroke himself off at the touch of her hand on his chest attracted.

Fuck. And she was nothing but bad news.

Wouldn't the town just love that, he thought with a wry twist of his mouth. Sweet, perfect Beth Ann, stolen away from handsome Allan Sunquist by one of the white-trash, no-good Waggoners.

Actually, he liked that thought very much, and his arms tightened around her, shifting her closer.

So this had started out as revenge, but it had changed at some point. Maybe when she'd laughed and apologized for being nasty to him. Maybe when she'd taken off her dress and shimmied into his shirt and even though he hadn't been looking, he'd been picturing it.

Either way, he was setting himself up for a world of hurt and a weekend full of blue balls. There were a lot of things girls like Beth Ann liked in this world, but blue collar, ex-military guys from trailer parks weren't one of them. Beth Ann's family had money. They mingled with Houston society. They held fund-raisers and held city offices and did stupid shit like that.

And even knowing all this, he wanted to tilt her face up from where it was buried against his chest, and slide his lips over her parted ones, and kiss the hell out of her. See if she'd respond to his kiss.

But he wasn't that big of a dick to molest a girl while she was sleeping. And Beth Ann wouldn't be interested in a guy like him. So he just lay his head back against the tree house wall and tried not to think about the curve of her hip resting against his cock, and how he could have her spun around and down on the floor, pushing her panties aside and sinking deep into her before she'd had time to fully awaken. Fuck her until that sleepy look in her eyes turned to desire.

Okay, so he was thinking about it a little.

Beth Ann slowly woke up, her front toasty and delicious, her feet incredibly cold. She shifted, wondering why her bottom felt so stiff. She was pressed up against something deliciously warm and hard, and her first thought was Allan. Except Allan didn't like to cuddle in bed with her, and there was definitely a large, warm hand cupping her ass. To her horror, she was drooling on a bare chest. Oh God. She suddenly knew whose chest that was, and she suspected he wouldn't like being drooled on. She sat up, surreptitiously wiping at her mouth, and then straightened the dog tags that had gotten stuck to her cheek, returning them to their usual spot on his chest.

"Mornin'," Colt said in a raspy drawl.

"Um, hi," she said, and ran a hand over her hair. It had dried sometime in the night into unruly waves. Lovely. She probably looked like a hot mess. "How'd you sleep?"

"Well enough considering the splinter up my ass," he said. "You?"

"Like a baby," she said. She laughed but it was kind of the truth. She'd slept well in his arms, given the circumstances. Almost too well. Of course, she'd never admit that to Colt. He didn't even like her.

"It's still raining," he pointed out.

"Still?" she said with dismay. "That means the river's still going to be too high to cross, then?"

"'Fraid so," he said, except she could have sworn he'd sounded pleased about it.

"You're having fun with all this, aren't you?"

"'Fraid so," he repeated with a grin. "This sort of thing's a challenge, but it's nice to push yourself against the elements, see who comes out on top."

"Right now it's the elements one, Beth Ann zero," she pointed out.

He simply smiled, one corner of his mouth tugging up. Through the day's growth of stubble, she saw a dimple. Heaven help her.

She stood up and stretched, then tugged the shirt down over her panties, remembering that her thong didn't cover much. He'd stood and began to put on his pants again, and she didn't watch, but she did notice what he was wearing. Tighty whities. She could see that. He was all business to the core.

Beth Ann reached out and grasped the hem of her dress and grimaced. "Still wet." Wet and cold to boot. The cloak was like one big soggy towel. She sighed and turned back to him. "So what's the plan?"

He put his hands on his hips and she noticed the marines symbol tattooed over one hard, flat pectoral. His stomach was flat and lean and his shoulders were hard with muscle. Had she really rested up against that all night? Mercy. She felt weak in the knees.

"You lead. I'm just here to make sure you don't get into trouble." His lean, predatory gaze stroked over her.

She was staring at him. She flushed and dropped her gaze, pretending to look at a fleck of mud on her big toe. "Well, seeing as how I have no clue of what I'm doing, I think it's your call."

"There's a supply shack the survival business keeps stocked in case of school emergency not too far from here," he admitted. "We could skirt the river and head toward it. Might not be drier than here, but there's some emergency supplies. And enough open area to build a fire."

"That sounds like as good a plan as any," Beth Ann said. Fire sounded awesome.

She leaned over and picked up her bag, and fished out one totally destroyed Louboutin. "I'm not going to be able to walk far in these." She stared at it, and then peered over at him. "I don't suppose you could snap the heels off?"

"Snap the heels?"

"Like in that movie." Beth Ann didn't remember which one. "So I can walk better." She held the shoe out to him.

He took it in hand and gave her an odd look. "Might not be a bad idea. Hope they aren't expensive."

"Twelve hundred dollars," she admitted, just as he snapped the first heel off and handed it to her.

He looked a little sick at the thought. "Twelve hundred?"

"Yup," she said cheerfully, and handed him the other shoe to destroy. "If it makes you feel any better, it wasn't my money."

"Allan?" he guessed, and snapped the other heel off and handed it back to her.

"He always thought I had a weakness for shoes," she admitted.

"And do you?" His keen gaze rested on her legs as she slid the shoes on. They were tilted at an odd angle to support the heel that was now missing, but she wouldn't sink in the mud anymore. That was a plus.

"Not really," Beth Ann said. "All I ever asked from him was faithfulness. Instead, I got expensive shoes, Coach handbags, and Tiffany jewelry."

"I don't know what any of that is," Colt drawled. "Expensive?"

She nodded. "Useless, too."

That dimple reappeared, and she felt like she'd suddenly said the right thing. "Keep the heels. Maybe you can get part of your money back."

She snorted, and then touched the hem of her damp dress. "I'll change back into this if you don't mind turning around."

He turned away from her, and she slipped his shirt off and her dress back on. She shivered as the damp, cold fabric slithered down her body, and then held his shirt out to him reluctantly. "Here you go."

He took it and turned, then frowned at her. "Cold already?"

"I didn't buy this because it was incredibly warm," she admitted.

He handed the shirt back to her. "Put this on over your dress."

"I—but you—"

He ran a hand over his own chest and her gaze was drawn there like a beacon. "I can stand a little cold."

She needed to quit staring at his far too nice pectorals. "Okay," she said weakly, and tugged the shirt back over her head. It helped, a lot. "Thank you."

He squinted at the sky, then at her. "It's letting up. We can grab some of those apples to eat and head out for the cabin before it starts to rain again. You sure you want to do this?"

"I'm good," she affirmed. "A little hike won't kill me. And your knee?"

Colt gave her a hard look. "If I avoided hiking because my knee hurt me, I wouldn't be much use as a survival instructor, would I?"

Ouch. She'd insulted him with her question. "Sorry. You're right. I wasn't trying to question your ability."

For some reason, his mouth quirked at that. "Oh, I'm perfectly capable of taking care of your needs."

A hot flush swept over her face at that. Oh mercy, he didn't mean that how she'd taken it. Did he? Because now she was thinking naughty things.

He handed her a few apples, oblivious to her blushing.

She took them and placed them in her plastic bag, along with another bottle of alcohol. Why not. She'd probably need a stiff drink by tonight. Her hand hesitated over the now-soggy box of condoms. She could toss them. Or she . . . could keep them. Beth Ann flushed even harder, thinking of his hand casually grazing over his chest, and how she'd wanted that to be her own hand.

I'm perfectly capable of taking care of your needs.

Wishful thinking, she told herself, but she left the box in. She was way too cowardly to make a move anyhow, and he likely saw her as an annoying burden for the weekend.

"Anyone looking for you?"

His sharp voice startled her out of her reverie and she clasped the bag tightly shut, cheeks flaming. "What?"

He gave her another one of those intense, narrow-eyed gazes that seemed to see right through her. "You didn't go home last night. Anyone going to be looking for you?"

"Oh." She thought for a moment. "My clients will be annoyed when they get to the salon and I'm not there, but I'll reschedule them and give a discount, and we should be okay."

"I meant family. Boyfriend?"

There went that flush again. "My parents will think I flounced back to the salon to hide out for the weekend. When I get mad at them, I do that. Living at home is too claustrophobic." She thought for a minute, and then grinned. "I've been doing a lot of weekend flouncing lately."

He gave her a slow, wicked smile in return that made the pit of her belly flutter with excitement. "Parents?"

"What?"

"You said you hide from your parents. Aren't you a little old for that?"

"I moved back in with them after I left Allan," she admitted. "Everyone thought it would be pretty temporary . . . except me."

She smiled over at him. "Eleven months later, here I am. Still living at home."

"Nothing to be ashamed of in that," he said, and she could have sworn that he was pleased.

"You?" she asked casually. "Anyone waiting at home for you?"

"Just Grant," he said with a drawl. "Probably wanting to go over class schedules again. So no."

"Ah," she said. So he was a total bachelor? It seemed weird and awkward to ask him if he had a girlfriend, but she suddenly really wanted to know.

"So no boyfriend?" His lazy drawl almost sounded interested, and her pulse fluttered.

"No boyfriend," she admitted, feeling as shy as a schoolgirl.

He grunted, then stared at the sky. "Come on," he said abruptly, interrupting her thoughts. "Let's get a move on before the rain comes down again."

FOUR

"Almost there," Colt told her as they crossed a low, muddy ridge. "In the next valley."

"I'll never be so happy to see a roof in my life," she said cheerfully, her breath coming in short pants.

He bit back his own smile in response. Colt was enjoying her company a little too much for his own good. It wasn't just that she was sexy and appealing, and that when the rain had started, his shirt had begun to cling to her like a second skin, or the fact that when she bent over, panting, to take a quick breather, that he thought very nasty things about having her bent over.

He . . . kind of liked her. And he'd be damned if that wasn't a surprise. Beth Ann's personality was cheerful and she was hardworking. The hike hadn't been a fun one—when the rain had returned, so had the mud, and it sucked at their feet at every step. She'd slipped and fallen twice, and he'd helped her back up. But instead of losing her shit about breaking a nail or whining about being tired, she'd simply given a self-conscious little laugh and cracked jokes about her now heel-less Louboutins.

When she'd asked him to show her which way was north, his curiosity had been piqued and he'd taken her aside for a few minutes to show her how to tell which direction was north when there was no sun and only cloud cover. He'd shown her how to make a compass with a needle and a bit of water. Not that he'd needed it, but she'd wanted to know. She'd seemed interested, and so he'd grudgingly demonstrated as they walked which branches made the best firewood, and how to cut pine bark from a tree to cook. She'd gamely taken a bite and laughed anew when he'd made a bitter face at the sour taste.

"I'm glad it wasn't just me, then," she'd exclaimed, and her gleeful delight had made his mouth tug up in a smile.

Dammit. She was supposed to be a spoiled princess. He remembered her in high school, always hanging on the arm of Allan Sunquist, jock and jackass. She'd seemed content back then to be arm candy, and he hadn't had much of an opinion of her. He thought of her when he'd first come back to town—his first sight of her had nearly knocked him flat. She'd been pretty in high school but she was flat-out amazing as an adult. Her blond hair was always perfectly styled, her clothing born to accentuate a long-legged figure. And she'd also been quick to cast him withering look after withering look that had quickly put his back up. He'd learned to avoid her after that.

Where had that vapid blond belle gone? He couldn't ask that, of course.

They moved over the ridge and he offered her a hand to slide down the steep side. She took it, and stepped down after him, her eyes scanning the horizon. "I thought I saw it."

"You did." He pointed off into the trees. "About fifty feet that way."

She gave a fist-pump and grinned at him. "If that thing doesn't have a roof, I'm going to cry," she told him, but her face wore a wide smile that made his lips itch to kiss.

"It has a roof," he told her. "I had to repair it when we moved in."

"Repair it?" she asked as they hiked forward. "So it's been here awhile?"

"A long while," he agreed, pushing past a low-hanging tree branch. "Probably before the emu farm that was here before we bought the place. It's an old hunter's cabin, so we don't use it much, but Brenna likes to keep it stocked in case of client emergency."

She visibly perked despite the rain trickling down over both of them. "Stocked?"

"Just a couple of MREs and some firewood. Nothing to get excited about."

"I'm already excited," she said. "I've never had an MRE and I'm already tired of apples." They'd eaten them along the way, but six apples later, and she was already looking for alternatives.

"We'll have a fire and I'll fix you a meal, then," Colt said. "But you have to ask nicely."

"I am excellent at pleading my case," she said in a silky, teasing voice. "I'm sure we can work something out."

Well damn. He'd just gone instantly hard. Luckily for him, the cabin came into view and she gasped at the sight of it. "We're here," he said.

It was also smaller than he'd remembered, he thought critically, looking at the little thing. The one window was caked with dirt and the old roof sagged on one side.

"I am so thrilled to see that thing right about now," she said with a laugh. "I can't wait to make a fire. It'll be so nice to be warm again. I'm going to have permanent goose bumps at this rate."

A twinge of guilt fired over him. It was his fault she was out here this weekend, just because he was a petty jackass. He squashed the feeling. "Why don't you check it out and I'll start gathering some firewood."

Maybe if he built her a nice big fire, he'd feel a little better about being a lying dick. Worth a shot.

There was wood in the cabin, but he didn't want to clean it out the first night they were there, so he went to forage in the woods. When he returned with an armful of wet tinder, he heard an enormous thwack from inside the cabin.

"Beth Ann?" he called out, warningly. "You okay in there?"

She came out a minute later, holding a stick like a club. Her breath came in rapid gasps and her blue eyes were lit up. "I just killed a rat the size of my foot."

"Probably more like a possum," he said, amused.

"Oh." She panted for a moment, then tilted her head at him. "Should we keep it?"

"Keep it?"

She nodded and wiped a hand over her brow, as if killing a creature had been a big effort. "You know, in case we have to eat it."

"We don't have to eat it," he drawled.

But she bristled at that. "We're surviving, right? You'd make your students eat it, wouldn't you?"

"First of all," he said, dumping the armful of wood. "I wouldn't make my students eat it, because it's most likely diseased. And second of all, we have MREs and we're only going to be stuck here for the weekend. You won't starve."

Her eyes gleamed with a challenging light and she studied her stick. "You don't think I can eat it, do you?"

"I don't think *I* can eat it," he pointed out. "And I've eaten a lot of disgusting things in the name of survival."

"I could eat it," she repeated.

He stepped up to her and looked down into her beautiful, clean face. She was just as pretty without a bit of makeup, he decided just then. Especially with that wicked gleam in her eye. "You tryin' to prove something to me, Beth Ann?"

"I'm tougher than I look," she said up to him, her gaze assessing. "And if I needed to eat a possum, I'd do it."

"Of that, I have no doubt," he drawled. "But I already know you're tougher than you look. You've already proved it."

Her eyes glittered with the compliment and her smile grew even wider, as if he'd just told her that she was the most beautiful woman on earth. "I could kiss you right about now for saying that," she said, smiling up at him.

You could, he thought.

But she didn't make a move. Just smiled.

Figured. Just girly talk. He gave her one of his lazy, "I don't give a shit" smiles and turned away. "I'm going to get some more wood."

Damn. She'd totally blown that moment. She'd been hitting on him hard and he hadn't even taken her up on it. Had she lost her mojo? Was she horribly unsexy? Or did Colt find her revolting? Weak? Both? She knew he was extremely disciplined and spent a lot of time in the woods, honing his craft. Was that why he was ignoring her feeble attempts at flirting?

Ugh. She didn't like to think that he might not respect her or was only tolerating her because he had to. Sure, they had to be together this weekend, but that didn't mean he had to loathe her company, right?

She didn't like to dwell on those sorts of things. That wasn't her style. But if she liked him, she needed to put it out there in the open or else he'd never get the hint.

Still, a little help on his end would not be amiss.

"Stay here. I'll be back," he said, without glancing over at her.

"Don't have to tell me twice," she said, and rubbed her calves. They'd done enough hiking today. The cabin was set up at a prime location, slightly raised off the ground and thick with grass, which meant less mud. She liked less mud.

As he disappeared back into the woods to get another armful of firewood, she gathered rocks to line the fire pit. She didn't know much about fires, but the ones in movies had rocks around the edges, right? So she'd do what she could. Her strappy shoes were just about destroyed from the day's hike anyhow. They'd cut into her feet for hours but she didn't have any other shoes, so it did no good to complain. Too bad she couldn't burn them, she thought with a grimace. She did find a water bucket that she put outside to collect rainwater.

After another armful of wood, Colt knelt beside the ring of rocks and began to set up the wood in a tepee fashion. She bent over to watch. He wasn't really instructing, but even she could pick up on the basics. He'd taken a handful of tinder out from the supplies in the cabin—she hadn't known what to make of the bucket of it, but now she was glad that they had it—and stuck it underneath the tepee of wood. Then, he pulled out an oversized pocket knife and flicked out a piece of square metal.

"What's that?"

"Magnesium. It's a fire starter." He took the other side of the knife and shaved the bar on one side, then began to flick the knife against the magnesium, letting it spark repeatedly until the tinder caught, and began to smoke. The entire process had taken minutes.

"Handy," she commented, impressed. "I should get me one of those."

He glanced over at her, the hint of a smile tugging at his mouth. "Probably not much use in a beauty salon."

"You're right. I'd be much better off arming myself with a curling iron."

Again that flash of an almost smile. It was encouraging. He nodded at the fire, barely more than a little spark in the middle of all that tepee wood. "Get me a little more tinder from the bucket, if you please."

She did so, quickly, and commented, "You guys sure have a lot of supplies in there. I thought it wouldn't be much of anything."

He grunted. "Grant feels that if we have clients on the land, in case of emergency, we need to have the supplies readily available for them to survive with. Last I checked, there's even a tackle box. Don't see why we don't just put a few cans in there with a can opener and a sign that says 'Here, eat this.' "

"You don't approve?"

He shrugged, feeding small twigs to the fire. "Not for me to approve or disapprove. It all boils down to the students. If they're willing to learn, we can teach them. If not, well . . . " He shrugged. "We have MREs and a pile of firewood at the ready."

She sat on her haunches near the fire, watching the smaller bits he fed into the fire take flame and grow. "Yes, but we're using the supplies, too."

He flicked a glance over at her. "We're different."

Not in a bad way, she hoped. As he leaned forward and fed twigs on the fire, she watched his bare chest flex. His chest was rock hard. A hint of a six pack rippled on his abdomen, and his shoulders were big and lean. Allan had stopped exercising in college and had put on a belly. She hadn't minded, of course, but all this lean, brawny muscle in front of her made her pulse flutter and she remembered how nice it was to dig her nails into a man's skin and feel the taut muscle underneath.

All thoughts she kept to herself, of course.

Soon enough, the fire was crackling. Colt dragged two of the larger pieces of wood out and laid them flat, and they served as seats. They curled up near the fire on their logs, and pulled out two of the MREs and a bottle of water to split between the two of them. Colt showed her how to pull the tab on her MRE to heat it. The meal itself was kind of hideous if she stopped and thought about it, but she didn't, and wolfed it down without complaint, noticing Colt did the same.

"Not the tastiest meal," he said casually.

"Better than apples," she said, and leaned over to nudge him with her shoulder teasingly. "Don't knock it."

At her casual brushing against him, he stiffened, and she internally winced. Okay, maybe she was striking out. He just wasn't into her. That was fine, really. They could be friends. Being enemies made hanging out with Miranda and Dane awkward, anyhow.

"So what's the plan?" she said, putting her hands on her knees and looking over at him.

He squinted at the skies. "It's probably going to rain again tonight. We'll stay here, warm up by the fire, and head into the cabin for the evening . . . once I get rid of your possum."

She rubbed her arms. "Sounds just fine to me."

He stood up and headed into the cabin. Well, while he was occupied, she could at least get rid of the shoes that had been paining her so much. For a few hours, anyway. She bent to wiggle one off her foot. The straps were caked with mud and when she pulled it off, she winced with pain, hissing as it felt like part of her skin came with it. Blisters, then. Or she'd rubbed her foot raw. With all that mud on her feet, it was impossible to tell. All she knew was that it hurt.

"Something wrong?" he said, startling her. She turned and looked over her shoulder and he hovered there, frowning down at her.

"Oh . . ." She turned back to her foot and began to pry the other strappy sandal off. "Just questioning my choice in footwear. They seemed fine when I didn't have to slog through a foot of mud cross country. I'm going to be feeling this for weeks."

"Hurts?" he asked.

She nodded.

He moved in front of her and sat on his knees. To her surprise, he reached for her foot and pulled it onto his lap.

She sucked in a breath of surprise at the feel of his strong, callused fingers against her foot, but winced when he grazed one of the raw spots on her foot.

"You tore them up pretty good," he said with a drawl.

"I didn't have another pair of feet to walk on," she said with a laugh, then winced when his fingers swept over her foot and grazed another tender spot.

He didn't seem to like her answer. His mouth compressed as he studied her muddy, dirty feet. "You should have said something."

"There was nothing to be done with it," she said calmly, and pulled her foot out of his grasp. "Complaining about it wouldn't have fixed it."

"Wait here," he said, and got up, heading back into the cabin. He returned a minute later with a water jug.

"Oh, now, you don't have to do that," she protested as he sat in front of her again and grabbed her foot once more, then began to pour water over it to rinse it. His fingers scrubbed away the mud carefully, and Beth Ann's job was to basically sit there, with her foot extended, as this big, muscular soldier cleaned her foot. It was silly. It was awkward.

It was . . . nice. He seemed determined to take care of her. When he placed her foot down and reached for the other, she didn't even protest. It was too enjoyable to get her feet cleaned. "You sure we should be spending the drinking water on that?"

"We'll leave the jug out overnight. It'll refill."

Good enough for her. She gave a sigh of pleasure as he swiped the mud off her ankle and calf, his fingers sliding up to stroke the mud off her smooth leg.

Once that was done, he took her other foot in his hands again and began to carefully knead the muscles.

A small moan of pleasure escaped her throat before she could bite it back.

His head jerked up at that, and he gave her a look of surprise.

"Sorry," she said, blushing. "My feet are, um, sensitive."

That, and she was finely attuned to his touch right about now.

His mouth quirked and she saw a flash of that dimple again. "I'll be careful, then." His fingers rubbed the ache in her foot even as he examined the places where her poor foot had been scraped raw and abused. She bit her lip as he continued to rub and brush his fingers over the skin. It was half massage, half medical examination. It shouldn't have made her pulse beat low in her pussy, sending shockwaves of heat through her body.

He leaned over her foot, then gave a snort of amusement and set it down, reaching for the other one. "You have a heart on your toe."

"Fourth one down," she agreed with a small smile. "It's my signature."

He looked up at her as he continued to stroke and rub her other foot. "Signature?"

Beth Ann shrugged her shoulders. "It sounds kind of stupid, but when I first started doing nails, I put a heart on mine because I liked it. I thought it was cute. Then when girls would come in, they'd ask for the same heart on their nails as mine. I didn't realize it, but apparently that's how people know that women in town get their nails done at my salon." She wiggled her fingers at him, showing the tiny heart on the tip of her short nails. "I like it. I always get a kick out of seeing people out and about and finding that small mark I made on them." God, now she was babbling on about manicures and nails. He was going to think she was the world's ditziest woman. "Kind of stupid, right?"

His thumb pressed into the arch of her foot and sent another pulse of pleasure thrumming through her body. "Nah. Smart branding. It was a clever idea."

Well what do you know. He thought she was clever. Between the foot rubbing and the compliments, she could have expired on the spot.

"All right, peas or carrots?"

She thought for a minute before responding. "I think I'd have to go with carrots."

He nodded, hands behind his head as he stretched out on his back. "I'd have picked that, too. Your turn."

"Hmm." She shifted on the slicker. The ground was still damp, so they had spread it out and used it as a makeshift picnic blanket in front of their fire. They lay there now, staring up at the starry sky overhead. Sometime in the afternoon, the clouds had begun to disappear, and tonight it was clear and brisk and lovely. The fire was warm, and even though the ground wasn't the softest, she was content. She also couldn't think of a thing to ask him. "Boxers or briefs?"

"Briefs. You already saw that."

So she had. They'd been playing versions of this sort of question game for hours. With nothing to do but hang around camp and feed their fire, they'd started on safe topics . . . such as spring or fall. It had gone on for hours.

She should be bored. Miserable. Annoyed as hell that her hair was tangled and she had dirt under her fingernails and her butt was mostly on grass that hadn't quite dried yet. But, looking up at the blanket of stars overhead, feeling the warm fire toasting their legs, and the warm press of Colt's shoulder against her own and she felt . . . curiously anything but miserable. She was enjoying herself. And that was odd.

"You kinda fixated on clothing?" He nudged her with his shoulder.

Only the ones covering his ass. Beth Ann shrugged. "I'm not good at this game."

"Nonsense," he drawled. "My turn. Supergirl or Wonder Woman?"

"Wonder Woman."

"How come?"

Beth Ann thought for a moment. "Because Wonder Woman doesn't live in anyone's shadow. Wonder Woman is her own woman. Supergirl is just Superman's kid sister or something."

"I don't know that she's Superman's sister," Colt said, twirling a blade of grass as he stared up at the sky. "Maybe his hot underage cousin or something."

"You're so into superheroes, then here's your question. Batman or Superman?"

"Batman."

"And why's that?"

Colt grinned up at the stars. "Because Superman's a reporter. Batman's a millionaire playboy. He gets all the pussy."

She rolled her eyes and laughed. "Typical man answer."

He grinned back over at her. "Cake or pie?"

"Cake," she answered promptly. "Definitely cake."

"Why definitely?"

"Because no one ever lets me eat it," she said with a smile up at the stars.

She felt him shift, sit up. His shadow blotted out the stars and he leaned over her, and his dog tags swayed close to her face. "What do you mean, no one lets you eat it?"

Beth Ann glanced over at him, her gaze straying to that bare expanse of chest. He didn't have a single hair on his chest. She liked that—neat, and clean, and allowed every muscle on his chest to show in blatant definition. She liked his tattoo, too. And the dog tags. Okay, she liked everything about him, which surprised her. "Oh, my parents were always very appearance conscious when I was growing up. Instead of a birthday cake, I got a fruit basket." At his snort, she laughed. "It's true. It wouldn't look good for the mayor to have a butterball for a daughter."

"Don't see why it mattered," he said in a low, angry rasp.

"It mattered very much to my parents. You've seen them about town. Have you ever seen a speck of dirt on my father's car? Never." Beth Ann supposed she should be annoyed with them, but their overbearing tendencies had been recently overshadowed by her newfound dislike for Allan. "They're nothing compared to my ex."

"Oh?" He lay back again, but still propped his head up on his bent arm, as if he wanted to watch her in the firelight.

The thought made her cheeks flush a little with excitement. "Allan always wanted me to look my best, of course. Anything other than a salad was greeted with 'You're going to eat all that?' or 'Will you be able to fit into your dress for the mixer on Friday?'

Allan very much wanted me to remain as thin and beautiful as I was in high school, in his eyes. Too many women let themselves go, he said, and he was determined to keep me looking just as perfect as I was then." She gave a bitter laugh. "I told myself that when I broke up with him for the last time, I was going to eat an entire birthday cake in revenge."

"And did you?"

She shook her head. "Nah. I think I was too upset to eat much of anything at the time, and by the time I remembered, it felt like I'd missed the point."

"He was a controlling bastard, wasn't he?"

This was getting uncomfortable. The last thing she wanted was a delicious, beautiful man leaning over her and talking about her ex. "Allan is Allan. He means well, but he has really high standards for everyone's behavior but his own. It took me a while to realize that, and then when I did figure it out, I kept hoping he'd change. He didn't, and I realized that I didn't trust him anymore." She looked over at him. "I've decided that I'm not having another relationship without trust."

He grunted.

She couldn't tell if that was agreement or disapproval, and felt the need to explain a bit more. "But no, I was oblivious to Allan's true nature for a long time. Sometimes we just have blinders to how certain people are, because we want them to be how they are in our minds. Don't you have anyone in your life like that? Your family?"

"Nope," he said abruptly. "We're not talking."

She remembered his big clan of brothers on the edge of town, all living in a doublewide. She saw one of the Waggoners every now and then, but she didn't run in the same circles as them. Most people didn't. She remembered the father as a Nascar-shirt-wearing, tobacco-spitting junkyard owner. "Ah," she said delicately.

His finger brushed her forehead, nudging aside a stray lock of her bangs. It sent a skitter of pleasure through her body. "If it makes you feel any better, I always thought Allan was a dick, even back in high school."

She laughed at that, smiling up at him. The moment felt so intimate—she didn't want to keep talking about Allan. "Let's just say that I don't regret our years together, but I also don't regret breaking up with him."

"Kinda thought I'd come back and see you still with him, and driving a minivan full of kids."

She'd always viewed herself with that, too. Funny how life worked out. Beth Ann's breath stopped for a moment as his finger brushed the lock of hair back to her hairline and lightly skimmed her brow. This was . . . incredibly sexy and intense all at once. And she felt like she had to make a little confession to him. "When I was with Allan, I was so focused on being the perfect girl—the perfect girlfriend, the perfect daughter, the perfect friend—that I didn't realize that I wasn't doing anything for myself. Allan didn't want me to work, so I stayed home and made him lunches and kept the house clean. And I volunteered for book clubs and charities and ran fund-raisers because he liked that. And at some point, I realized, I stopped being me." Her hand went to her heart, and her throat rasped just a little in remembrance. "I wasn't Beth Ann anymore. Not to anyone. People didn't see me as Beth Ann—they just saw me as that nice girl that Allan was going to someday make an honest woman out of. Not *me*. An extension of him. And it was partially my fault, because I'd been so focused on building him up in everyone's eyes. All my hobbies were designed to make him look good."

Colt said nothing, simply watched her, his fingertip still smoothing stray hairs back on her hairline.

"Do you know," she said with a wry twist of her mouth, "that when I broke up with Allan for the last time, people in town kept coming up to me to give me advice. At first I thought it was sweet that they were so concerned with my happiness. And then I realized that they were giving me advice because they'd felt I'd done something wrong. That I'd been the one that somehow screwed up. And that with their guidance, they were sure they could make him love me again." The laugh that escaped her throat was bitter.

"Does it help much if I say I always hated everyone in town, too?"

A tiny laugh escaped her, and she smothered it with a hand. "No. Well, a little. I'm sorry to unload on you about Allan."

"Don't be," he said, his voice a low, soft drawl. "I always thought he was a jackass, but I didn't realize how much of one."

She smiled and shook her head. "It's not his fault. Or I should say, it's only half his fault. He made me half a person because I let him. After we broke up, I decided I was going to be Beth Ann from now on. I was going to do things that people didn't expect Allan's fiancée to do. I was going to say what I thought, and do what I wanted."

A tiny flash of dimple appeared in his cheek. "And have you?"

"I opened my salon," she admitted. "Everyone thought I

should go to college, but I didn't want to spend four years waiting for my life to start again. I wanted to start it right away, and I'd been taking beautician classes on the side. Hair and makeup has always been something I was good at, and I loved making other people feel special. It just seemed like the right move for me—to open a salon and run my own business, doing my own thing. Not dependent on anyone for anything. My father didn't approve of his oldest daughter being something as common as a hair-dresser. He thinks 'trophy wife' is an acceptable occupation. And I thought Allan was going to have a fit over that. He didn't think I could do it. But I am, and I'm doing just fine," she said proudly. "And I dress how I want, not how I thought Allan's fiancée should dress."

His fingers slid to the strap of her dress. His T-shirt was hanging on a hastily erected frame, drying near the fire. She was wearing her dress, of course, but for the first time today, she was acutely aware of how much skin it exposed. And it was exciting.

"This?" he asked, and tugged on the strap.

She could have sworn his voice dropped a husky note that made her pulse flutter with longing. "This," she agreed. "I'm going to be me, and if it takes twenty years, I'm going to do all kinds of things that no one would expect from me."

His fingertip lightly traced the skin under the thin strap of her dress. "Such as?" he said huskily.

Her entire world now seemed to be focused on that graze of his finger over her skin. It felt wonderful and ticklish and exciting and utterly alarming all at once. Beth Ann suddenly felt like a teenager on her first date again.

And she rather liked the feeling. "All kinds of things," she whispered.

"Like what?" He grinned down at her. "What does Bluebonnet not expect sweet Beth Ann Williamson to do?"

She looked up at him leaning over her, beautiful and hard in the shadows, his face all angles. Her body was aching with need—need that hopefully wasn't one-sided. She gathered her courage—she'd never know unless she asked. "I've never had a one-night stand."

FIVE

Colt stared down at her, surprised. His erection was rock hard in his pants, yet he paused. What the hell was she thinking? Beth Ann was beautiful, and funny, and so incredibly sweet she made his entire body ache with need.

And here she was propositioning him?

Below him, she licked her lips and looked suddenly uncertain. "I'm guessing that request was not a flattering one?"

What, was she crazy? "Ain't that," he said softly. "Just trying to figure out what's going through this thing right about now." He tapped a fingertip to her temple.

He liked her. He liked her a lot. But he sure as hell didn't want to be part of some revenge plot to get even with her ex-boyfriend.

Even if he did hate the guy.

Beth Ann suddenly looked chagrined. "You can tell me no, you know. You won't hurt my feelings."

God, she thought he was turning her down?

"I mean, I don't normally proposition men," she began in a rush.

He put a finger over her lips, silencing her. "I just want to make sure . . ." Well, hell. How to put it delicately. "That this isn't something you're going to regret."

She gave him a wide-eyed look. "I'll regret it if you're lousy at it."

He snorted, amused. "You know what I mean. Didn't you say you didn't want a relationship without trust?"

"This is a one-night stand. That's different."

So she wanted no-strings sex with him? Avoid the relationship thing entirely? He stared at her dubiously.

"I know what you're trying to ask me," she said, and reached for him. Her fingers danced along his shoulder, and slid down his arm, tracing a vein in his biceps, and he was effectively distracted once more. "You want to make sure I'm not doing this to get back at Allan."

"The thought did cross my mind," he admitted. He wanted to touch her back, explore her the way she was exploring him. But until she told him what he wanted to hear, it was a no-go. He wasn't that big of a dick.

"It's not about Allan," she said softly. "It's about me, wanting things and actually going after them instead of caring what others think."

"And you want a one-night stand?" Damn, if his dick got any harder, he was going to lose his mind.

"I want you," she admitted. "We can start with one night and see how it turns out. But if you're not interested, let me know."

"You slept curled up against my hard-on last night, and you're going to sit here and tell me that you're not sure if I'm interested?" He could feel the smile stretching his mouth. "Platonic, not dead, remember?"

Her hand slid to his tattoo, and she brushed her fingertips over it. "So is that a yes?"

Of course it was a yes. Hell, he wasn't stupid. A beautiful woman that he found himself intensely attracted to was offering him no-strings-attached sex. Of course he was interested. He'd been thinking about her mouth all day, or how it'd feel to have her legs wrap around his hips and sink deep into her warmth. Feel her pussy tighten around him as she came.

He'd been thinking about that sort of shit all night, even as she talked about peas and carrots and things like that.

But she looked flustered, and he had to admit that he liked seeing her a little off guard. "We haven't even kissed yet," he teased her. "Don't you want to try before you buy?"

"We can start with a kiss," she said, almost eagerly. Her hands went to the sides of his neck and she pulled him down toward her slowly, not wasting any time. But just before she pulled him in for the kiss, she hesitated, her nose brushing against his lightly, as if trying to make sure this was, in fact, what he wanted.

He'd just have to show her, then. He leaned in, closing the distance between the two of them, and brushed his lips against hers. They were warm and soft, just barely slick from when she'd licked them in her nervousness.

At the feel of his lips against hers, he felt her body tense slightly, and he liked that. He kissed her gently, simply pressing his lips against hers in small, polite kisses. Because that wasn't what she'd expect from him, and he liked surprising her. Her lips began to part a little more under each kiss, and on the last one, he grazed his tongue against the parted seam of her mouth. He felt her intake of breath, felt her fingers tighten against his neck. And he leaned in to press another soft kiss against her mouth.

This time it was her tongue that stroked against his lips. It shot a bolt of heat straight to his cock, and he suddenly wanted to push her back in the dirt and fuck the living daylights out of her, until she was crying out his name, and she'd lost track of everything but his cock thrusting inside her.

His tongue found hers, and he stroked into her mouth. When she made a small noise of pleasure in her throat, he slanted his head slightly and began to kiss her even more fiercely. If they were going to be together tonight, she wasn't going to think of anyone but him.

He was going to fucking *ruin* her for Allan and any other man, he decided. And he realized that was a dumbass territorial thing to be thinking, and he didn't give a shit. He thrust his tongue into her mouth, mimicking the thrust he wanted to do into her sweet warmth, and he felt a full-body tremble sweep over her.

That was more like it.

He broke off the kiss and noted with pleasure that she'd been reluctant to do so. Her mouth lingered on his even as he pulled away, as if she craved his mouth on her own. He liked that. Her eyes opened and she had a glazed, almost sleepy look that was incredibly sexy. Her mouth was full and pouting and wet with his kiss, too.

"How was that for a test drive?"

Beth Ann gave a small sigh of pleasure and smiled up at him. "I'm pretty convinced, but I might need another round before I decide for sure."

And her gaze fell back to his mouth.

He didn't need to be told twice. He kissed her again, this time lingering on her full lips. He tugged at her lower one, teasing the plumpness with his mouth until he'd had enough, and licked deep into her mouth again. This time, she whimpered, and he could have sworn her hips rose up off the ground. Nice. She was responsive. He liked that about her.

"And now?" he murmured against her mouth.

"Sold."

"Good," he replied, and placed his hand back on her shoulder. That thin, slinky strap to her dress was tormenting him—had been tormenting him all day. He slid his fingers under it, feeling the softness of her skin even as he dipped low for another kiss. She arched under his touch.

He kissed her until she was breathless and panting, making small little noises of excitement every time his tongue thrust against her own. He moved down to her chin, tasting her there, then traveled along her jaw. He moved to the shell of her ear, and heard her gratifying intake of breath when his tongue traced it.

"Oh, that feels good," she murmured, her fingers finding his hair and rubbing the short, stubbled hair on the back of his head, where his hair was closely shaved.

His hand slid down, skimming along her thigh. Not heading straight for her pussy, but exploring her legs, the smooth feel of them, the curve of her knee. He lifted his head as he touched her, watching her face.

Her eyes had fluttered shut, but she was incredibly expressive, and he loved observing every flicker of desire flash across her face. Loved watching that flush sweep over her cheeks when his fingertips grazed the inside of her thigh. That flick of disappointment when he moved back to her knee again.

Oh yeah, he liked seeing that disappointment. Because it meant that she wanted this as badly as he did. He did it a second time, just to watch that fleeting glimpse of frustration pass over her face.

Her knee nudged against his fingers, and he knew she was spreading her legs wider. "Want to lose the dress?" he asked her huskily.

"If you promise to lose your pants."

That he could do. He stood up abruptly, watched her prop up on her elbows so she could watch him undress in the firelight, her lips gleaming from his kisses, her legs sprawled open as if waiting for him. He groaned at the sight of her, so eager, and rubbed his hand against the front of his pants. "You are fucking beautiful."

She smiled up at him. "Don't distract me. I want to see this."

He undid his belt—pretty much ruined from the rain anyhow—and flung it aside. His hand went to his zipper and he noticed her eyes flash with excitement. He slowly tugged it down, and dropped his trousers. Her eyes went wide with appreciation at the sight of his erection jutting from his briefs. "Very nice," she said lightly.

So he dropped his briefs, too.

Her gasp of delight turned into a purr of pleasure. She sat up, and her hands reached for him. "Your cock . . . is gorgeous." Her hands reached for him, and then she pulled back, clasping them to her chest, as if concerned. "May I?"

He gave a short, clipped nod. Colt wasn't stupid. If she wanted to put her hands all over him, he'd gladly let her. The breath in his chest went tight as she sat on her knees and lightly brushed her fingertips over his cock. It bucked against her touch, and it took everything Colt had not to grab her by the hair and force her mouth down on it, fucking her lips and mouth the way he'd daydreamed about all day today as they'd walked.

Time for that later. So he gritted his teeth and thought about other things while she explored him.

"It's so . . . thick."

A guy could get used to a girl saying things like that. "You'll like how thick it is," he told her, unable to resist brushing the hair off her shoulder and exposing those thin dress straps again. Those straps were just fucking with his head. He was going to get rid of them, and soon.

As if sensing his thoughts, Beth Ann sat back on her haunches and smiled up at him. "Deal's a deal." She tugged at the hem of her dress and pulled the entire thing over her head. As he watched, her breasts were revealed. Small but tight, he stared at them, then reached out to brush his fingers over one erect nipple. "Gorgeous," he growled. "Thought you were beautiful before, but this is the prettiest thing I've ever seen."

She smiled up at him, and gave a shy little laugh. Was she . . . nervous? At being with him?

He wondered if she'd ever slept with anyone other than that

dick Allan. He didn't want to think about that cockroach touching her. Colt took her by the hands and lifted her to her feet.

"It's not too late to back out," he told her softly, brushing a stray lock of hair from her shoulder.

She gave a small, anxious chuckle and reached down to grasp his cock in her hand. "Something tells me that this part of you won't understand if I say no."

He took her hand and placed it over his heart. "This part of me will, though."

Her mouth trembled a little and she smiled up at him. "I want this," she admitted. "I'm just a little . . ."

"Nervous?"

"Can you tell?"

Oh yeah, he could tell. But he suspected she'd be mortified to hear that. So he said, "Nah." And leaned in to kiss her again. Her hand squeezed on his cock as his tongue slicked into her mouth and he groaned. "We gotta kiss like this more often," he said against her mouth. "Your hands on my cock and your tongue in my mouth."

"Oh?" she said breathlessly, and squeezed his cock again. "Feel good? Why don't you tell me about it?"

"I'll show you," he said, and slid his hand to the front of her small thong, and slipped his fingers under the fabric. She was slick and wet, and his entire body jolted at her gasp of surprise. He parted the lips of her pussy with his fingers and slid them to the front of her sex, searching for her clit. When he lit upon it, her fingers spasmed on his cock and she whimpered.

"Feel good?" he asked, unable to stop licking at her mouth. The woman was so fucking erotic.

"Y-yes," she breathed, her voice coming out in little gasps and whimpers. He leaned in to kiss her again, and when he lightly pressed a kiss against her full, parted mouth, he tapped his finger against her clit. Her lips parted in response, even as her fingers clenched around his cock, subconsciously squeezing and milking it as she responded to her own pleasure. She was so slick and hot that he wanted to bury his face there. Watch her responses when his mouth was deep in her pussy. Would he get those gasps of delight that he was getting right now? He couldn't wait to find out.

He flicked at her clit again, and she nearly buckled against him.

"Why don't we lay you back down on the jacket?" he said softly, giving that sweet pussy a little pat before releasing it. He could have sworn she looked disappointed when his fingers left her body.

But she nodded and slid back down to the raincoat, lying back down. Her tight little breasts jutted into the air, her nipples like pink pearls on her chest, her tangled hair like a cloud around her head. God. He wanted to run his mouth all over her body.

But first, he had to search the goddamn shed for condoms. They sometimes kept them in the first-aid kits, since they made great water skins in an emergency, but Colt was pretty sure that he hadn't seen an extra med kit in the cabin. Damn. Of all the things to be out of. They had goddamn buckets of tinder and not one fucking med kit?

"What's wrong?" she asked, the sensual, glazed look flicking off her face again, replaced with uncertainty. He immediately wanted to push her down and kiss her until it returned, but he needed this first.

"Condoms," he said, and ran a hand down his face in frustration, feeling the stubble growing in there.

"Oh," she said, and that soft, secretive smile lit her face again. "I have a whole box of them."

He looked down at her, eyes narrowing. "What?"

She waved a hand in the air. "That QuestMaster party. When you paid at the gate, they gave you a bottle of rum and condoms. Most messed up party favors ever."

"The next time I see one of those guys, I'm going to hug him," he declared. "Where'd you leave the box?"

"In my bag," she said with a wiggle, and her fingertips slid to her breasts, playing with her nipples.

He paused to stare down at her, dumbfounded, as she touched herself. Fuck, that was gorgeous. He wanted to be doing that for her, though. So he headed quickly to the cabin and got the box. Sure enough. It was soggy from the rain, but the foil-sealed packets inside were intact. He grabbed a few and headed back out to the fire, where Beth Ann was waiting. Sexy, sensual, fucking amazing Beth Ann that he was going to fuck all over that rain slicker in about five minutes.

Provided he could last that long. He was incredibly hard and aching just thinking about what she'd feel like, the tip of his cock wet with need.

He tossed the condoms down on the ground nearby and moved back to her. Beth Ann's arms lifted as he knelt beside her, and her hands caressed his shoulders, then glided over his pecs. She seemed to enjoy touching him. That was good, seeing as how he almost nutted every time he touched her.

"Found them?" she asked breathlessly.

He gave a curt nod. "No more interruptions." And with that, he kissed her until she was breathless all over again, until she was making those soft noises in her throat. He pulled away for a moment, gazing down at her, at the flush on her face, the tangle of her hair.

"What is it?" she whispered.

"Just looking at you. You're mighty nice to look at."

The smile returned to her mouth and she arched her back under him. "I taste pretty good, too."

"Let's find out," he whispered huskily, and dipped down to taste one beaded nipple. Her little gasp of shock was incredibly erotic. And fuck, but she tasted sweet. The tiny bud was tight and hard, and he licked it, enjoying the feel of it against his tongue, and her little panting responses. His hand moved to her other breast and plumped it, cupping the slight weight and then skimming his thumb over the curve of it.

She moaned and arched underneath him. "Colt . . . your mouth."

"Like it?" He lightly kissed the tip of her breast, and then slid to the valley between them, nuzzling the soft flesh there, before moving to her other breast and nipping the tip of it, ready to give it just as much attention as its companion.

Beth Ann's nails raked over his shoulders, digging into his skin, and she whimpered. Firelight flickered over her creamy skin, and her bellybutton was dipped in shadow. He suddenly wanted to touch it, and brushed his knuckle over it, even as he scored her nipple with his teeth again.

Her hips lifted in response. "Please," she murmured. "Colt,

please. I need you." As he watched, her hand began to slide down to her pussy, to tease her clit as he feasted on her breasts.

"Naughty girl," he murmured, and his hand moved to cover hers.

She froze in place, her hand fluttering under his as she tried to pull away. "Sorry," she said, and her voice was mortified.

"Don't be sorry," he said, and leaned in to kiss her once more, wanting that anxiety to disappear from her face. With his hand, he pushed her fingers between her legs. "Just wanted to remind you that this is a joint effort, darlin'."

His fingers pushed against hers, and together, they parted the hot, wet folds of her sex, delving deep. She inhaled sharply and her hand relaxed under his. She was going to let him guide her. Her eyes were open wide, and she stared up at him, even as he kissed that full, delicious mouth.

Colt pressed her fingers over her clit. Pushed, and then stroked back and forth, rolling the small nub with the movement. Her eyes fluttered shut for a moment and an aching, intense look swept over her face. "Oh, sweet lord."

He gently moved her fingers back and forth, his fingers using hers to stroke that sensitive bud. Her mouth parted, her eyes shut, her head tilted back as he rubbed her clit slowly, surely, evenly. The movements were measured and precise, and he knew that would drive her crazy over time as she wanted more, needed more. And fuck if she wasn't beautiful in her intensity. He watched her, writhing, hips raising in response to each measured stroke of his fingers. Her breath was coming in sharp little pants of need. He leaned down and kissed her neck, enjoying the tremors that rocked through her body. Her legs had fallen open wide, and she lay splayed beneath him, totally open to his touch, his cock—whatever he wanted to do to her, she'd let him. He liked the thought of that.

Her hand jerked under his, her fingers flexing. She made a soft, little circling motion with her fingers over her clit, and he felt her body stiffen. Ah. She was going to come. He wanted to watch this. Colt raised his head and his fingers pressed down harder on hers, and he mimicked the swirling motion she'd done. Her breath caught. He forced her to rub harder, faster, and then she bit her lip. She inhaled sharply, then exhaled hard, and the circles she was rubbing grew tighter, and harder, her eyes squeezed shut. He felt her legs tighten a little, felt her quiver, and then she let out a long, slow breath, a sigh of relief. Her legs relaxed and her fingers stopped their rubbing.

She'd come while biting her lip and being entirely silent. Another habit she'd picked up from good ol' Allan? He didn't want that. He wanted her screaming his name to the stars. So he continued to rub, enjoying that her body trembled with an aftershock as he stroked her fingers over her sensitive clit again. Her hand tried to pull away, but he kept it there, and rubbed again. Again, another aftershock trembled through her. Beth Ann's eyes opened, and she gave him a dazed look of surprise, and he leaned in and kissed her hard, possessively, even as he continued to rub her clit. This time he went straight for the small, circling motions she seemed to like. Her hips tilted in response and she moaned softly.

That was better. "Keep rubbing yourself, darlin'."

"But, Colt . . . I—"

"Came. I know." He kissed her again to silence her protest, and continued to rub. She squirmed a little under him. "You can do it again for me. Keep rubbing."

Her fingers twitched, and then she took up the rubbing again, her gaze flicking over him with hot need. He liked that she watched him while she rubbed herself, as if she was thinking about how he'd feel deep inside her. And fuck if he wasn't thinking about that now, too.

"Keep rubbing," he rasped. His hand slid away from hers and his fingers trailed down the slick valley of her pussy, to where she was silky and damp with need. Her sharp little breaths jerked as he rubbed his finger against the opening of her sex, teasing her. She was so wet and hot underneath him. He slid a finger in, and was surprised to find her tighter than he'd thought. Had she not had sex in a long time? Oddly enough, that pleased him. He stroked his finger deep inside her and was rewarded with her little gasp. With his next stroke, he added another finger and then another, stretching her. His cock was thick, and he didn't want to hurt her.

He felt a tremor pulse through her legs, her pussy. "Colt," she gasped. "I'm going to—"

He thrust his fingers inside her again, hard, and she gave a small, broken moan in response, her hand trembling over her clit. The tremor rocked through her body and he knew she'd come again. The moan had been an improvement, at least. Her hand slowed, her fingers toying with her gleaming, wet flesh. He leaned down to taste the slickness and she moaned anew at the feel of his mouth and tongue flicking against her fingertips, her pussy. She was delicious and so, so wet.

"Keep rubbing," he told her.

Her small moan sounded like a protest. He slid his fingers from her body, reached for the condoms and tore one off. He ripped it open and rolled it down the length of his cock, noticing that her gaze followed his movements, suddenly hungry again. Her fingers began to circle once more, her eyes avid as she watched him. As he looked down at her, she licked her lips, and the sight of that pink tongue drove him insane with need. He grabbed her by the waist and hauled her up against him, pulled her in for a searing, hot kiss. She kissed him back, and her hand slid away.

"No," he said softly. "Keep touching yourself."

"But—" The look she gave him was clouded with desire and confusion.

"Turn around," he said. "On your knees. Cheek on the ground. And keep touching yourself."

She trembled at that, but obeyed. His hands slid over her beautiful, soft skin as she turned, presenting him with a full, lush ass. He couldn't resist the urge and lightly slapped one full buttock. She jumped.

"Still touching yourself?" He slid a hand to her damp sex, feeling for her fingers, and was pleased to notice that she was.

"Yes," she said breathlessly.

"Good," he murmured. His fingers moved over the small of her back—fuckin' beautiful, that little spot of flesh—and gently pushed her downward. "You ready, darlin'?"

As he watched, she nodded and pressed her cheek to the rain slicker. Her entire body quivered, and she was biting her lip again.

He moved behind her and with his knee, gently nudged her own apart. "I can't see your face this way, darlin'. You're going to have to tell me if it's good or not, okay? We won't go on until it's good for you."

"O-okay," she breathed, and shifted a little, parting her legs even more for him. Good girl.

His hands rested on her ass for a moment—so sweet and plump. Damn, she had a nice ass. Even though his cock was killing him and he wanted nothing more in the world than to sink it deep inside her, he forced himself to stop, stroking the smooth flesh of her buttocks. So damn lovely. She liked that, too, judging by the soft little sound of pleasure that came from her throat. He ran one hand down her spine. "You still touching yourself, darlin'?"

"Yes," she said, and the sound came out as a half-breathless sob. Her hips rolled a little at the response, as if seeking his cock. His hand went to the base of his shaft and he guided the head against her wet, waiting heat. Her entrance was slick and so hot that he nearly came right then. His fingers clenched against her ass. Her hips did that little roll again and she moaned.

He stopped.

"Colt, please," she said in a low voice.

"Tell me what you need, Beth Ann." It was sheer torture not sinking deep inside her, but he wanted to hear her voice. Wanted to know that she was with him all the way. So he nudged the crown of his cock against her tight opening and waited.

She wiggled below him, another moan rising from her throat. "Please . . ."

He tapped a hand lightly on her ass. "Tell me."

"Push," she panted. "Push deep."

He pushed in, groaning low in his own throat as her tight warmth threatened to suck him deeper. One nice, hard thrust and he'd be seated to the hilt inside her, her pussy so tight and hot around him. Fuck. Why was he torturing her—and himself—with this?

"Deeper, Colt," she moaned, reminding him. Ah, yes. There was nothing fucking sweeter than her moaning his name. And since she'd asked so damn nicely, he pushed deeper, until he was about halfway in. His teeth were gritted with restraint, and he gave her a shallow thrust, only to feel her entire pussy spasm around him. And oh fuck, that felt so good that his eyes nearly rolled back in his head.

"Deeper, Colt," she panted. "Oh please . . . deep . . . hard . . ."

"Still touching yourself?"

"Y-yes," she sobbed. "Oh, Colt . . ."

"What is it?" he asked, thrusting shallowly again, torturing her with only a taste of what he could give her. "Tell me what you need."

"Colt, please." Her voice quivered and then a moment later, she said, "I need you in me."

He growled and slammed deep into her, pushing all the way in, hard. His breath exited his throat in a hiss. Goddamn. She felt amazing. Her pussy clenched around him like a hot little fist, squeezing his cock. She was incredibly tight. "Like that, darlin'?"

She gasped, inhaling sharply.

He froze, worried he'd hurt her. She was so tight.

"Again," she moaned. "Again, Colt. Please!"

His hands dug into the flesh of her soft hips and he growled low in his throat, thrusting hard once more. She felt so good he wanted to keep thrusting and thrusting until he filled her up. Pound into her until she was seeing stars, blissed out of her mind.

She cried out again, and this time he realized she was calling out his name.

And fuck if that didn't cause him to nearly lose it. He slammed into her, over and over again. Thrusting hard. Pounding into her.

And she kept repeating his name, her voice broken and gasping, every word moaned almost incoherently. And she didn't stop moaning. "Again, Colt. Again. Oh God, again."

As if he was *ever* fucking stopping. He thrust into her, his entire body moving with the force of each pumping thrust, and he watched her hips rising to meet his thrusts, her blond hair spread out on the rain slicker, her eyes squeezed shut as she moaned, and she still rubbed and rubbed between her hips, even as he thrust into her. So he thrust harder, and faster, because he wanted to fuck her until she couldn't do anything but yell his name.

And then she screamed. Her pussy clenched around him, milking him tight, and her entire body shuddered. Her hips jerked—she was coming. And she was screaming.

And it was the hottest fucking thing he'd ever heard. His own orgasm roared through him. His cock jerked deep inside her and he bit out her name as he came, his release pouring forth with a rush. He ground his hips into her plush ass as he came, letting the wave of sensation carry him.

Damn.

That had been intense. Amazing. Mind-blowingly hot. He ran a hand over her ass one last time, and then slipped out of her, turning away to roll off the condom and toss it into the fire.

When he turned back to look at her, she was still in the same place, sprawled, her ass in the air, as if she didn't have the energy to move.

He chuckled at that. He'd fucked her into a stupor. He liked that. Colt lay down beside her and pulled her against him, and she snuggled close, still breathing as hard as he was.

"You okay?" he asked, panting. He ran a hand down his chest. He was all sweaty. Too bad there wasn't a shower—or a river nearby. Of course, he couldn't take her to the damn river. She'd know he'd been lying to her, and then he'd have some serious explaining to do.

"I think I died just then," she said in an exhausted voice. "Died and all my bones turned to water."

He leaned in and kissed her temple. "You're welcome."

She thumped his chest lightly, seeming to recover a little. "You're so arrogant."

"Of course I am," he said, just a bit smug as his hand ran over her ass and cupped one cheek, tugging her even closer to him. Her skin, even sweaty, was as silky as the rest of her. He wanted all of it against him. "You were screaming my name just a minute ago and calling me your 'sweet lord.' It's enough to bolster any man's ego."

"Oh lord," she said, burying her face against him.

"There you go again."

"I'm so sorry," she said, cupping a hand over her mouth. "I didn't realize I was being so loud. I tried to stay quiet."

"Quiet's for nuns. If I want you to be silent, I'll give you something big and hard to shove into your mouth."

She laughed and thumped him again. "You're terrible."

"I know." He wouldn't mind seeing how much noise she

made with his dick in her mouth anyhow. Maybe tomorrow, if she was amenable. He certainly was, and he'd be more than willing to reciprocate. "So," he said, running a hand up and down her bare arm. "As one-night stands go, how'd that do?"

"It pretty much rocked my world," she said dreamily.

Fuckin' right it did.

Her hand slid to his stomach and stole to his side, and then he felt her fingers dance along his ass. "Night's not over yet, though."

"We seem to be on the same page, darlin'," he said with a grin.

She smiled and snuggled close, and he tucked her chin against his chest, content to hold her for a few minutes and let his dick recover. That had been some of the best sex he'd ever had. And she was right; the night was young yet. Damn, but this was turning out to be a good day, rain and all.

Not what he'd expected from the weekend, but he'd been more than happy to be proven wrong about a great many things.

"You want to go inside the cabin?" he whispered against her hair. "We might be able to find a clear spot next to the woodpile."

She didn't answer.

He glanced down and saw her eyes were closed, her breathing regular, her mouth slightly slack with sleep. Her hand still clasped his ass, as if he were a prized possession she was afraid to let go of, even in her sleep.

And even when he chuckled, he didn't wake her up.

Well, plenty of time for morning-after sex, too, he supposed.

SIX

Beth Ann was cold. She'd been so warm moments before, and so she turned in her sleep, reaching for the warm body that had been there before. "Colt?"

"Here, darlin'," he said softly, and then she was pulled back against a warm, broad chest. Her hands slid between them, instinctively looking to slide into the warmth between their bodies, and encountered his cock, hard and erect.

That caused her to wake up. Beth Ann opened her eyes, blinked, and stared up into Colt's angular face.

"Mornin'," he said, and that dimple appeared under two days' worth of beard stubble.

She blushed, realizing she still had her hand curled around his cock, and her bare breasts were pressed against his chest. Her nipples hardened even as she thought about it. "Hi."

He leaned in to kiss her, and she grimaced, turning her head. "I probably have morning breath."

"Here," he said, and reached over her to grab a bottle of water. She took it from him and swished her mouth, and then swallowed a couple mouthfuls before handing it back to him.

"All better?" he asked.

She nodded.

"Good." And he rolled onto her, bearing her down to the ground. His mouth was on hers and his tongue thrust into her mouth, claiming her quickly, and she sighed in response. Oh God. The man should not be able to kiss like that. She should be feeling dirty and ashamed this morning. She'd done something cheap and tawdry and she'd jumped this beautiful, hard man . . . and she wanted to do it again. As he sucked on her lower lip, she moaned, remembering last night and all the delicious, naughty things they'd done.

That had been amazing. Sex with Allan had never even been close to that, and he'd been her first—and only. With him, sex was usually missionary, and only minutes long. When they'd been in high school, he'd taken time with her breasts and to kiss her, but as the years had worn on, it had basically turned into an endless string of quickies. He'd give her a cursory kiss, a flick on the breasts, and then fuck her for an unexciting minute or two, and then they'd go on with their day.

She hadn't realized until last night just how much she'd missed being kissed and teased. Her hand stroked his cock, and she was pleased with the way he groaned against her mouth. "Someone's awake and alert this morning," she said softly.

"Reveille," he muttered, moving to her ear and licking the shell of it.

When his tongue dipped into her ear, it shot a bolt of pleasure through her body and she whimpered. "Reveille?"

"Up at dawn," he murmured.

"Every dawn? Lucky me." Her hands moved to his buttocks and then up his back, and she hooked one leg behind him, trying to pull him down against her.

He groaned, still kissing her fiercely. His beard stubble scratched her face, but she didn't care. Her fingers slid to the front of his chest and she plucked at his nipples, liking how flat and hard they were. Just like the rest of him. When she raised her hips, she felt the hard length of him against her pussy and she suddenly wanted him deep inside her again.

"Wait," he said, and fumbled for something nearby. "Condoms," he said between kisses.

"Hurry," she said softly. Her fingertips grazed his nipples. She didn't want to lose this moment. She wanted to make love to him and go back to that place of madness and desire all over again. She wanted to see if he could take her there again this morning, or if it'd be disappointing now that the edge had been taken off her desire.

She heard the crinkle of the wrapper, and then he shifted, rolling the condom on. He continued to kiss her, though his kiss had become a little distracted, turning into small nibbles against her lips instead.

And then he was over her, sliding between her widespread thighs. Oh. They were going to do missionary, then? She experienced a stab of disappointment . . . that just as quickly vanished as he pushed deep into her, seating to the hilt. She gasped, her hands clasping his slim hips. Oh God. He was buried deep so fast, and the stretch of his girth had given her a little tight twinge, but now that he was deep inside her, it was . . . really nice. He leaned down and kissed her again, deep, hard, and oh, she liked that. And he thrust.

She could feel every inch of him sinking deep inside her. "Oh," she murmured, half surprised. That had been so *good*.

Over her, he gave her a wicked, half smile, his dog tags fluttering in her face. That look on his face almost said "I know," and then he thrust again. On the third thrust, she raised her hips, and felt every inch of him slide out, and then bury deep again. And oh . . . that was really good.

"How's that little clit of yours?" he whispered against her, kissing her throat as he thrust again.

She gasped. That was such a . . . direct thing to say. He seemed to know just how to shock her. It aroused her at the same time. "I . . . I don't know."

"Why don't you touch it and find out?"

A full-body tremble swept through her. God, that was so naughty. It was daylight, and he could see all of her. Was he going to watch? Her eyes slid open even as her hand slid down between the two of them, brushing through the wet curls. She pushed between the lips of her sex, finding her clit, and gasped at how sensitive it felt. She must have tried to rub the darn thing off last night. Beth Ann could feel her cheeks flushing. "Tender," she said in a low voice.

His gaze watched her face. "What if you touch it lightly?" Thrust.

She gave a low whimper, and his eyes gleamed.

"Touch yourself, Beth Ann," he said, and she did. She stroked the little nub with gentle fingers, and sensation raced through her hips. She clenched tight around him, and he groaned in response. "Just like that." He sat up on the next thrust, and tugged her forward, so he was sitting up as she lay in the ground, resting on his legs, her hips cradled in his lap.

So he could watch her touch herself as he fucked her. Her entire body flushed even as her nipples got harder and tighter at the thought. His next thrust was shallower thanks to her tilted position, but the gleam in his eyes told her he was still enjoying himself. Her hand moved back down to her sex and she stroked her clit lightly, and bit her lip.

"Don't," he said. "Don't bite it back. I want you to tell me how it feels."

She froze under him. "I . . ."

"Is your clit soft?" he asked, his voice husky, his gaze intense. Oh mercy, she loved that intense look on his face. As if he could devour her whole with his eyes.

"Soft," she admitted, and stroked the pad of her finger over her clit again, moaning when he gave another shallow thrust.

"And how does it feel?"

She swallowed, hard. Forced herself to squeak the words out. "Like . . . lightning racing through me . . . when you thrust."

"Keep touching yourself, then," he murmured. "Until you come. Want to watch you."

She stroked her clit again. It was swollen to touch, so she was delicate and light with her fingers, but it was also extremely sensitive. She whimpered when he thrust again, and rubbed harder.

"Touch your nipples," he said, and she did. She flicked one and then twisted it, hissing out a breath when it sent a bolt of sensation rocketing through her again.

He rolled his hips slightly, and she felt the ripples of pleasure all through her body. Another moan erupted from her.

"So fucking beautiful," he bit out. "Watching you touch yourself with my cock deep inside you."

She whimpered again, as just his words were making her crazy with need. Her pussy pulsed with desire, and her fingers stroked faster, harder. Her hand teased her nipple and she began to pant.

"You like the feel of my cock deep inside you?"

That was so incredibly dirty. Here she was, a woman that didn't even cuss, and he was saying all these dirty things to her. Worse, it was arousing her. A thrill shot through her and she flicked her clit harder. "Yes," she whimpered.

"Then tell me."

"I like it," she managed to say, even as she rubbed harder. God, he was impaling her, his cock was so hard and thick. And she was saying dirty things back to him, and didn't even care. She felt her pussy shiver all around his thick length deep inside her.

"What do you like?"

"I love your cock," she panted, rubbing. Oh mercy, she was so close. "Deep inside me. Making me . . . come." Her last word ended in a moan as an orgasm blasted through her and she clenched hard. He swore and pushed her forward, and then he was over her, fucking her hard and thrusting deep, and her orgasm continued to build.

She cried out as he slammed into her. And oh God, she was still coming, and he kept thrusting into her, and she couldn't think, and her legs were so tight with her orgasm that she was going to shatter and oh my God—

And then he shouted a word that sounded like her name mashed together, and gave one last, hard thrust, and fell over her, panting.

Dazed, she wrapped her arms around him. This was totally not her—dirty talking, "one-night stand Beth Ann" was not "demure town Beth Ann." Her mission to be different had just headed off on a major U-turn.

And she was not complaining.

He lifted up off her and looked down at her face. "You are amazing."

She smiled. "Flatterer."

"I speak the truth," he said, and leaned in to kiss her again.

"So what now?" she asked.

He glanced up at the sky. Crystal clear, and orange with dawn. "Breakfast, and then I guess we can see about heading back into town."

"Great," she said with a smile. But for some reason, she didn't feel all that enthusiastic about it.

"Thank you for a wonderful weekend," Colt said. "Have to say that I enjoyed myself."

"A wonderful weekend?" she said with a laugh, gesturing at the ground. "Even with all this mud and rain?"

He gave her a hot look. "A *very* wonderful weekend."

A blush crept over her cheeks. "I'll make a note to get stranded more often, so you can come rescue me more often."

For some reason, the look on his face became a little more forced. "You do that, and I promise to come after you." He gave her an intense look. "No regrets, I hope?"

"I regret all the dirt under my nails," she admitted, and then added, "But nothing else." And she kissed his hard mouth to prove it.

Her pulse fluttered at the sight of that dimple when he smiled.

They cleaned up the small campsite as best they could when the sun was high. Colt banked the fire while she straightened up the cabin and gathered trash. She hadn't realized that they had any trash, but empty MRE bags and open condom wrappers qualified. So she'd stashed it all and tied the bag tight, tucking it into a corner of the shed. "Should we take it with us?"

"Nah. I'll send Brenna out for it tomorrow, and she can resupply the cabin. Don't worry about it."

Beth Ann hefted the bottles of rum and stared at them thoughtfully. "Seems a shame not to at least taste our alcohol."

Colt grimaced. "That's a cheap brand of rum. You're probably lucky you didn't taste it."

"Oh?" She studied the bottle.

"You're probably used to drinking some fancy shit anyhow," he said, using the side of his boot to rake mud and leaves over the remains of the fire pit.

"Actually I've never been drunk," she admitted. "I kind of wanted to try it."

"Never?" He looked down at her, incredulous, then picked up a bottle. "We'll save one for you then. Maybe see what you're like when you're plastered. You've led a pretty sad life if you've never been drunk off of cheap alcohol, Miss Beth Ann."

She grinned with wickedness. "I know." It was like Allan's wants and needs had ruled her life for the last nine years. Longer than that—they'd gotten together when she was in high school.

So much time wasted trying to please a man that couldn't be pleased.

"Tired of being the good girl?"

"Not that," she said, tugging one muddy, horrid shoe back on her foot. After this, she was going to wear sneakers for a week. "Tired of doing what everyone expects me to do. That's all. I did it and it got me nowhere. I'm doing what I want to do, and if that means trying new, occasionally stupid things, I'm going to do it."

"Atta girl," he said, and then gestured at the woods. "Come on. Let's see if we can make it back while the day is young enough."

And to her surprise, he held out his hand. A warm feeling swept through her, and Beth Ann smiled. She took his hand and glanced around. "Where's your slicker?" She was still wearing his shirt over her dress, and his chest was still bare. Streaks of mud dotted his skin, and she could have sworn that those were claw-marks from her nails on his back.

She could only imagine what she looked like.

"It's pretty destroyed," he admitted, and he glanced over at her, giving her a blade-sharp smile that made the dimple in his cheek appear. "Someone got carried away last night."

She nudged him with her shoulder, blushing. "Two some-ones."

"True enough," he said with a chuckle.

He was cold, wet, tired, muddy, needed a shower and a shave . . . and he didn't want the day to end. The woman at his side held his hand, and her tangle of hair brushed against his arm occasionally as they walked. She looked like a mess, too, but she seemed content. There was a sensual look in her eyes when she glanced over at him and it fired his blood all over again.

Last night had been incredibly hot. This morning had been incredibly hot, too. Here in the woods, she was all his. When they got back to civilization, she'd turn into pink and blond proper Beth Ann Williamson, queen bee of Bluebonnet, and he'd turn back into that white-trash Waggoner boy. She'd thank him for getting her out of the woods and the one-night stand would just be a dirty little secret between the two of them.

And for some reason, that didn't sit right with him. Maybe it was because he needed another night of sex with her to get last night's experience out of his mind. Maybe it wouldn't be as good and she wouldn't be as responsive, and he'd be done with her and could go back to work with an itch scratched. That'd be all right. But they didn't have another night. After they got out of the woods, he was going to borrow Grant's car (since his was supposed to be stranded along with hers), drive her home, and not think about her again.

But he kept thinking about last night, and her, as they walked.

He knew exactly where they were, of course. They were on Daughtry Ranch land, and he knew every acre by heart. He'd crawled over and under every shrub in the area in the past six months or so with their survival classes. And so he deliberately tracked back, circling over to one of the many creeks that cut through the area. The water was high, but not swollen and rushing. They crossed at a shallow point, and after they crossed, Beth Ann shivered with cold, and he pulled her in close to him for a minute.

"You going to be okay?" He could stand to hold her for a little while if she needed. When he pulled her close, he could smell the wood smoke in her hair, and her tight little nipples brushed against his chest.

She nodded, biting her lip. "I'm glad we waited to cross," she said with relief. "Just imagine how bad it would have been yesterday."

Still crossable, he thought to himself, but only drawled a "Yup." Then, he rubbed her back. "Let's get going. Not too much farther now."

The ground began to level out, the trees thinning, and he led her toward one of the trails. She promptly took off her shoes, smiling over at him and wiggling her toes in the still-damp earth. "Thank goodness. Those shoes are killing my feet."

And here he felt all guilty again. "Almost there."

It was another hour of walking until they reached the edge of the land, and the trail forked ahead of them. The trees were thick, but the branches overhead were clearing a bit more, and he knew this area by heart now. They were on the edge of the ranch proper, with the cozy group of cabins up ahead. Almost home. Almost back to reality.

"Which way?" she asked, turning to him. He noticed dark circles under her eyes. She was tired. Another thing he had to blame himself for. Damn. He hated feeling guilty, so he ignored it. "If we head left, we'll run into Dane's cabin. Mine is on the right fork of the trail." Straight ahead would take them to the main house, and behind that was Grant's cabin, and Brenna's, and the spare that they'd had built.

Her eyes brightened at the mention of his cabin. "You mean we're almost out of here?"

"Almost," he said dryly, hating that enthusiasm in her voice.

"Could . . . could I borrow your shower? I hate to impose."

Beth Ann wet, naked, and sudsy in his cabin? "Impose."

She grinned. "Lead the way."

Everyone that worked at the survival business had a small cabin built for themselves. It was one of the perks of being employees, and Grant had insisted. They were always nearby if needed, though the occasion hadn't happened often. Dane's cabin was the most remote, and he didn't have electricity running to his cabin. If he wanted electricity, he'd explained to them, he'd have gotten a place in town. Dane was just intense about the survival stuff like that. His shower and water was hooked up to a well, too.

Neither Colt nor Grant was quite so fastidious about that sort of thing. Grant's cabin was twice as big as anyone else's, and full of luxuries. They'd even built a spare cabin for another instructor, should the need arise, and Brenna was currently staying there. Colt had the smallest cabin of the lot, but fully wired for electricity. His cabin was one large square room, but that was fine, because he didn't need much.

The grass was slightly overgrown in the area—since it was a

wilderness ranch, they didn't bother with mowing except around the main cabin. Trees loomed overhead—he'd insisted on some shade. He knew it looked small from the outside, though, and wondered what Beth Ann was thinking.

He walked up the three short steps and opened the door, flicking on the light. Hard, bright lights shone and he moved to the side, gesturing for Beth Ann to enter. "Here we go."

She stepped in, looking around. "Wow." She blinked, then looked back at him with a smile. "You sure you live here?"

He looked around at his small cabin. The kitchenette was clean, all the dishes neatly put away in their places. He had a compact fridge off to one side, and across the room was his bed. A chair sat in one corner, and the TV perched atop his dresser, though he didn't watch much here. If he wanted to watch TV or play video games, he'd go to the main lodge. They all hung out there. "There a problem?"

She laughed lightly and stepped farther in, her arms crossed over her chest. "Where's all your stuff?"

He frowned at that little laugh. "Put away."

She continued to pace inside, smiling as if amused. "This is how you live?"

He glanced around, then back at her. What was she getting at?

She gestured at his bed. "You made your bed?" She moved to the sink and peered in. "No dirty dishes. If I look in your sock drawer, are they all organized by color?"

He scowled. "I like things neat. Tidy. In their place."

She chewed on her lip, studying the room. "I almost feel bad for trailing our dirt into here. We're going to mess up the cabin."

"It'll clean," he said gruffly.

Her gaze wandered to the fridge, where he had two pictures stuck there with magnets. She moved toward it and peered at them. "Who's this?"

He knew what she was looking at, pushed down the ache in his throat. The only picture he'd kept of his time in the marines. Him and his buddies in his regiment, standing in front of a Humvee in Iraq. They'd all posed with their guns and helmets while in wife-beaters, just being a bunch of idiots, cigarettes dangling from their mouths. "Just a bunch of Devil Dogs."

"Devil Dogs?" She turned to look at him and smiled. "Is that what you called each other?"

He nodded.

"Which one are you?"

"I'm the one in front. With the sunglasses."

She smiled with delight, leaning in to squint at the picture. "You look so cute and young in this picture. Did you smoke back then?"

"Nah. Just for that picture."

"You keep in contact with any of your friends?"

"Nah," he said again.

Her face fell. "Are they . . ."

"Nah," he said again. "They're fine. Just scattered to the four winds. When I left I sorta fell off the radar. Spent some time in Alaska."

Her face brightened and she turned back to the other picture. "Is this where you were?"

He moved to stand over her shoulder, staring down at the picture of the small log cabin with its plume of smoke rising from the chimney. It was a little blot of humanity tucked into the wild, nearly covered by the lush pine trees. In the distance, tall mountains rose. "Yup. I stayed there for over a year. Dane stayed with me for a while. That's him in the picture."

Beth Ann peered. "Wow, check out that beard."

He smiled a little. "ZZ Top would have been jealous."

"Did you grow one, too?"

"Nah. Kept it neat and clean."

"Just like when you were in the military, I take it? I noticed you still wear your dog tags."

"Once a marine, always a marine."

She smiled over at him, and continued her tour of his cabin, turning toward the corner of his cabin that held the vanity. Beth Ann froze at the sight of herself in the mirror. Her hand went to her cheek. "Lord have mercy. I look awful."

She looked beautiful. But at least now they were talking about something other than his past. He stepped forward and knelt in front of the vanity and pulled out a fluffy white towel, handing it back to her. "Shower's through that door."

She took the towel with gratitude, then hesitated. "It's your place. Did you want to shower first?"

"Go ahead," he drawled, and thought it was worth it to see her face light up with pleasure. She stepped inside the door and disappeared, and a moment later, the water started.

Colt sat back in his chair, scratching his chest, his gaze fixed on the line of light underneath the bathroom door. By now she'd have stripped off his shirt. She would be sliding out of that slippery, spangled dress, letting it pool around her feet. She'd kick it to the side and step into the shower, naked, and let the water slide down her body. She'd raise her arms to push back her hair, and those tight little breasts would raise up. And the look on her face would be ecstatic.

And fuck all if he didn't want to go in there and shove his way into the shower. Roll on a quick condom, brace her hands against the tile wall, and fuck her all over again. His cock twitched in response at the thought, and he brushed his hand down the front of his pants, then stopped.

And if he did that, she'd think he was a fucking psycho pervert that couldn't keep his hands off of her. He'd scare her off, jumping her every time she turned around. She deserved to have a goddamn shower in peace, didn't she? Christ, he was a Neanderthal. He ran a hand down his face and groaned.

She just wanted to borrow his shower. She hadn't indicated that she wanted more sex. Hell, he'd more or less pressed it on her this morning. If he jumped her now she'd think he constantly walked around with a goddamn boner.

He'd control himself. He'd let her shower, clean up, change into something warm, and then he'd go and shower, too.

And then he'd jerk off to the thought of her soaping up the slick lips of her pussy, of her fingers skimming over her breasts.

He was going to take a nice, *long* shower.

SEVEN

When he came out of the shower, she sat curled up on the center of his bed, dressed in one of his T-shirts, her legs tucked against her chest. Her wet hair tumbled over her shoulders and her face was scrubbed pink and clean. "I borrowed some clothes. I hope that's okay."

"Fine with me." He'd have been fine with her remaining naked, too. He stood there for a moment, towel wrapped around his hips, and glanced at the neat stack of clothes she'd placed on the vanity for him. "Thanks."

Beth Ann gave a shy little smile, reminding him a bit of a skittish colt. "Least I can do."

He took the clothes and moved back into the bathroom to change, lest he alarm her by dropping his towel. It was too warm in the small cabin for a shirt, so he skipped it and pulled on briefs and a pair of pajama pants instead. Odd that she hadn't picked out jeans for him.

Odd that she hadn't taken the pants for herself.

He reemerged from the bathroom and found her leaning into his fridge. Her shirt—his shirt—had ridden up, revealing her curvy ass cupped in a pair of his briefs. They were a little tight over her rounded buttocks. He approved of that. "Hungry?"

She jerked up at his voice and gave him a sheepish look. "Starving. Your fridge doesn't have much."

That was because he normally didn't eat in. "Suppose I'd better drive you home, then."

She bit her lip.

"What?"

Beth Ann gestured to the bottle on the counter, then sauntered toward him, running her fingers down over his chest in a blatant gesture. "I kinda hate to get drunk for the first time all by myself."

"You propositioning me?"

She looked up at him, tilted her head. "Maybe."

His hands slid to her hips, grasped her ass, and pulled her tight against him so she could feel the erection that was returning even though he'd stroked one out in the shower. "Now's not the time to be shy."

Her thumbs brushed over his nipples and she bit her lip again. "I just thought, you know . . . I don't have anywhere to be until tomorrow. And even then, it's my day off. If you're not busy . . ."

Damn but she was having a hard time spitting out what she

wanted. He decided to supply her with the question. "You mean, if I'm not busy, could I please toss you down on the bed and lick you until you scream my name?"

Her jaw dropped a little.

"Again?" he reminded her. "Repeat of last night?"

Her eyes gleamed and she grinned, wrapping her arms around his waist and leaning in to lick his tattoo. "Something like that."

Well hell yes, he was all about that. "Anyone going to be missing you tonight if I keep you here and fuck the daylights out of you?"

She sighed and lay her head against his chest, her fingers trailing up and down his back in ticklish motions. She was a cuddler. He liked that. More opportunity to press her body against him. "I guess I should check my messages."

"Me, too."

She reluctantly pulled from his arms and crossed the room to where she'd left her tiny purse. "It didn't have service out in the woods, so I'm not sure if it'll have service here." She pulled it out of the purse and water dripped from it. She wiped the screen with a finger, then sighed and dropped it back into her purse. "Or I could need to replace it entirely."

He gestured at the phone hanging on the wall. "Use mine."

She smiled at him, then picked up the phone and dialed her voicemail. He watched her face as she listened to the first message. Was she going to hear something that was going to take her away for the evening? Admit it was a mistake?

He wanted to rip the phone out of her hand and throw her back down on his bed and kiss the daylights out of her.

But all she did was wince as she listened, her head cocked.

"One of my Saturday appointments called. She's pissed. Guess I'm going to have to squeeze her in on Tuesday when I open again." She tapped a button on the phone, deleting the message, then listened to the next. "Another client." Tap. "Another." Tap.

When she got to the next message, her demeanor changed and she hastily deleted the message as soon as the loud voice on the other end started to talk. She hung up the phone.

"Another client?" he asked, even though it wasn't his damn business.

"Allan," she said shortly, and offered nothing else.

"Your parents ain't much worried about you, are they?" She'd disappeared for the weekend and they hadn't even bothered to call? Pricks.

She shrugged. "They probably think I'm hiding from them at the salon again." Her gaze slid to her ruined dress and her purse, and he could almost see the thoughts turning in her head.

She should leave. Go back to reality. Say goodbye to her one-night stand. Be the responsible, upstanding Beth Ann everyone thought she was.

"You want to order pizza?" he found himself volunteering.

A smile lit her face. "Does that go well with cheap rum?"

"Absolutely." He grinned.

"You've got to actually get the quarter *into* the shot glass," Colt pointed out.

Beth Ann giggled and tried to bounce it across his table again. The quarter smacked into the wall. "Do I get to drink now?"

"Not exactly," he said, trying not to smile as she stood up and trotted across the room to get the only quarter they had between the two of them. When she bent over, her luscious ass looked damn hot in his briefs. She eyed the quarter, then eyed the glass again.

"Maybe we'd better take a break on the drinking games," he told her, grabbing the shot and swigging it down so she wouldn't drink it.

She pouted up at him, sticking out her lower lip like a child. "Cheater."

"You've had enough to drink, darlin'." She was giggling at everything. It was incredibly cute, but he could tell she was drunk. When she walked, she weaved.

And judging from the way her face was lit up, she was having a grand time, too. He'd only drank a little of the alcohol, more to keep her company than to get drunk himself. He had a feeling that if they were both drunk, well . . . he didn't want to scare her off. Drunken declarations tended to do that.

"You know what would be fun?"

"What?"

"We should go skinny dipping," she said, smiling at him as she moved to sit back down in his lap. She'd been sitting there to play quarters, oblivious to the hard on that had been killing him for the past few hours. But she was drunk, and he wasn't going to take advantage of that. If she wanted him, he wanted her to want him while sober. Not when plastered on cheap-ass rum.

"You want to?" She looked at him expectantly, her eyelids heavy with drunkenness. "We could get naked together and slip and slide against each other like fishes. It'd be fun. I've never been skinny dipping."

"Not tonight," he said. Damn. "You should probably drink a glass of water and sleep this off so you don't have a headache in the morning."

"Oh, Colt," she said, slapping his bare chest. "You're so silly."

"Silly," he agreed, then grabbed her by the ass and stood up, cradling her against him. Her arms latched around his neck and she cuddled close. One hand pulled his dog tags, and her mouth was suddenly on his neck, hot and wet. And fuck if his cock didn't jerk in response.

"Time for you to go to bed, Beth Ann," he said, laying her down on top of the blankets.

She rolled her eyes at him but when he lay her down, she grabbed his pillow and hugged it close. "I'm only a little tired."

He went to the sink, got a glass of water, and then returned to her. "Drink this first."

She drank it and immediately lay back down. He put the glass back on the counter and glanced over at his chair. Seemed like a good a place as any to spend the night.

Beth Ann patted the bed. "Come lay beside me?"

"You need to sleep—"

"I will," she said quickly. "If you come lay next to me."

Colt knew he should tell her no, but she looked sweet and soft and inviting. He lay on the side of the bed and she immediately snuggled up alongside him. He wrapped a loose arm around her and was absurdly pleased with her sigh of contentment.

"Get some sleep," he murmured.

"Aye, aye, Captain," she muttered.

He smiled as he lay back and closed his eyes. He was tired, too, even if he didn't like to admit it. His knee throbbed a little and felt tight, but he could work that out in the morning. The few shots he'd had weren't enough to send him under, but it definitely made him tired. It wasn't long before he fell asleep himself.

He woke up a short time later and stared into the darkness, disoriented. What—

A hot, wet mouth closed over the head of his cock. Need unfurled within him, and he groaned, a mixture of frustration and desire. "Beth Ann."

Her fingers tickled his balls, grazing over them, and her mouth continued to suck, her tongue running under the head of his cock. Oh fuck, that was good. Oh *fuck*, a drunk woman was giving him head. Not good.

"Beth Ann," he said again, firmly, and tried to push her away.

Her mouth slid over the head of his cock, pressing light kisses there and he nearly lost control as she licked the shaft. "You are so thick, Colt. God, I love that. Wanted to know how it felt in my mouth."

"You can figure that out in the morning, darlin', when you're sober." He pulled at her, trying to tug her off of him. Fuck his principles. He should just lie back and let her suck his dick, tangle his hands in her hair and fuck her pretty, soft mouth like she wanted.

But then she giggled, and it was that same, silly drunken giggle. And slid her mouth over his cock again.

"No, darlin'," he said hoarsely. How in the hell had she gotten his pants down to his knees without waking him up? He tried to sit up, but she was laying over his abdomen.

She sat up and gave him a sad look. "Don't you want me, Colt?"

"I do, Beth Ann. So damn bad."

She leaned in to kiss him, and her kiss was off center. "I'm really good at blow jobs."

"Oh, I just bet you are." Damn.

But she cuddled down next to him again. Her fingers went to his chest and she traced his nipples. He'd let her do that, as long as she didn't reach for his dick again. "We're consenting adults, Colt."

"I know. But it's not right."

"You can't take advantage of me," she pointed out, her words slurred. "We had sex last night. And this morning."

"Still not right. Get some sleep."

"You know what I haven't done?" she said, leaning over to press kisses on his chest. On his tattoo. She was fascinated with it.

"What's that?"

"I haven't had anal."

He groaned. Hard.

"Have you?" she asked.

"Yes."

"Did you like it?"

"Go to sleep, Beth Ann."

"If I asked you to do it to me, would you?"

He was about thirty seconds away from throwing her down on the mattress and showing her just what she was asking for. "Ask me when you're sober, and yes."

She pinched his nipple, hard. "Fine then, I will. So there."

"Good night, Beth Ann," he said dryly.

"You're no fun," she said sleepily. Her hand reached for his cock, and he moved it back away again.

"No fun at all," he agreed, and vehemently wished that wasn't the case.

When Beth Ann woke up, it was still dark. She rolled over in bed, trying to figure out her surroundings. Her hand encountered a warm chest, and she heard the faint sound of snoring. Her mouth was fuzzy with a weird taste, and her head throbbed a little.

Colt. She laid her head back on his chest again, remembering last night. She hadn't drank too much rum—he'd been very careful with how much she could have—but she'd still been tipsy right away. In the past, she'd drank a glass of wine here and there, and the occasional champagne, but it hadn't hit her quite like the rum. She'd been drunk, and it had been silly, and fun. And then he'd dragged her to bed and . . .

Her eyes flew open. She looked down at his cock, but his pajama pants were back up around his waist. Oh lord, she'd told him she wanted to have *anal* sex.

How mortifying.

And he hadn't touched her, either. She didn't know what to make of that. True, she'd been tipsy, but they'd had sex the night before. Why hadn't he touched her? Was he that much of a gentleman? The thought was endearing and frustrating all at once. She looked up at his sleeping face. All the hard angles and frown lines were eased when he was sleeping. He looked adorable. The longer hair on top of his head was sticking straight up in cowlicks. His chest was warm and delicious, too. She still rested her cheek on it. She supposed she should wake him up.

Her hand strayed to the drawstring of his pajama pants. Tugged at the bow, and felt it loosen. She sat up slowly and watched him, waiting for him to awaken. He didn't.

A heavy sleeper, then. Nice. She slid down the bed and eased his pants down his legs, revealing his briefs. Mmm, he filled them out nicely. Much better than she did. The pair she'd borrowed out of necessity were too small across the behind, and she was pretty sure half of her butt was sticking out over the top.

Her fingers eased along the elastic waistband, and she watched his face, waiting for him to wake up. Nothing. Holding the elastic taut, she slid his briefs down his legs, exposing his cock.

He was already half hard, and she looked down at it with pleasure. He really did have an amazing set of equipment. Just long enough and really thick. Oh mercy, she liked that. She bit her lip, thinking about how he'd felt deep inside her. Apparently she'd woken up aroused this morning. She leaned over him, bracing her hands on either side of the bed, and leaned to take him into her mouth. Her tongue lightly whirled on the head, lapping and licking.

And teasing him. He groaned and shifted underneath her, his cock hardening, swelling even larger. Oh yes. It was just as big and thick as she remembered. She wrapped her fingers around the girth of him and continued to tongue the head, dipping against the sweet indentation that was beaded with pre-cum. He tasted so good in her mouth. She closed her lips over him, sinking lower on the root of his cock and taking him deep into her throat. He was fully erect now, and hard, and she sucked, pulling up and then sliding back down over his cock. She repeated the motion, feeling her own pussy get slick and wet with need. She drew harder on him, and slid his cock out of her mouth to run her tongue along the thick crown again.

A hand twisted in her hair—not hard. Firm. She moaned as his hand pushed her mouth back down over his cock, and her gaze flicked up to him. He was watching her with slitted eyes. As she looked up at him, she took the head of his cock back in her mouth and let it rub along her tongue. He thrust, the head of his cock butting against the back of her throat. And she made a noise of pleasure that echoed his own.

"Goddamn, Beth Ann," he rasped. "I hope to God you're not drunk any longer."

She slid her mouth up and gave his cock head a playful lick. "Not drunk."

"Good," he growled, and pushed her head back down on his cock.

She sucked him deep again, her pussy clenching with the erotic sound of the groan he made when she pulled him all the way into her mouth. He was so big and full in her mouth. Lord, that was making her hot.

He thrust into her mouth again, his fingers digging into the back of her head, and she heard a hard, rasping breath jerk from him. She sucked harder, humming a little in the back of her throat. He pumped quicker now, his hips rising to thrust into her mouth over and over.

And then he froze. She looked up at him and saw his face was tight, and he pulled her back off of him. "I'm going to come, darlin'," he said. He pulled her off his cock, allowing her to abandon her efforts in case she didn't want to swallow his seed.

But that wasn't what she wanted. "Then come," she said softly, and leaned down to take him back into her mouth again. The groan he gave after that was low and filled with need, and his fingers twined in her thick hair. He began to thrust into her mouth again, shallow, rapid jolts that matched the panting of his breath. She took him deeper, though, encouraging him. He drove into her mouth wildly and then his body tightened under her.

"Fuck," he bit out, and she felt the hot flood of his cum in the back of her throat. She swallowed even as he thrust again, more shallowly. He gave a ragged breath, exhaling as she released him, then sat up and wiped at the corners of her mouth.

"Good morning," she said softly, and couldn't resist the smile that curved her lips.

"You are going to drive me crazy, you know that?" he panted.

"Good," she said with a smile.

"That's a helluva lot more effective than a cup of coffee," he said, still panting. He grabbed her leg and tugged until she fell into bed beside him. "Your turn."

Her eyes went wide with surprise. "Oh?"

"Absolutely," he said, and slid down her body, his hands going to her hips. He tugged at the briefs and slid them down her legs. She shifted slightly under him, doing her best not to wiggle—or tremble. She felt exposed, uncertain. This was incredibly intimate for her. Allan hadn't been a fan of going down on her, and she could count the times she'd had oral with him on one hand.

Great, now she was thinking about Allan again.

And then he tugged at her leg, asking her to part them. His hand stroked along her inner thigh. She waited for him to say something. She hadn't gotten a Brazilian in forever, and, well, the carpet didn't match the drapes, if she was going to be blunt. And sure, he'd seen her naked and they'd had sex, but this was the first time he was getting up close and personal, and in broad daylight. It made her anxious.

But all he said was, "Pretty."

And that made her flush with pleasure.

His fingers brushed over the curls of her pussy. One slid deep, brushing against her clit and eliciting a gasp from her.

"Pretty, and very wet," he murmured. "Did you like having my cock in your mouth?"

She nodded.

But he waited, and looked up at her. "Tell me."

A hot flush crept over Beth Ann's cheeks as he eased one of her bent knees back toward the bed, then the other, splaying her. "I . . . liked waking you up like that."

"Gonna spoil me for alarm clocks," he said with a hint of a smile, and continued to run his finger along the wet slit of her pussy. "I want you to tell me what you like, Beth Ann."

"Okay."

As she watched, he dipped his head and nuzzled at her sex. A moan rose from her throat and her legs jerked involuntarily at the sight. Lord have mercy, but that was erotic. She felt his tongue slide out, part the seam of her pussy, and stroke along her clit. Her breath sucked in.

He lifted his head, and she saw his lips were wet with her own juices. "Didn't like that?"

"I did."

That dimple flashed. "Then tell me."

"I will. I promise."

"We're going to make a demanding woman out of you yet, Beth Ann Williamson."

She simply grinned at that, and ran her hands over his short, spiky hair. "Mmm, I like this."

"Then keep rubbing it," he said, and bent and licked her sex again. His fingers parted it, revealing her clit, and he glanced up at her as he gave it another long, slow lick.

She moaned. God, was he going to watch her responses the entire time he was licking her? It made her body flush and her nipples grow tight.

But then he moved away again, kissing around where she wanted him to be, and pressing his mouth to the curve of her hip. She shivered and rubbed her fingers on his head. It felt good, but not nearly as wonderful as his mouth on her clit. "Colt . . . go—go back."

He moved his mouth and flicked his gaze up to her, hovering just over her slit. "Here?"

He was so close she felt his breath there. She nodded, biting her lip.

"Tell me."

"O-on my clit. Please." Why was it so hard to say? She felt so vulnerable and exposed having to tell him what she wanted.

But he descended back on her clit, and she forgot about being exposed as he gave it a long, slow lick with his tongue. Her hips pressed against his mouth. "Oooh."

His hands grasped her hips, holding her steady, and paused, waiting.

"L-lick me again," she said, her breath shuddering.

He did again, long, slow and exquisite, and she felt every moment of it singing through her entire body. Her toes curled. "Don't stop. Keep licking me."

He began to flick his tongue against her clit then, the movements slow, languid. Lapping at her like she was a favorite dish. Slow, measured strokes. Her hips lifted again, but she was pinned down by his hands. "Oh mercy, just like that." With every flick of his tongue on her clit, her hips bucked, trying to follow.

But he was going so very slow. Each flick of his tongue seemed more like a tease than a promise. "Faster," she breathed. "Lick . . . faster." And lord, if that wasn't a naughty thing to be demanding of him. But oh, he did begin to lick faster, and she moaned, throwing her head back as he continued, his tongue now flicking against her clit in a faster staccato. "Oh, that's good," she murmured. "Keep going." Her short nails raked over his head, and she caught the barest sound of his growl of pleasure. Was he enjoying this, too? Liquid heat rushed through her at the thought, and she shivered, her skin prickling. Was he just as turned on licking her as she was when she'd taken his cock in her mouth? Enjoying the power he had over her? She squeezed her eyes open again. His fingers held her pussy spread open, and as she watched, his tongue slid out and flicked over her flesh, over and over again. And oh lord, that was intensely erotic.

A jolt of lust flared through her, and she felt herself become even wetter. The tension in her body began to build, her hips trying to rise off the bed. She wanted to look away. She couldn't look away. All she could see was that dark sweep of lashes as his gaze was on her pussy, concentrating, his tongue flicking over her clit over and over again. "Faster, please," she panted. "Need more."

She shifted her hips in a little circle, trying to buck up against his tongue.

He nuzzled deep as she watched, swiveling his tongue over her clit and she whimpered. Oh God, that had felt good. "Again," she cried. He did, and she clenched hard. She needed more. Needed something—

"Fingers," she gasped.

A thick one thrust deep into her, eliciting a small cry of pleasure from her throat. He didn't stop, his tongue continuing to flick at that same measured pace.

"Faster," she cried again, undulating her hips. "More. Please. Give me more."

The finger thrust inside her, harder, fiercer, and his mouth sped up. She cried out, writhing underneath him. She was so close. Needed more. "Please," she panted. "Please. More. More."

Faster he thrust with his fingers, and she heard the low moan in his throat as she flexed her hips against him, trying to push over the edge. "Please," she said, her voice an almost sob. "Colt. Please."

But then he was lifting his mouth from her, and bit back a curse. She gave a whimpering sound of distress as he left her. God, she was so close and he was leaving her like this? But then she heard the crackle of a condom wrapper, and then he grabbed her leg, and she opened her eyes again just as he slid his cock deep into her.

She screamed, her entire body locking in orgasm.

He bit out another curse, thrusting into her hard. Her knees were pushed into her chest, hitting her breasts as he pounded into her, and waves of the orgasm kept hitting her. Her scream had bubbled into a keening cry that seemed to go on and on, just like her orgasm. Wave after wave of it crashed over her, and every time he pounded into her, it cascaded all over again.

And then she was gasping for breath, and he jerked against her, and it was her name he bit out. His body stiffened and then he fell forward and kissed her, hard. Branding her. She could still taste her own sex on his lips, felt him seated deep in her body. Her knees were still pressed to her breasts, and her pulse was pounding so hard that she thought she might pass out. Didn't care. That had been intense.

He rolled off of her after a moment and he leaned over the side of the bed, tossing the used condom into a nearby wastebasket. Then, he pulled her against him. "Definitely ruined me for coffee."

She grinned and burrowed against him. Her legs felt like Jell-O. Good, wonderful, blissful Jell-O.

His fingers trailed up her shirt and danced along her spine. "Guess we should take you home soon."

All her languid contentment vanished, replaced with uncertainty. Was he just trying to get rid of her and here she was throwing herself at him? How embarrassing. Of course he was going to take a blow job if it was offered.

But then he leaned in and kissed her again, fiercely, and she didn't know what to think.

One-night stand, dummy, she told herself. Of course she knew what to think. She felt stupid. So it had turned into a two-night stand. How silly of her. It had been great sex, but that's all it was. No-strings-attached sex, and now she'd go back to her salon and he'd go back to his survival classes, and they'd be totally awkward around each other when they ran into each other in town.

Totally normal.

She sat up, pushing at her hair. It was a frizzy, tangled mop. That was going to be fun to detangle later. "I suppose I should go back before people start wondering where I am."

"All right, then," he said.

They dressed in silence and left the small cabin. Her feet were bare—the Louboutins tossed into the garbage once and for all—and her dress that had once been cute and swingy was now saggy and a sad shade of muddy gray. She had no idea where her panties were, either, but was too embarrassed to admit that to Colt.

He borrowed a Jeep from the school and she climbed in. "Where to?"

"My salon," she said, and ran her fingers through her tangled hair again. "While I would love to go and give my smirky little sister a piece of my mind, I can't really go back to my parents' house looking like this."

He grunted. "You're an adult."

"It's not them I'm worried about." She thought for a moment, then paused.

"What?"

Beth Ann glanced over at him, then bit her lip. "It's just that . . . if it got back to Allan, he'd be worried, and then he'd swing by the house to make sure I'm okay, and I just don't feel like the hassle."

His hands tightened on the steering wheel, and she wondered if she'd said the wrong thing. "All right then."

They rode back to town, awkwardly silent. Beth Ann was almost disappointed to see the bright, cheery pink sign of California Dreamin'. Her wild little weekend was over. No more mud, no more hiking.

No more Colt.

Just Lucy, who wouldn't feel guilty in the slightest that her big sister got stuck in the woods all weekend. Just her parents, who would shake their heads, puzzled at her need for independence at the age of twenty-seven. Just Allan, who would come by on an almost-daily basis to give her sad puppy-dog eyes and hope that enough guilt would make her go back to him.

She sighed as he pulled into the space in front of the salon. "Thanks again for the ride," she said. "I'll see you around town?"

He gave a crisp nod.

She opened her door and began to slide out.

His hand caught hers and she looked back at him, hopeful.

"Keys," he said.

"Keys?"

"To your car. I'll bring it by when it's towed with the others."

Oh. "Of course," she said hastily and dug into her ruined little purse. Her keys were muddy, too, and she tugged the Volkswagen key off of the key ring. "Here you go."

Colt nodded at her, and she thought she caught a glimpse of dimple. And then she shut the car door, and he pulled out.

And he was gone. Good-bye weekend, hello reality.

She sighed, unlocked the door to her salon, and stepped inside. Her answering machine light was flickering—no surprise. She ignored it and went to the big mirror in front of the barber chair. Sure enough, she looked like a wreck. She set to work—

once her hair was detangled, she pulled it into a braid and curled her bangs. Her nails had little rings of dirt under them, so she fixed that and repainted both fingers and toes, and then moisturized her feet because they'd had a rough weekend. She flipped through the magazines she kept stacked in the salon, even though she'd read them all before. When she could stall no longer, she headed to the back storage room where she kept her air mattress and a few changes of clothes. She switched out, tossing her dress into the garbage—it was ruined. Then she changed clothes, put on a pair of disposable flip-flops, and called her parents' house, hating that she had to do so.

Lucy picked up.

"It's me," Beth Ann said. "Come and pick me up at the salon."

EIGHT

Lucy had been all apologies, and was still apologizing when she dropped by the salon to pick up Beth Ann a few minutes later. "Mom and Dad totally grounded me. I can't see Colossus anymore," Lucy said with a frown, her blue-streaked braids swinging as she shook her head. "It's such bullshit."

"That's too bad," Beth Ann murmured, lost in thought. Her brain was still focused on that morning, waking Colt up with her mouth. She'd loved that electric moment when he'd wrapped his hand in her hair and she'd realized he was conscious and could feel everything she was doing. That had been so . . . delicious.

"So where you been all weekend?" Lucy asked, giving Beth Ann a narrow-eyed stare. "You get evacuated, too? I tried calling your cell but you didn't answer. I thought you were pissed at me."

"I *was* mad. I'm still mad," Beth Ann said lightly, and pulled out her waterlogged phone. "And you owe me a new iPhone."

Lucy looked over and sighed. "Were you at the motel, too? They made us sleep girls with girls. So lame."

"No," Beth Ann said, and then paused. "I had one of the volunteers drive me to the salon so I could cool off."

A total lie, but she didn't want to tell Lucy that she'd spent the weekend with Colt. That was a little too personal.

"Huh," Lucy said. "I could have sworn I left with the last batch of volunteers. I stuck around to see if you were going to make it out, you know. I wouldn't leave you behind. I didn't realize you'd deliberately *wanted* to be left behind."

Lucy looked over and gave her sister an obvious wink.

Ha. "Nothing like that. I left a little after the last group," Beth Ann said.

"Sure you did."

Beth Ann gritted her teeth. "I left a little after the last group, honey," she repeated. "And if you don't want me telling Mom and Dad that they were handing out alcohol and condoms at the gate, I think we should just end this conversation right now."

"Ending conversation," Lucy said with an impish grin made all the more roguish by her nose ring. "We won't talk about anyone's hookups."

"Do not mention hookups, Lucinda Janelle Williamson," Beth Ann hissed. "If this gets back to Allan—"

"I know, I know," Lucy said, turning the car up the long, winding drive to their parents' house. "Then his crazy ass will start stalking you again. Don't worry. The last person I'd tell about your hookup is that jerk. Your secret is safe with me."

"Thanks, Luce."

Lucy examined her fingernails. "Don't suppose you'd hook a sister up with a mani?"

She had a feeling there'd be a lot of free manicures in Lucy's future, just to keep her mouth shut. "You know I can."

When Colt got back from dropping Beth Ann off, he returned to his cabin. The sheets were still rumpled, the floor tracked with mud from the night before. He moved to the bed and ran his hand over it. Still smelled like her—and him—together. Damn. He didn't want to sit here all day, ruminating on their weekend together. It had been hot and intense and mind-blowing.

And it was over.

He left the cabin and hiked over to the main lodge. He swung in and of course both Brenna and Grant sat at their desks, working. They looked up at the sight of him, and Brenna smiled. He gave her a half wave and ignored the desk he shared with Dane. Why Grant thought that two survival instructors needed a desk, he didn't know. He headed to the rec room in the back and turned on the TV, picking up the Xbox controller. A mindless game would distract him.

"Hey," Brenna protested in the other room. "Where've you been?"

He ignored her, too.

She pushed into the room a moment later. Her hair was pulled into two buns perched high on top of her head, both speared with pencils. Brenna crossed her arms over her chest. "I saw your truck parked on the side of the highway all weekend. What gives?"

His truck. He supposed he should go get it. "I was busy after the rescue. You wanna be a dear and go retrieve it for me?"

She gave him an exasperated look, then put her hand out. "Keys?"

He tossed them to her, and she gave him a wink, then left.

Good. Maybe now he'd get some peace and quiet.

As soon as Brenna left, Grant entered the room. Fuck. Not what he wanted at the moment. He tilted his head back and closed his eyes, waiting for him to start in.

It didn't take long.

"You are not going to believe the shit Brenna pulled this time," Grant began. "Remember I asked her to log all the receipts from the camping goods store? She logged them all in a spreadsheet as 'camping stuff.' One hundred and eighty-two lines of data. No dates. No dollar amounts. Nothing but 'camping stuff.' How am I supposed to write that off?"

Here we go.

"I'm positive she's doing it just to fuck with me."

Colt was pretty sure that Grant was right. He and Brenna seemed to have an antagonistic relationship—they were pleasant enough in person, but Grant constantly picked apart everything Brenna did, and Brenna turned around and deliberately did things to irritate Grant.

Sometimes, Dane speculated that it was like working with two children that couldn't get along. Personally, Colt just thought the two of them needed to fuck and get it over with. He wouldn't say that to Grant, though. The man still had issues, even five years after his wife had passed away.

So Colt said nothing. He clicked on the remote.

"Speaking of fucking," Grant said slowly, and Colt looked over at his buddy. Grant had grabbed a coke from the fridge and twisted the cap off. Too early for beer, then. "You disappeared all weekend after that big rescue mission on Friday. You find some hot little piece in need of rescuing and hookup?"

Every muscle in his body tensed. He forced himself to give a light, careless shrug. "Maybe."

"Out in the woods all weekend?" Grant shook his head. "Too much rain and mud for me. You are stone cold, Waggoner."

"River washed out the way back," Colt said after a moment, but even the lie tasted bad on his lips. "Had to hike our way back to the ranch."

"Bullshit," Grant said, kicking the side of his chair with a grin. "I don't know the area half as well as you and Dane, but even I know the river doesn't come anywhere near the road, dumbass."

Colt said nothing.

"Hot damn. You lucky dog," Grant said with a grin, and swigged his drink. "Don't tell Brenna."

"I ain't even tellin' you, bro."

"Who was it? Someone we know?"

Colt turned up the volume on the TV.

"Fine," Grant said, still amused. He picked up the other controller. "It's a small town, though. It's bound to get out."

It *was* bound to get out, Colt realized. It was just a matter of time before someone pointed out the flaws in his story and knew that he'd deliberately detained Beth Ann—though not originally for the reason they'd think.

And then she'd be furious at him. Good thing she'd only

wanted a one-night stand. If she never brought it up again, he wouldn't, either, and no one need know the truth.

Beth Ann had said she couldn't have a relationship that wasn't built on trust, after all. And their little fling had been built on a foundation of solid lies—all his.

Grant casually added, "Your brother, Marlin, stopped by a few hours ago."

Damn it. "What the fuck does he want?"

"Said he wanted you to go by and visit your dad. Old man wants to talk to you."

Hell. Colt didn't want to talk to him. Henry Waggoner lived on the trashiest plot of land on the outskirts of Bluebonnet, in a double-wide that was so torn up it had holes in the floor. His front yard was covered in broken-down trucks, washing machines, and various bits of scrap metal. It looked like a junkyard.

His dad insisted it was all stuff that had value. All Colt saw was garbage. And that garbage had been there for the entire twenty-seven years his dad had been living in that trailer. He hadn't even bothered to clean it up when Colt's mother got fed up and ran off for parts unknown back when he and his brothers were just little boys.

White-trash Waggoners. The entire town called them that. He'd worked hard to pull himself out of that misery. He'd trained hard, joined the marines, trained harder . . . and then with one lousy shot to his fucking knee, he'd lost it all again.

"If he comes by again, tell him to fuck off," Colt said in a hard voice. "I don't want anything to do with them."

• • •

Tuesday was a hell of a day. In addition to Beth Ann's booked appointments, she was still trying to squeeze in her Saturday clients. Most of them were upset that she'd been a no-show, but she'd mentioned the word *migraine* and most of the women had been sympathetic.

All except nasty Mrs. Potter. She came in every Saturday to have her hair teased and curled for Saturday night bingo two towns over.

"It's not responsible for you to just not show up, Beth Ann," Mrs. Potter said for the seventh time on the call.

"I know. And I'm very sorry, honey," Beth Ann said soothingly, resting the phone on her cheek as she shampooed someone's hair. "It won't happen again. Did you want me to squeeze you in today? Or tomorrow?"

"No," Mrs. Potter said in a sour voice. "I went to that new place instead."

"New . . . place?"

"That one down the street. Next to the hardware store. She just moved in. Lovely girl. She used to do hair in Dallas, you know. She cut Troy Aikman's hair once."

"You don't say," Beth Ann murmured. She grabbed the spray nozzle and began to rinse her client's hair. "Well, I'll see you for your Saturday appointment as usual, then?"

"Or maybe I'll just go there," Mrs. Potter said nastily. "We'll see on Saturday, won't we?" She hung up.

Jeez. Beth Ann put the phone on the counter and wrapped a

towel around her client's wet hair as the woman sat up. "So you wanted to take off two inches?"

As she began to rattle off about what she wanted done to her hair, Beth Ann listened halfheartedly. When the woman sat in the barber chair, Beth Ann moved to the big storefront window and peeked out the mini blinds. The shop next to the hardware store had been closed for a while. Had someone moved in, or was Mrs. Potter just being her usual snide self?

But then she saw a customer walk in. And there was a sign in the window, though it was too far away to make out.

"What do you think? Two inches?" the woman in her chair was saying.

Beth Ann forced herself to turn away from the window and smiled. "Two inches is a little shorter than you normally wear it, but I think it'd be cute."

No matter how curious she was, she was *not* going to look out the window again.

After her last appointment left for the day, Beth Ann sat down and sighed. She'd been on her feet all day straight. Normally she didn't mind, but today she'd been juggling clients on top of clients, and it had been exhausting. She needed a few minutes off her feet. Better yet, she needed someone to come in here and give her a pedicure and a foot massage herself, instead of being the one to give them. She closed her eyes and rubbed her forehead.

The cowbell on the door clanged, indicating a new customer.

"No walk-ins today, sorry," Beth Ann said in as pleasant a

voice as she could . . . and then had to stifle her groan at the sight of the man that had just walked in.

Allan. He smiled over at her, his boyish face handsome. “I sold two BMWs today, Bethy-babe. Thought I’d come by and see if you wanted to go out to dinner to celebrate.”

Ugh. “That’s nice, Allan,” she said politely. “Congratulations.”

“Get your purse and let’s go. I made dinner reservations at that Italian place you like over in Huntsville.”

Annoyance swept over her. He made reservations? Without asking her? And she didn’t like that Italian place—he did. Typical. “Allan, listen, that’s very nice but I’m too tired to go out.” *Especially with you.*

“Nonsense,” he said cheerfully. “My treat.”

“Allan, no—”

A car horn honked out front.

That sounded like *her* car. Beth Ann’s heart began to thud rapidly, and she felt her nipples grow tight. Colt. Oh.

She’d been thinking about him nonstop since they’d parted. So she was kind of not doing so hot with the “no strings attached one night stand” sort of thing. She wanted to see him again. Of course she couldn’t ask. She’d been the one insisting that it be a brief, meaningless fling. It wasn’t his fault that he’d been so flat-out amazing in bed that she was craving more. She was a junkie. A Colt junkie. How silly.

But she still found herself pushing past Allan to step out the front door of her salon, straightening her hair and smoothing her skirt. She smiled in delight at the sight of her green VW, shining and clean.

Colt stood up from the driver's side and grinned at her. "Hey, darlin'."

"Hey," she said breathlessly, feeling like a teenager. "You brought my car. Thank you."

"Got it all cleaned up for you." He shut the door and began to stroll toward her, his hands in his pockets, and she felt a little thrill at the sight of him. His white shirt was tight across his pectorals and tucked neatly into his dark green BDUs. She could almost make out his dog tags underneath, and remembered them smacking her in the cheek as he'd been deep inside her.

Warmth flushed through her body at the thought. "You're a good man," she said softly, and was rewarded with a flash of his dimple as he approached.

"The best," he said in a low, husky voice.

Oh mercy, he was sexy. Her nipples pricked and she smiled widely at him, her cheeks hot with excitement. She was glad she'd dressed pretty today, in a light blue dress with a full skirt that swished at her knees. Feminine. She looked her best. And he was smiling at her. And maybe he'd want to see her again. That dimple gave her hope.

"Beth Ann?" called Allan from behind her.

She gritted her teeth, crossing her arms over her chest in frustration. The playful, sensual look on Colt's face had disappeared, replaced by intense dislike.

"I can see this is a bad time," Colt drawled.

"It's not," she said hastily. "I assure you. I—"

"Bethy-babe," Allan said, coming up behind her and putting his arm around her waist. "We need to go if we're going to make those reservations."

As she watched, Colt's eyes narrowed to slits. Just like that, Allan was going to ruin her hopes with Colt. He was going to shove his way in and make Colt think that she was with him. And the thought horrified her.

She had to do something.

"No," she said, stepping away from Allan, her gaze on Colt for a moment longer before turning to frown at Allan. "I told you, I'm not going out with you. You shouldn't have made reservations without asking me first. I'm too tired to go out."

Allan gave her a wounded look, as if she'd crushed him. She was very familiar with that look. Whenever she did something that didn't please him, she got the hurt stare. As if she were the unreasonable one.

Colt was watching the two of them closely. Beth Ann kept her arms crossed over her chest, her chin firm. Allan had to learn.

"Bethy-babe," he began.

"Allan, please," she said in exasperation.

"There a problem?" Colt asked, stepping toward her. He gave another menacing look to Allan.

"No problem," Beth Ann said pointedly. "Allan was just leaving."

Allan hesitated, gave her another wounded flash, and then raised his phone and shook it. "I'll call you tomorrow. We need to talk."

"No, we don't," she said, but he'd already turned away and was getting into his car.

She remained frozen in place until he drove away, and then she exhaled, furious.

"You okay?" Colt asked.

"As soon as I punch something, yes," she said lightly.

Colt gave a wry snort and glanced back in the direction of where Allan had left. "You guys broke up, huh?"

"Ten months ago. He can't seem to get it through his head. For that matter, neither can half the town." Was that bitter voice hers? "He's driving me crazy."

"He stalking you?" Colt's voice was hard, unforgiving.

"Nothing as bad as that. He seems to think he can win me back, and that it's just a matter of time." She shook her head. "I'm sorry. This looks horrible, doesn't it? Trust is so important and here I am looking like I'm two-timing."

"Can't two-time if it's a one-night stand," he said slowly.

She flinched. Ouch. "You're right. How silly of me."

"Wasn't meaning to offend you," he said. "Just stating a fact."

"Well, thanks for dropping off my car," she bit out. "It was real nice of you."

He stepped a bit closer to her, and she could smell campfire smoke on him. He'd had a class today then? He smelled like their weekend together. God, she hadn't realized how smoke could smell so erotic.

"I'm doing this all wrong, aren't I?" he said softly. He took her hand in his. "I didn't come here to drop off your car. I came here to give you these."

He pressed her panties into her hand.

"Oh." A hot blush covered her face and she reached into the front of her dress and hastily shoved the panties into her bra. "Thank you."

He was so close that she could see that miniscule curve of his mouth, as if he were about to smile.

She waited for a minute. This was so oddly tense and awkward. They hadn't been tense together when they were together. It was this bizarre in-between state that they weren't handling very well. She looked down at her keys, then back at her car. "You need a ride?"

"Nah. Dane's over at the library to harass Miranda for a few minutes. He's giving me a ride back to the ranch."

"I see."

"And you're not with that douche bag?" he asked abruptly.

Oh. "I'm not with anybody," she answered honestly, peeking up at him through her eyelashes.

"Good," he said and the word was husky and made her panties wet all over again. "You want to go out?"

"When?" She sounded breathless, even to her own ears.

"This weekend? I have an overnight trip for the next few days. ROTC team-building exercise. But then I'm free this weekend."

"I work on Saturday until three," she said, smiling back at him. "I'm free after that."

"Saturday night, then? Dinner? I can pick you up here."

"Sounds good."

"Good."

He stared at her for a moment longer, then gave her that crisp, military nod. "See you then."

"Okay."

He turned away, took two steps toward the street, then turned back to her. Before she could ask if anything was wrong, he put his hands on the sides of her neck and pulled her in for a hard, fierce kiss.

Her mouth had barely parted under his when he pulled back slightly and licked at her lips, eliciting a moan from her.

"Saturday. If you want, you can leave those at my place again," he said, and nodded at the panties.

"Rascal," she said with a laugh.

He winked at her and then headed down the street.

NINE

The week passed incredibly slowly at times. Miranda had dropped by to have lunch one day, but Beth Ann hadn't brought herself to confess her fling with Colt just yet. She wanted to see how the date on Saturday was going to go. After all, there was no point in talking it up if they didn't go out again, right? And she didn't want Miranda getting her hopes up for Beth Ann and Colt being together.

Because hey, Beth Ann's hopes were up already. No sense in disappointing two people if it didn't work out.

She liked Colt. She trusted him—so far. And he was amazing in bed. So yeah, her hopes were up, just a little.

Mrs. Potter hadn't come in for her Saturday appointment after all. Neither had another one of her Saturdays. The salon down the street still didn't have a permanent sign, but she'd strolled past the window to read the one taped up on the glass. It was a list of services offered—waxes, perms, highlights, blow-outs, everything that Beth Ann offered. And she was charging three times as much. Beth Ann had gaped, even more so when she'd noticed the small salon had people waiting.

Was Bluebonnet big enough for two salons? She didn't know. Either way, it made her stomach gnaw with nervousness. Her business had to succeed. Had to. She was never going back to being the stay-at-home "little woman" ever again.

She'd stayed in her salon every night that week. Her mother protested once, but then she'd asked Beth Ann to pick up her dry cleaning while she was in town. Naturally. Jeanette didn't care what Beth Ann did as long as it didn't inconvenience Jeanette. So Beth Ann took a larger stack of her clothes to the salon that week and vowed to get an apartment just as soon as she could afford it. She dropped by her parents' house to shower, but other than that, she kept to her salon.

And every night, in the back of the salon on her air mattress, she masturbated, thinking about Colt. Yet another reason to be glad for her privacy. She couldn't wait for their date. It was stupid to be so excited—it could be totally wrong and awkward and they'd part ways and never speak again. They'd go back to adversaries, actively disliking each other.

Or they might hit it off and spend the evening making love.

She decided to get waxed, just in case. Instead of a Brazilian, she went totally nude. The sensation was erotic—her pussy felt bare and soft and everything brushed up against her skin.

She couldn't wait to see the look on Colt's face when he noticed. And she flushed at the thought.

On Saturday night, she took care with her hair, blowing it out so it'd fall perfectly down her back. Her nails were a pale pink, the signature heart carefully placed on the fourth finger of each hand and foot. She'd decided on a tight black sweater with short sleeves and a high collar, and a flowing, short red gauze skirt and black peep-toe heels. It was a little bold for a night out in Bluebonnet, but that was why she liked it. She'd worn black lacy lingerie and garters underneath, too. Just in case.

And she really, really hoped for that just in case.

"You look very pretty today," Mrs. Doolittle told her as Beth Ann arranged her soft, white curls.

She smiled at Mrs. D—her last appointment of the day. "Thank you. I just thought I'd dress up today."

"You going out with that nice Allan Sunquist tonight?"

Beth Ann's face fell. "We're not going out anymore, Mrs. D. I'm seeing someone else now."

"Such a shame," Mrs. D said, and shook her head, ruining Beth Ann's careful arranging.

"Not a shame, honey," Beth Ann said lightly. "You remember Colt Waggoner?"

"One of those white-trash Waggoner boys?" The old woman harrumphed. "He came back with that lewd hockey player, didn't he?"

"Lewd?" Beth Ann asked, blinking. Her hands had stopped.

"The one that showed his delicates to everyone in town just to impress that little Miranda Hill." She gave a harrumph. "As if showing her his bits would impress her."

Beth Ann smothered her laugh. "I'm sure she knew better than that to be impressed by a man waving his bits at her," she assured Mrs. D. as the woman paid and left.

Poor, poor Miranda and Dane. At first Miranda's boobs had been legendary about town. Now all anyone talked about was Dane's lily white butt. And Dane was a good natured guy—he didn't mind in the slightest, because Dane's naked stroll made everyone talk about his photos rather than Miranda's. She smothered a laugh at the memory of him walking down Main Street, wearing nothing but a hockey helmet over his junk.

The doorbell to her shop clanged and Beth Ann looked up. Her breath caught in her throat at the sight of Colt.

Well damn. There was Beth Ann, looking like one of his wet dreams in a tight black sweater and a short red skirt. She lit up at the sight of him, and Colt turned and flipped the sign on her door to "closed."

"Hey," he said.

"Hey yourself," she said with a smile, and moved past him to turn the lights off on the big sign. He said nothing, watching her. She looked damn pretty. Her ass looked amazing in that skirt, and those shoes made her legs look long and slim. She looked perfect.

She looked untouchable again. Out of his league.

Damn. What was he thinking? She'd had a weekend of sex with him, but she belonged with someone with money. She was the belle of the town—no one'd want to see her with trash like him. Williamsons didn't mix with Waggoners.

She looked over at him, and her fingers reached up and brushed his hair, just above his ear. "You're getting shaggy," she said lightly. "Want me to fix that up for you?"

"If you like," he said, content to watch her movements. After all, she wasn't kicking him out the door yet.

She grinned and gestured back at her chair. "Come sit down."

He sat, and glared into the mirror when she pulled out a pink cape to cover him. "Not that shit again."

The last time he'd gotten his hair cut at her place, she'd put that pink cape on him deliberately, he'd suspected.

She gave him an exasperated look. "Pink's the only color I've got."

"Buy a black one. You can cut my hair then."

She rolled her eyes at him in the mirror and reached to pull it around him. "You need a haircut."

"I don't need to look like a sissy." He caught her hand in his.

Beth Ann froze against him, and they stared at each other. They were awkward now. Tense. He wanted to go back to where she was warm and soft in his bed, and smiling up at him.

Had to do something. He didn't want her glaring at him. He wanted her soft, and sweet, and ready to wrap her legs around him again.

So he caught her hand and pressed a kiss to the palm. "Do you trust me?"

She softened as she looked down at him. "You kept me safe in the woods, didn't you?"

Well, yeah, but it was his fault she'd been stuck there. That wasn't a conversation he wanted to get into today, though, so he decided to distract her. He nipped at one of her fingertips, then looked up at her. "You said you wanted to be the woman nobody in town expects you to be. I bet no one expects you to have sex with me. Here. If you trust me, of course."

Her mouth parted a little.

Colt waited for her to protest. To be shocked by his suggestion.

But her eyes got soft and she licked her lips, and he felt the tremor that raced through her. "No, they wouldn't expect me to do that at all, would they?" she said huskily. She ran her free hand over the back of his hair, as if she found the buzz of his short haircut just as erotic as touching the rest of him.

Hell, yes. His cock got hard immediately. He took the pink cape from her and tossed it down on the ground. He tugged her hand and pulled her across his lap. Her smile was soft and seductive, and he kissed her because he needed to taste her lips again.

She tasted just as sweet as he'd remembered. He'd thought about her all week, and their date. He didn't expect sex from her, of course. But if he suggested it and she was willing? Well, they could base a relationship on a lot worse things than sex, he supposed.

She broke away from the kiss with a gasp and tried to pull out of his lap. "The windows—"

His entire body stiffened with anger. "You ashamed to be seen kissing me?"

She gave him a confused look. "What do you mean?"

"Cause I'm one of those white-trash Waggoners," he gritted out.

"Actually," she said softly, "I thought if I was going to take my clothes off, we should shut the windows."

"Ah," he said, since an apology was not going to cross his mouth.

Beth Ann leaned up and kissed him. "Silly." She slid out of

his lap and went to the front door, locked it, then turned to the long panel of windows that made up the front of the salon. They looked out over Main Street, and they'd given everyone a glimpse of their kissing.

Probably a good call to close them. He stood up and ran a hand along the back of her chair, then pumped his foot on the bar a few times to raise it higher.

When all the blinds were closed, she turned to look back at him with a puzzled frown. "What are you doing?"

"Raising your chair up," he said. "I'm going to make love to you in it."

She licked her lips, and he liked the sight of that. "Oh," she said, the word soft and husky. "Sounds lovely."

He pulled her toward him again and kissed her, enjoying how sweetly she wrapped her arms around his neck, and how her mouth parted under the thrusts of his tongue. "Been thinking about you all week, Beth Ann."

"I've been thinking about you, too," she admitted, and her hand stroked down the front of his shirt. He'd worn a button up shirt—his only one—and slacks for the date. Didn't feel like him, but he didn't want to look like a pity date when they went out. He wanted to impress her, and a T-shirt and BDUs wouldn't do it.

"You look good tonight," she said softly.

"You look better."

Beth Ann smiled at him and took a step back. Her hands went to her sweater and she pulled it over her head, tossing it aside. Her high, tight little breasts—breasts he'd been seeing in his sleep, they were so perfect—were cupped by black lace so sheer that he could see her little nipples through them. He wanted them in his mouth already, to feel them beading on his tongue, to feel her hands stroking the buzz on the back of his head as she moaned under him.

Her fingers went to the buttons on his shirt, and he pulled it over his head, tossing it over to where her sweater lay on a nearby magazine rack.

She gave a small sigh of pleasure at the sight of his undershirt. Her finger ran along the chain of his dog tags. "Oh, this looks sinful with your muscles."

"Should I take it off?"

"God no," she said, and grinned up at him. "I like it far too much." Her hands slid down to the belt of his pants. "These, however . . ."

He slid off his shoes, undid his belt and dropped it to the ground. His briefs followed a moment later.

She groaned and dropped to her knees in front of him. "Mercy, I love the sight of this," she said with a little sigh of pleasure that did crazy things to his insides. "I kept wondering if it was as thick in reality as it was in my memory."

His hand moved to her hair, caressed her cheek. "And?"

"Much better than my memories," she said, and leaned forward and gave the thick crown a little swipe with her tongue.

He groaned and hauled her back to her feet. "Not tonight, darlin'. I want to fuck you first."

She smiled at him and leaned in to kiss him again as his hands went to the tiny zipper at the side of her skirt and tugged it down. The garters surprised him. And so did the little scrap of panties. "Nice." He ran his hands down the curve of her ass. "Very nice."

"You like?" She still wore a mischievous smile.

"I do," he said, lifting a hand to brush against one of her nipples, still tight through the fabric of the thin bra. "Want to get a better look at them."

"I'd better take off my panties first," she said, and bent to tug at one of the straps of her garters.

"You keep those on," he said, his voice husky. He wanted to fuck her with them on, her legs encased in the silky, erotic fabric.

"I will." She grinned and turned away, bending over to undo the straps. As she did, she presented him with her ass, sweet and round. He groaned and ran his hands over those cheeks, enjoying the creamy flesh hidden by tantalizing scraps of lace. A moment later, she pushed her panties down to the ground, stepped out of them, and then began to hook her garters back once more. When she was done, she turned back to him expectantly.

"On the chair," he said.

"The shoes?"

"Stay on."

"Naughty," she said with a grin, and slid over to the chair, then crossed her legs daintily in it and waited. Her pose hid everything but her smooth thighs, and while she was a lovely picture like that, he had other plans. His hand moved to her leg and skimmed along the thigh, stroking her soft skin. He then hooked his hand under her knee and tugged her leg outward until it was straight. She arched her foot as he did, and he remembered that she liked to be kissed there. His mouth went to her ankle, and he lightly kissed the flesh through the silky hose, enjoying her shivers. Her hands brushed over his cock as he did, as if she couldn't resist touching him.

His hands stroked down that smooth length of leg, so straight, and then tilted it back. At her gasp, he reached for her other leg, straightened it, and then tilted it back, too, until her legs were a vee straight in the air, and she was forced to clutch the arms of the chair to keep her balance. Her breath was coming in short, spiky pants that pleased him.

Not nearly as much as when he looked down and discovered that she was completely bare. Her sweet little pussy was pink, the slit gleaming with moisture.

"Well I'll be damned," he said, his cock hard as steel at the sight.

"I wanted to surprise you," she said softly, then chuckled. "Surprise."

He knelt in front of the chair. "Now that's just beggin' for a taste."

At her sharply inhaled breath, he knew she liked the thought, and he tugged at her hips, pulling her close. "Hands on your legs. Keep them straight up in the air," he said. "Gotta show off those gorgeous legs."

She trembled but did as she was told, and he leaned in and brushed his mouth over the tender flesh. He felt the shiver that coursed through her, heard the moan she bit back. He licked the wet seam of her, felt her hips jerking in response. She was entirely open like this, her legs arching high in the air, her hands locked behind each knee, her bare sex exposed to him. Trusting him. Wanting him as much as he wanted her.

He needed her, right then. With a low groan in his throat, he kissed her right on the plumpest part of her pussy. "Stay there, darlin'."

A moment later, he returned, condom in hand. He quickly put it on and watched her biting her lip, her eyes hot with need.

He couldn't resist teasing her a moment more, though. With a lazy finger, he slid it through the damp folds, trailing back and forth in her slickness. "Are you wet enough?"

She nodded, a high-pitched whimper emerging from her throat.

"Should I lick you a little more? Just to be sure?"

"No," she breathed, but trembled at his words. "Take me now. Please."

"You want me deep inside you?" He moved forward, his hands on her thighs, pulling her a few inches forward, to the edge of the chair. She was perfectly lined up with the height of his cock, and he placed the thick head of it at her wet, hot entrance, and nudged it in, just a little.

She moaned.

He stopped, though he thought his balls were going to explode with need. "Tell me that you want me, Beth Ann."

"Please, Colt," she said softly, her fingers digging into her silky stockings. As he watched, her legs trembled. "I need you."

"Need this?" he asked, and thrust shallowly against her entrance.

She whimpered. "Yes."

"Convince me," he said softly.

She whimpered again, tugging at her legs, as if dying to pull her hands from where they were anchored.

"Tell me."

"Please," she panted, the words rushing forth from her. "I ache for you."

"You do?" He ran a hand down one beautiful leg. "Did you think about me this week? Think about fucking me again?"

She nodded, then bit her lip. "I want to feel your thickness deep inside me."

Holy hell. He pushed deeper, into her tight warmth. She was so incredibly wet and snug around him, and judging by her little keening gasps, it felt just as good to her as it did to him. He slowly pushed in, inch by inch, until he was seated deep within her. And then he stopped again.

She writhed against him, and he felt that tight pussy clench all around his cock. Tight, slick, and totally bare. He stroked one hand over her mound, his thumb dipping to flick her wet clit.

Beth Ann shuddered, gasping. Her legs jolted involuntarily.

He pushed forward, until those sexy shoes were pushing against his shoulders, her legs long, sweet spikes that lay against his body. And still he didn't move inside her. He wanted her to ask for it, because there was nothing fucking hotter than that.

"Colt," she said softly, breathing his name. "Colt, I need—"

"Tell me."

Her hips flexed. "Move."

"Move?" He gave a small little flex of his hips in return. "You mean . . . you want me to fuck you?"

She nodded, her blond hair cascading over her shoulders. "Please."

"Darlin'," he said softly, and leaned in to kiss her pretty, parted mouth. He was in her so deep, her shoes almost grazing his ears. "You need to ask me for that."

Her eyelids fluttered. Her mouth worked, as if she was having a hard time expressing the words. This was a woman that said "fiddlesticks" after wandering hours in the rain and mud. But he knew he could make her ask for more.

"Colt," she panted.

"Yes, darlin'."

"Fuck . . . me . . ." She gasped. "I need you to fuck me."

Most erotic thing he'd ever heard. He grasped her thighs, pulled back until only the head of his cock was still seated in her warmth, and then slammed deep back into her.

A loud moan tore from her throat. "Like that. Oh, like that."

He buried himself deep in her again, pumping hard. Her moans were fucking beautiful, and they were mixed with wild, needy words as he stroked deep inside her. Over and over, he thrust hard, into that hot, slick, welcome warmth. Her calves against his shoulders trembled and she bucked her hips with every little thrust.

"Like that." She kept breathing with every stroke, as if she had to keep instructing him. "Oh, like that."

And damn if it didn't make him want to fuck her harder. He slammed into her with every thrust, the chair rocking and shaking with every slap of their skin meeting. She tensed under him, and the whimpers escalated, her eyes squeezed shut.

He was going to come soon, and she hadn't come yet. Her pussy was clenching him tight, like a vise, and he wasn't going to last. But she needed to come first.

"Touch yourself, darlin'. Touch that bare pussy for me."

Her gasps turned into small cries that matched his thrusts. "Colt . . . I need . . ."

"Touch," he said with a thrust.

Her hand slid down her belly, her fingers sliding to her sex as he watched. They parted the slick flesh, swiped over her clit. She stiffened, her mouth forming a small O of ecstasy.

"Keep touching," he gritted, his thrusts into her wild now, jerky. Christ, watching her touch herself as he pumped into her was going to make his control disappear entirely.

She whimpered out his name, her fingers jerking on her clit, and his name turned into a sob as her legs stiffened, and he felt her pussy shiver around his cock, clamping around it.

He came with a hoarse shout, his fingers dug into her hips, slamming against her in the chair.

Fucking hell. Did every round of sex with her have to be more mind-blowing than the last? He exhaled slowly, bracing himself on the arms of the chair while he recovered. Her legs twitched against him, calves still propped on his shoulders, and he heard her soft panting.

He staggered backward, almost regretting that he had to pull out of her delicious warmth, and turned away to dispose of the condom. When he turned back, she'd curled her legs down against herself and still sat in the chair, dazed.

Her hair was a mess. Her mouth was red in the corners from where he'd kissed her too fiercely and left stubble burn.

She looked gorgeous. And here he'd jumped on her like some horny teenager as soon as he saw her. Allan would have taken her out for a nice dinner, romanced her, and then brought her home and made love to her in a nice big bed.

Hell, Colt just threw her down in her barber chair and fucked her. He ran a hand down his face. "I'm sorry."

She sat up, stiffening, her face suddenly guarded. "Sorry?"

"This," he said, gesturing at the salon. Their clothes had been thrown all over the small room. "Probably isn't what you wanted. I should have taken you out for a nice dinner like a civilized human being."

She laughed and got up from the chair. "*This* is exactly what I wanted, Colt Waggoner." Her hands went to his undershirt and flicked down his nipples. "Now that we've gotten all the sex out of the way, we can be together and not worry about being tense or weird about anything."

He leaned down and kissed her fiercely. "Two things," he said, when he pulled away from her mouth.

"What's that?"

"First of all, this is not all the sex gotten out of the way. This is the first round of sex gotten out of the way."

She laughed, and her hands stole to his buttocks, squeezed. "And the second?"

"The second is that you're the most beautiful thing I've ever seen, Beth Ann Williamson."

Her mouth got all soft and she stared up at him with a smile. She squeezed his ass again. "I'm still game to go out if you are. Night's early. Where did you want to go?"

He shrugged, remembering what Allan had mentioned. "You like Italian?"

She made a face. "Not really."

He thought for a minute more. "Wings? There's a sports bar next town over. Great wings. Private booths."

She laughed and twirled away. "You just want to see me licking my fingers all night, don't you?"

"The thought did cross my mind," he said with a smile.

They cleaned up with towels and her rinsing sink, redressed, and drove to the next town over. In the car, Beth Ann chatted with him about her week—the new salon that had moved in down the street, her customers, her sister being grounded for a month after being caught at the Arcane Forest with Lord Colossus.

He'd told her about the class he'd had, and how they'd gotten lost almost immediately. She'd laughed at all the things he thought were amusing, and listened to his camping stories. Boring shit for a girl that liked hair and makeup, but she didn't seem bored by them at all. And when they got to the bar, she'd sat on the same side of the booth as him so she could watch the TV, too. He spent most of the night watching her lick her fingers as she ate wings—and damn it if that wasn't one of the hottest things he'd ever seen—and explaining hockey to her. He'd become a fan ever since Dane had been drafted, and she seemed eager to learn more.

They'd ended the night with a sweet kiss on her salon doorstep. Then, she'd murmured naughty things into his ear, and they'd stumbled back to the air mattress she had in the back storage room, and made love twice more before he'd kissed her good night and headed back to the ranch.

All in all, not a bad first date.

TEN

Beth Ann saw Colt three times that week, and regularly for the next three weeks. Twice he'd swung by to see her to bring lunch, or have dinner, and once she'd headed by the ranch just because she'd been thinking about him, and brought him dinner. They kept tabs on each other's schedules, since his job had varying hours and he wanted to make sure that her schedule matched up with his at least a few times during the week. The nights he was gone on overnight trips and she didn't get to see him, she missed him. Stupid to be so far gone over a guy she'd only been seeing for a month, but there it was. And every time he got back from a trip, he'd swing by the salon on the pretense of a haircut, and they'd end up in the back room with her ankles on his shoulders and his cock deep inside her.

Beth Ann flushed at the thought. So far, so good on the relationship. They'd gone out of town to date more often than they'd stayed in, and no one in Bluebonnet had seemed to pick up on the fact that they were seeing each other. They weren't hiding it, after all. But no one seemed to notice, and Beth Ann was still frequently asked when she was going to get back together with Allan.

She didn't know what to make of it. She didn't mind if people thought she was dating Colt—not in the slightest. But when people asked, she didn't say she was dating anyone. Colt hadn't mentioned if he wanted it to be known or not. And the longer Allan was kept in the dark about how serious they were, the easier it was for her. She liked things how they were.

Well, she'd have liked them more if they had a real bed, she amended. The last time Colt had been over, they'd busted the air mattress and ended up on the floor. He'd bought her a new one and promised to accompany her apartment hunting his next Saturday off.

Which was today, and just as soon as she was done with her appointments, they'd be heading out the door. She smiled at the thought and had dressed to please him. A white backless sundress covered in a cherry pattern with a swingy skirt. Heels. No panties. And bare again, because she knew he liked that. She glanced at her watch. Her last appointment was running late. Annoying. Her Saturday hadn't been great so far—she'd had another client defect to Cutz, the new salon across the street. It was ridiculous. She'd heard the woman was horribly unfriendly, the prices sky-high, and Beth Ann still lost clients on a regular basis.

It was going to drive her crazy. She had to do something about it, but what, she didn't know.

The mailman dropped by with a nod and a wave, handing her

a stack of magazines. "Thanks, Doug." She took them and flipped through the mail, frowning at a personalized envelope. From her landlord? Beth Ann pushed the stack of magazines aside and tore open the envelope.

Her rent was going up. A full six hundred dollars a month. That was ridiculous. Her landlord had included an apologetic note, citing property tax rates and how she understood if Beth Ann needed to break her lease.

Tears of frustration pricked at her eyes. Drat. What was she going to do? She was trying to save money to afford an apartment of her own so she could stop having to go to her parents to shower and do laundry. She wanted her own home, not hiding out in the back room of her salon. If her landlord knew she was doing that, she'd probably get booted for that, too. An extra six hundred a month was going to cut her savings to zero, especially now that she was losing clients to the rival down the street. She pinched the bridge of her nose in frustration, willing the tears away.

The cowbell on the door clanged, announcing a customer. She looked up with a smile of greeting. It faded as Allan entered, carrying a bouquet of pale pink roses—her favorite.

"Hi, Allan," she said, softly.

"Got time for a walk-in?" He smiled at her. "We haven't talked much in the past few days and I thought this would be a good chance to say hello."

"Actually, I have a two thirty," she said. "Mrs. Patmore."

He smiled. "I saw her on the street, actually. She was heading to that other salon."

"She was?" she said with a gasp, hating that broken little sound in her throat. "Well that's just freaking great."

Allan brightened, stepping forward. "So you have time to take one walk-in, then?"

She gestured to the barber chair, feeling helpless. With her rent going up, she couldn't really afford to turn a paying customer away. Maybe she could work extra hours. Run a sale on mani/pedi combos, work on her days off, bring in some extra clients . . .

"So how is work going?" Allan asked as she settled the cape over him and pulled out her scissors.

She began to cut, thinking hard. She could do Allan's haircut by heart—she'd been doing it for him for years, even before she had her salon. Even when they'd been between engagements in the past, she'd cut his hair for him. Then he'd smile at her, buy her something expensive, then beg for forgiveness. Losing her had changed him, he'd tell her. It had made him rethink his priorities and what he wanted was her. And yet every time they'd get back together, she'd find out about another girl, and nothing would change.

And it all started with another haircut. Beth Ann gave Allan's smiling face a wary glance.

"I miss you," he said softly as she began to cut.

"Don't, Allan," she said. "I don't want to hear it."

"It's true. We were good together. You know we were."

If we were so good together, how come you kept cheating on me? she wanted to say, but bit the words back. Instead, she just continued to cut, lifting thick strands of his hair and snipping. Allan had always had thick, beautiful hair. Curse that it should be on such an unfaithful man.

"Huh."

"What?" She glanced up at him, cutting carefully.

"Your dress. It's rather low cut in the back, don't you think?"

It was rather low cut. That was why she liked it. "Is it?" she said lightly. "I hadn't noticed."

"It's not like you." He frowned at her reflection for a moment, and then his easy smile returned. "You know what Mrs. D said to me last week?"

"No, but I'm sure you'll tell me."

"She told me that she missed seeing you with me. And you know what, Bethy-babe? I miss seeing you with me, too."

"Allan, if you don't stop it, I'm going to cut you a bald spot," she warned, shaking her scissors at him.

"But . . ." He gave her a hurt look, one that had never failed to wring her heart in the past. "I don't understand why you won't give me another chance."

"Because every time I give you another chance, you hurt me again, Allan. I'm tired of being hurt. It's time that I have someone I trust in my life."

And her entire body flushed just thinking about Colt. She had him, didn't she? A man that pulled her into his arms and held her close, a man that protected her. Made her feel safe. Secure. Adored. She glanced in the mirror, saw Allan's devastated look, and sighed. "This isn't good, Allan. I've moved on. You need to move on, too."

"I can't move on. You're the love of my life." His voice dropped into a low whisper that cracked. "My life is no good without you, Bethy-babe. Please come back to me."

She stopped. Put down her scissors. There was a dull ache in her chest. She'd loved Allan for so long. And when he was good to her, he was very good. But she didn't matter to him. She had never mattered to him. She was just his favorite accessory. When her feelings were hurt, he hadn't noticed. When he'd slept with other women, he'd thought that it was a problem that could be easily fixed with enough apologizing and gifts. He didn't understand her.

"I need a minute, Allan," she murmured, and headed to the back room.

"I'll be here," he called after her, his voice sad with longing.

That just made her feel worse. She closed the door to the back room and leaned against it, willing the guilt to go away. Beth Ann breathed deep, rubbing her temples. Allan pressed her relentlessly whenever he saw her. It gave her such a headache. She popped a few Tylenol, then tucked the rest into her purse, and brought it back into the main room with her. Colt'd be picking her up soon enough. She just had to put up with Allan for a bit longer and then boot him out of the shop.

When she emerged, he was still looking at her with sad eyes. "Will you take me back?"

"Allan, please. You know I can't have a relationship without trust. I won't do that to myself again. Ever again. And I can't trust you. And I won't be in a relationship with you anymore."

He caught her hand, stared at her in the mirror. "Then let me rebuild your trust. One step at a time."

"There is no rebuilding," she said. "You lied to me one too many times. I won't be with someone who lies to me and acts like what I want means nothing."

"And I'm working hard to change my ways," he said, and as she watched, he pulled a long, velvet box out of his pocket and held it out to her.

Beth Ann moved to the counter and threw her scissors down. "Good lord, Allan. Not again."

"It's for you. I thought of you and wanted you to have it. No strings attached."

No strings attached, her lily white butt. Beth Ann shook her head, didn't move toward the jewelry. "I don't want it. Even if I took it, I'd just pawn it for money."

He brightened, and she knew she'd said the wrong thing. "I can take care of you if you're having money trouble. Let me help you."

"I don't want help," she gritted. "Allan, please. Just stop it."

He reached for her hand again, but she sidled away. "Not until you promise to come back to me," he said stubbornly. "I'll change your mind."

"She can't come back to you if she's with me," Colt drawled, and stepped into the salon.

She looked up in surprise. When did he get here? She hadn't heard. He must have sat in one of the two waiting area chairs, listening to the conversation with Allan. She froze. What had he heard? Was he mad at her?

But Colt came forward and pressed a kiss to her temple, and looked down at Allan. There was a possessive look on his face as he casually laid a hand on the small of her exposed back.

Allan looked at Colt, then back to Beth Ann. Shock and hurt flickered across his face. "I don't understand."

"Well," Beth Ann said, wishing this wasn't so tense and uncomfortable. "I'm seeing someone."

"Me," Colt said flatly.

"But . . . what about me?" Allan tugged the pink cape off, let it fall to his lap.

"Guess you'll have to find someone else to sleep with. Sounds like you're good at doing that," Colt said, the words tense. His hand tightened against the small of her back, as if he wanted to pull her away from Allan.

Beth Ann flushed. Ouch. Allan's face grew flushed with anger under his tan. He stood. "You're sleeping with this man, Beth Ann?"

Lord, her cheeks were going to catch fire if they got any redder. "I don't see what business it is of yours if I am or not."

"It's my business because I care about you. I don't want to see you with someone that's not . . . that's not . . ." He paused, as if almost afraid to spit out the words. "You deserve better," he finally bit out.

"Like you?" she said in a hard, bitter laugh. "Twenty dollars for the cut, Allan. You can see yourself out the door."

He grabbed a twenty from his pocket and held it out to her. When she reached for it, he pulled it back, infuriating her. "So this is the man you 'trust'? The one you feel that you can trust more than me?" He gave a hard laugh. "You're kidding, right?"

She held her hand out for the money. "Just stop it, Allan."

"Yeah, well, you'll come to your senses soon enough, Beth Ann. Because we both know you deserve so much better than him. And when you do, I'll be waiting."

She snatched the twenty from him. "Don't hold your breath."

He gave Colt a hateful glare and shoved out of the room, casting her one last wounded look. Beth Ann didn't follow. She didn't want to follow. That was what Allan wanted.

He paused in the doorway of the shop and turned to look back at her. "Your father wanted me to tell you that the Halloween committee meeting is tonight. He needs you to be there."

He slammed the door.

"Fuck!" Beth Ann said, clenching her hands into fists.

Colt looked at her in surprise.

"Sorry," she said, and then bit her fist in frustration. "That man makes me so mad that I want to spit nails."

"Do I need to scare him off?" The look in Colt's eyes was deadly serious.

She shook her head. She could only imagine what Colt would do, and Allan would call the cops in a heartbeat. "He just needs to get it in his head once and for all that I'm not with him."

Colt pulled her close, his hand sliding against her back. He pressed a light kiss to her mouth. "Maybe we should be more public with our relationship."

"Sex in the football bleachers?" she asked wryly. "We could ask Allan to hold the condoms and he still wouldn't grasp that I don't want to be with him."

He chuckled, brushed a hand down her back. "Nothing quite so public as that, I don't think. We could start with your committee tonight."

She groaned, leaning against him as if the thought sapped her will to live. "I don't want to go. Don't make me go."

"I won't make you go," he said, his hands cupping her ass through her skirts.

Beth Ann sighed. "And if I don't go, my father will thunder in like a hurricane and want to know why I'm sabotaging his campaign for reelection by being so publicly unhelpful when he needs me now more than ever." She rolled her eyes. "He trots out those excuses every other year around this time." Her arms wrapped around his neck and she lifted her face for another kiss. "I have to go to this stupid meeting."

"I'll go with you. If that dickhead is going to be there, I'm not leaving your side."

A warm, fuzzy feeling crept down her belly. So protective of her. She loved that. But he had to know what he was getting into. "I'm warning you. It'll be boring."

"I'll think of new ways to make love to you. I'll make a list. They'll think I'm taking notes."

She laughed and her hand slid to the front of his pants. "Well, I wasn't entirely against the sex on the bleachers idea. I've never made love in public."

"I'll put that as number one on the list," Colt drawled, smiling down at her. "Though it's probably not as scandalous if everyone thinks we're in a relationship."

She kissed him again, her heart fluttering. He'd said *relationship* twice now. Is that where they were going with this? They hadn't put a name on what they had yet. And she was afraid to ask, for fear she might ruin it.

After all, Allan had showed that she wasn't good with relationships. But she trusted Colt, and he knew how important that trust was to her. So maybe she could hope, just a little.

The committee meeting was every bit as boring as she'd thought it would be. She'd been assigned the costume bash in the town square, and it was her task to set guidelines for costumes, contests, awards, and sponsors. Easy enough—why did they have to have four more committee meetings before Halloween to determine things? She complained as much to Colt on the way home, who agreed.

He'd been a perfect gentleman that night, she'd decided. He'd sat at the back of the room, just enough of a reminder for Allan to be quiet about his proclamations of love. Others had seen her enter with Colt, and the looks they'd given her were disapproving to downright confused. Wasn't she supposed to be with Allan? They had to be thinking it.

She'd take their confusion. Eventually people would get the picture, and if she had to trot Colt out everywhere she went, she would.

The meeting went on for three hours, killing any hopes she'd had of going out with Colt after the meeting had ended.

His expression when they met afterward was grim. "They don't like me with you."

"That's crazy."

He shook his head. "It's not crazy. You saw the way they were all looking at me. Like I'd come between the two of you." His jaw was clenched with fury. "So we either fuck in secret like we have something to hide, or when we're together, people act like I'm the bad guy."

"I don't care what other people think," she told him. Her voice echoed in the halls of the school and she quieted. "They'll get used to it."

"Will they?" The look he gave her was shuttered with anger. "This entire town thinks you belong to *him*."

She stopped, took his hand in hers. "But I'm with you," she said softly.

He turned her, then, pushing her up against the lockers with a bang. His mouth dove on hers, kissing her with fierce intensity. She gasped as his tongue thrust into her mouth, the sensation pouring liquid need through her body. She moaned against him, her hand sliding to the front of his pants to cup his cock.

"I need you, Beth Ann," he whispered against her mouth. "Let's go back to my place. Or yours. Whichever gets me deep inside you the fastest."

A thrill pulsed through her. She gave him another kiss, then gave a shaky laugh as a rather scandalous idea occurred to her. "No one would ever think I'm the kind of girl to have sex on a desk," she said softly, then nipped at his lower lip.

He groaned. "Here?"

"Why not?"

Colt glanced around, then took her hand and they moved to one of the doors along the school hallway. The first one was locked, but the second was not. He pulled her inside, and stared at the surroundings. High school classes—good. The walls were covered with posters of Einstein and other scientists. No kid stuff, or that might have weirded her out. He left the lights off, and pulled her forward, and picked her up and sat her down on top of a desk in the front row, and began to kiss her again. "You sure you want to do this here?"

"We can do the bleachers, if you'd rather," she said softly, then linked her legs around his, tugging him into the vee of her legs. "But we're already here."

He groaned and his tongue thrust deep into her mouth as he kissed her, stroking and rubbing against her tongue. "You amaze me," he said, his hands moving to the tie at the back of her neck. His fingers swiftly undid it and the straps fell forward. He tugged them down, exposing her breasts to his gaze.

She shivered with the sheer naughtiness of it, her nipples prickling. He rubbed his thumbs over both of the small peaks, enjoying her whimpers of delight, then tugged on one before leaning down to take it into his mouth.

"Colt," she breathed, groaning with need as his tongue flicked over the tip. Oh heavens, that felt so amazing. "Oh, mercy, that feels so good."

He bit her nipple, eliciting a sharp, soft little cry from her throat. His mouth immediately moved to cover hers, kissing away the sounds she made. "Someone might be hanging around, darlin'," he said. " You want them to hear you getting pleasured?" His fingers twirled around one peak even as he whispered to her, driving her mad with need.

"I'll be quiet," she whispered, and when he leaned down to bite her other nipple, she whimpered, biting down on her lip. His hand moved under her skirts, finding her panties, and she parted her thighs wider to allow him access to her pussy.

"So slick and wet," he murmured against the peak of her breast, and gave it a lick even as he brushed his thumb over her clit.

She gasped, moaning, her fingers digging into his shirt. "Colt—"

"Sounds like you *do* want them to hear you," he said, though the sound was a low chuckle, as if he were pleased she couldn't quite keep herself as quiet as she wanted. His mouth tugged at her nipple, rolling it against his tongue and then lightly biting it, and each new sensation was accompanied by a flick over her clit. She cried out, bucking against his hand. God, she was so wet, so full of need for him. His fingers rubbed along her clit faster, even as he turned his attentions to her other breast, nipping at the peak. She clung to his shoulders, her heels wrapped around his hips, locked together.

The door clicked. The light came on.

"Beth Ann?" Allan stood there in the doorway.

Beth Ann gasped, unlocking her legs from around Colt's waist, struggling to pull her dress back to cover her breasts. "Get out of here, Allan!"

Allan stared at the two of them in shock. He didn't move. "What the hell is this?"

Colt stepped in front of her, blocking her from Allan's view. "Get the fuck out of here."

"This is a public building," Allan said, furious. He looked at Beth Ann, scandalized, then back to Colt. "You son of a bitch. You're taking advantage of her while she's hurting."

She rolled her eyes. "Allan, go away—"

"Get the fuck out of here," Colt repeated again, his voice low and dangerous. His hand went backward to her, as if he could shield her from Allan.

But Allan looked at the two of them, furious. "Disgusting, trashy behavior. I should have guessed that was why she'd want to go slumming with you. Well, newsflash, Waggoner, she's a shitty lay—"

Colt launched himself at Allan. He tackled the other man to the ground with a crash, and she barely had time to scream before

Colt was straddling Allan. He slammed a fist into the other man's face.

"Colt!" Her shrill cry didn't make either man pause. As she watched, Allan's fist aimed for Colt's face, missed, then slammed into his jaw. "Both of you! Stop it!" She hopped down from the desk, clutching her dress to her.

Colt's fist slammed into Allan's face again, and she grew afraid. Oh lord, if he beat the snot out of Allan, Allan would call the cops on him. She tugged at Colt's arm. "Colt, please, stop it."

"Yeah, Colt," Allan said with a sneer, blood streaming down his face. "She doesn't want you to hurt me."

But Colt had stopped, and he panted, still straddling Allan, and cast a bleak look at Beth Ann, as if betrayed that she would stop him.

"I'd put my shoe through your damn face myself, Allan," she said in a hard voice, and continued to tug at Colt's arm. "But this is enough. Colt. Please."

He lowered his fist. Slowly got off Allan. Blood trickled from the corner of his mouth, blood that he ignored.

Allan got to his feet, pressed his sleeve to his nose, then snarled at Colt, "I'm calling the police."

"No, you're not," Beth Ann said calmly, and she was surprised at how calm she was. "Or I'll tell them you were stalking me, and Colt was defending me."

"I know the police. They're my friends," Allan said smugly.

"They used to be my friends, too," she pointed out, moving toward Colt. "And they know you won't leave me alone. If you file one charge against him, it's going to be your word against both of ours."

Allan glared. He wiped his face with his sleeve, smearing blood. "We'll discuss this some other time."

"No we won't," she said, but the door had slammed shut.

Colt followed him to the door, and for a moment, she thought he was going to chase Allan down the hallway and beat him some more. Her heart thundered in her chest. But Colt only turned the light back off, locked the door, and returned to her.

"You okay?" she breathed.

He leaned down and kissed her, hard. His teeth ground against her own and she tasted his blood in her mouth. His tongue thrust once, twice, and then he was pressing hard kisses down her neck and throat. "Colt?"

He growled against her skin. "I fucking hate that dirtbag."

"I'm sorry," she said softly.

He turned back to her and his hands went to her cheeks. "Don't tell me you're sorry," he said in a hard voice. "Just tell me you're never going to go back to him again."

"I'm not—"

"And tell me that you're mine." His eyes glittered in the moonlight, and she felt him press his erection against her.

"I'm yours," she said softly. The fight had brought out his protective streak. "All yours."

He tugged at the straps of her dress, pulling them from her hands to let them fall back around her waist once more, exposing her breasts. His fingers moved to the nipple, pinched it. He watched her face.

Her breath inhaled sharply. "Do you—should we . . ."

"Turn around, darlin'," he said softly.

A dangerous, erotic thrill shot through her. She moved slowly, turning until her back was to him. He moved forward, his hand skimming along her back, and she arched against those wonderful, callused fingers. She loved his touch.

"Bend over the desk," he rasped, and his hand went to her neck. He didn't exert pressure—it was just there to remind her of what he wanted. And she bent over the desk, gasping when the cold wood surface hit her fevered nipples. Her belly clenched as it hit the wood, and she shuddered in anticipation.

"Do you want me, Beth Ann?" Colt's voice was low, possessive. "Right here? Right now? Say no, and I can just walk away right now."

Say no, and I can just walk away right now. For some reason, she suspected that had a lot more meaning than to just right now. As in, forever. But she was in this too deep—and currently too turned on—to even think about leaving. "I'm staying."

"Because no one would expect you to fuck me after we'd been found out?"

"Because I want you," she said softly. "Only you."

His hands pushed up her cherry skirt—no panties. She spread her legs, steadying herself. Her hands clamped onto the front of the desk and she waited, her body rigid with anticipation. The crinkle of the condom wrapper alerted her, but she still wasn't prepared for the feel of him when he surged into her. She sucked in a breath. She'd been wet, but not as soaked as she normally was when he finally thrust into her. There was a bit of sting, and tightness to her, and she wiggled, trying to adjust.

His hands gripped her hips and he rocked deep, groaning with need. "Beth Ann."

"I'm here," she said softly.

He thrust again, and this time it didn't hurt. Pleasure began to strum through her—his cock was so thick that it rubbed against all of her when he stroked in, and rubbed even more when he moved out. It was an exquisite sensation—she felt filled with lust when he stroked between her legs. It was like her entire core was one big g-spot. Amazing, that. He began to thrust hard, fast, his hand stealing to her shoulder to anchor her down. This was not a soft, tender exploration of bodies. This was hard, possessive sex. He was claiming her as his, branding her, making his mark on her.

And she loved it.

Soft little cries began to break from her with every hard, punishing thrust. The desk slammed back and forth with every motion as he rocked into her. His balls slapped against her with every thrust, and his thighs smacked against her own every time. This was the hardest they'd ever fucked, and instead of scaring her, she reveled in it. She wanted him to thrust deeper, harder. Lose all control. Her fingers dug against the side of the desk. She reached up, pulled his face down to her own, and whispered, "Fuck me harder, Colt."

He groaned, an animal noise, and his body slammed into her. Once, twice, and then he bit out her name, and his entire body clenched. She felt him spasm deep inside her, and she panted, motionless. He'd come before her. That hadn't happened before, but she understood it. He'd needed her—needed this so bad. He rocked into her one more time, as if reluctant to leave her body, and then exhaled sharply. "Turn over."

She sat up, turned around, flushed, and leaned in to kiss him.

He stopped her. "Back on the desk."

"But—"

He grabbed her by the hips and hauled her back up. "On your elbows."

She did, though she was in danger of falling off the desk. Again, he pushed up her skirts, and to her shock, he buried his face in her pussy. "Colt," she gasped. "But—"

"Want to hear you come, darlin'," he murmured against her flesh, and the vibrations of his low, husky voice sent shockwaves skittering through her. She moaned, and when his tongue began to lap at her, her hips quivered in response.

A finger sank deep inside her—not nearly as exciting as his cock—and was joined by two others. He fucked her with his fingers, even as he bent to her clit and began to lick it with slow, measured strokes.

"Oh mercy," she moaned, forgetting all about being quiet. "Oh, Colt, yes, please . . ."

"You taste sweet, Beth Ann," he said, and she moaned anew, wishing her skirts weren't blocking her view. His fingers continued to thrust into her, even as his tongue worked her clit over. Her hips began to undulate with need, and her cries ripped through the air as she came with a wet rush, the orgasm ripping through her with intensity.

When she'd come down again, he took her by the hand and pulled her off the desk, and gave her a kiss that tasted like her sex. "Turn around."

She did as she was told, still panting.

"Lift your hair." When she did, he pressed a kiss to the back of her neck, and she smiled. "Come to my place tonight," he said softly, tying the straps of her dress behind her neck for her again.

He hadn't invited her back since that first night after they'd gotten out of the woods. She felt a little flutter in her chest. "You sure?"

When she turned, he nodded, and kissed her again, and she touched the cut on the corner of his mouth with concern. "Doesn't hurt," he said. "Will you stay?"

"Is this because you want me with you, or because you're afraid Allan's going to come by and harass me again?"

"Both," he said. "Plus, I like the way you wake a man up. Ruined me for coffee, remember?"

She laughed. "Let's stop by my place and get my things first."

They swung by her salon while she packed a quick overnight bag, and then headed out to the ranch in his car. Once in his cabin, they'd made love again—this time tender, sweet love—before going to sleep in each other's arms, naked.

ELEVEN

The front door banged open, startling Beth Ann awake.

"Sorry to barge in, Colt," Miranda sang out, and Beth Ann heard a cord dragging. "But you're the closest cabin and the closest outlet, and I need to curl my hair before we meet Dane's parents today, and I—"

Beth Ann sat up, pushing aside a nest of blond hair that had fallen into her face.

Colt sat up, too, and his voice was amused. "Mornin', Miranda."

Beth Ann's best friend stared at the two of them in bed together in horror. Her jaw went slack with surprise, and then she dropped the curling iron in her hand. "Oh." She scooped it up and then tilted her head, staring at them. "I came over to borrow an outlet. I, uh, didn't realize Colt had company."

"Hey, honey," Beth Ann said softly, her cheeks flushing. "How are you?"

"Holy shit!" Miranda exclaimed, the sight of her friend finally sinking in. "Beth Ann! What the hell? You never said a word to me!"

Beth Ann bit her lip and looked over at Colt.

"Miranda," he said, "can I get you to turn around so I can get some pants?"

"Oh my *God*. You're both naked," Miranda squeaked. "Oh God, I'm scarred for life. I'll go to the big lodge—"

"It's okay," Colt said. "Just give me two minutes for pants, and then you and Beth Ann can talk—"

Before he could finish, Miranda was back out the door. Colt chuckled and glanced over at Beth Ann. "Didn't realize she was that skittish."

"She's probably in shock," Beth Ann admitted, hugging Colt's blankets to her.

"Not half as shocked as she'd be if we told her what we were doing last night."

Beth Ann flushed.

He grinned, pulled her toward him and kissed her temple, then crawled out of bed over her. She admired his ass as he dressed, pulling on briefs, and then a pair of jeans. He turned as he tugged a shirt over his head, and his hair—that sexy high and tight haircut—was sticking up in tufts from sleep. "You want coffee, darlin'?"

"Coffee sounds good," she admitted.

He grinned and tossed a shirt at her. "I'll get some from the lodge and will be back. Don't go anywhere."

"You're my ride," she pointed out. Plus, she was pretty sure she'd forgotten to pack panties in their haste last night. She tugged on Colt's T-shirt and a pair of his sweatpants, and opened the door to the cabin to let Miranda in. "It's safe now, honey. No more naked people."

Miranda climbed up the steps and reentered with her curling iron. She plugged it into the wall, and then whirled to look at Beth Ann. "Well, I suppose this is a blessing," she said lightly. "You can fix my hair so I don't look like an idiot when I meet Dane's parents for lunch."

"Are they in town?" Beth Ann asked politely.

"They are," Miranda said stiffly. "We're having lunch with them to talk about the wedding and—oh hell, Beth Ann. You're sleeping with Colt?" Her friend's voice was scandalized. "You two hate each other. Like cats and dogs hate. Cats and water hate. Brenna and Grant hate." Her eyes widened. "Is this a hate-sex relationship? Is that what you need after Allan? Someone to make you feel like—"

"Nothing like that," Beth Ann said hastily. She moved to the curling iron and picked it up, then gestured for Miranda to sit in the sole chair in the cabin. "You bring clips?"

Miranda handed her one as Beth Ann separated a lock of her hair with her fingers. "Don't change the subject. How did you and Colt get together?"

"It's kind of complicated."

"And that's why you should tell your best friend," Miranda pointed out. "I should be terribly hurt that you never said a peep to me, but frankly—wow. Now I don't have to plan my wedding around whether or not you two can be civilized to each other. I can just plan it around whether or not you two need separate rooms or not."

Beth Ann blushed and wrapped the curling iron around a long, dark lock of Miranda's thick hair. "Don't read too much into it yet, honey. We're still casual."

Miranda twisted in her seat, jerking at the curling iron. "Oh my God. You guys are just fuck buddies?"

Lord. "We're dating. I just don't know if it'll last. I'm trying not to read too much into it just yet."

"Because Allan's going to try and chase him off?"

The thought had crossed Beth Ann's mind.

Miranda turned again. "Have you thought about Allan? What's he going to say?"

"He kind of found out the hard way," Beth Ann said lightly. "He walked in on us."

Miranda gasped, her hands going to the high collar of her dress. "What? How on earth did that happen?"

"Um." Beth Ann curled another long strand. "Same way you did."

Miranda wiggled in the seat. "Tell me everything. I'm your best friend. You know all my secrets."

She was pretty sure she didn't know all of Miranda's secrets, but this one was bound to get out. "He caught us. On one of the desks at the school. After a Halloween committee meeting."

Miranda gave another scandalized gasp. "Oh my God. Beth Ann! On a desk? In the school? That is so not like you!"

For some reason, that made Beth Ann's mouth curl up in a smile. "I know."

"I'm thinking he's a bad influence on you," Miranda said darkly. Her arms crossed over her chest.

"I'm thinking I like that bad influence, honey," Beth Ann said with a smile. "I like it a lot."

To Beth Ann's surprise, Miranda reached backward and took Beth Ann's free hand. She squeezed it. "I want you to be happy, girl. I'm tired of seeing you get hurt."

Tears pricked Beth Ann's eyes, and she resisted the urge to drop the curling iron and hug the pants off of her best friend. "Me, too, honey. Me, too."

"You realize I have to tell Dane this."

"Oh, I know."

"Man, he is going to flip out. He thought you guys hated each other."

"We did," Beth Ann mused. "Until we got stranded together."

Miranda released Beth Ann's hand and gestured at her hair. "You keep curling. And tell me all the gory details. Well, most of the gory details. I don't want to know the nasty stuff."

"You don't want to know how big and thick his man parts are, then?" Beth Ann drawled, teasing.

"Ugh! God no. I have to look him in the eye, you know. I don't want to imagine anyone's man parts but Dane's."

Beth Ann told her the story of their weekend together, skipping over the details of their physical relationship. Miranda made sympathetic noises at all the rain and mud, and gasped with horror at the Louboutins being destroyed. "I loved those shoes!"

"I didn't," Beth Ann said dryly. "I have two more pairs sitting in my closet that Allan gave me. You want them?"

"Heck yes. They're a little out of a librarian's salary, you know."

"A beautician's salary, too," Beth Ann said with a grin.

Miranda turned to look back at her again. "Won't Allan be mad that you gave them to me?"

She didn't care if he was. "Allan—and everyone else in this town—needs to learn that he doesn't own me."

Now that Miranda knew about Colt and Beth Ann, it was just a matter of time before Grant and Dane descended on him with questions.

He'd managed to avoid both of them so far, thanks to a three-day beginner class in survival. He'd taken them deep into the woods to his favorite spot, and kept the focus on teaching them how to make fires and fish with few to no supplies. He most definitely was not thinking about Beth Ann or if Allan was harassing her. Or if Dane and Grant were trying to squeeze details from her. Or if she laid on that sad air mattress in the back of her little salon and thought about him. Did she masturbate thinking about him? Touch herself because she needed him? Or did she just go blissfully about her day?

Brenna had called his satellite phone repeatedly, making kissy noises, so he'd turned the damn thing off so he could concentrate. But when he took his class in for their graduation, Grant was there to take their pictures, and he wore a knowing smile.

Brenna saw him and immediately started singing a nursery rhyme under her breath. "Colt and Beth Ann sitting in a tree . . . *F-U-C-K-I-N-G—*"

"Both of you can go to hell," he said, as soon as the class was sent on their way.

Brenna's green eyes widened. "Someone's a little touchy."

He should have guessed they'd be so childish about the whole damn thing. They knew Beth Ann. Had laughed and commented on how they didn't get along. And now they were laughing and commenting about how much they *were* getting along.

"Laugh it up, you two jackasses," he said, pointing at Brenna and Grant. "Just a matter of time."

Grant scowled at him, while Brenna looked confused. "Matter of time for what?"

Before you two start fucking, Colt wanted to say, but it'd drive them crazier to wonder, so he simply smiled and headed back to the main lodge to log his class records.

Dane was sitting at their desk when he came in, feet kicked up on the desk, hands behind his head. "Just the man I wanted to see."

Colt ripped the log book out from under Dane's feet. "Not you, too."

But Dane grinned, all boyish enthusiasm. "You're nailing Beth Ann Williamson? She's so sweet and proper. I didn't take her for your type."

"And what is my type?" he drawled, moving to Grant's desk and sitting down.

Dane shrugged, turning his chair so he could continue his conversation with Colt. "Little trashy. Little easy. One fuck and gone."

Great. So Beth Ann wasn't his type because she wasn't trash? That crawled under his skin. Did not even his friends think that he deserved someone classy like her? "Just fuck off about it, man."

Dane looked surprised at Colt's irritation. "I'm just trying to warn you, bro. She's bad news. She may sleep with you now, but she's going to run right back to Allan the moment she feels like he's suffered enough. She can't stay away from him. They've been together since high school. Remember?"

Oh, he remembered all right. She'd been laughing and popular and completely dismissive of him back in high school. He hadn't existed for her—her tiny world had included Allan, Allan's friends, and her friends. Colt hadn't even been a blip on her radar, even in a graduating class of only fifty students. He'd been a loner, kept to himself. Hadn't touched a girl until he got in the military. Then, they'd been falling all over the uniform. He'd been nobody in Bluebonnet.

And Allan had had everything. Fuck Allan. Colt had Beth Ann now. "She's not going back to him."

Dane shrugged. "I'll believe it when I see it. Miranda says she keeps going back to him over and over again. She hopes that Beth Ann's kicked him for good, but I think Miranda's worried that she'll go back again. I'm supposed to tell you not to break Beth Ann's heart, or my girl will come after you with a knife." And he grinned like that was adorable.

Colt rolled his eyes and bent low over the books. Goddamn it. He wished they'd all quit asking like he was doomed to somehow screw this up. He wasn't aware that by dating Beth Ann, he was somehow ruining the American dream for the whole fucking town.

Well, okay, maybe he'd known that a little. It just gave him a bit of added pleasure.

The door to the lodge opened and Colt glanced up, then groaned.

His younger brother, Berry, stood there. He wore a dirty

T-shirt that hung from his lanky frame, and jeans that were so ripped and stained that they should have been tossed out. Unkempt, shaggy hair stuck out from under the John Deere cap on his head.

Colt threw down the pencil in his hand. He was tired, annoyed, and the last thing he needed was one of his brothers showing up and starting shit.

"Hey, Berry," Dane said easily. "How you doing? Long time no see."

"Howdy, Dane. Good to see you here." Berry leaned over and clapped hands with Dane, his expression easy. "I should be asking for your autograph."

Dane grinned. "Nah, man. It's all good. I'm old and retired now."

Brenna entered a moment later, and Berry's gaze turned to her as she sat down at her desk. She wore a short, hot pink skirt that he could have sworn she'd worn as a tube top last week, and had tied a flannel T-shirt at her waist. Her curling, crazy hair was loose around her shoulders. He was pretty sure she was wearing bunny slippers, too. Brenna was odd, but cute enough. "Grant'll be back in a minute, guys. He's taking a few final pictures to update the brochures."

"Well, hello," Berry said, moving to Brenna's desk.

She gave him a cheerful, oblivious smile. "Hello."

"I'm Berry."

She looked up and tilted her head, her smile confused. "Like . . . the flavor?"

"It's short for Beretta," Dane said cheerfully. "Go on, ask what his other brother's names are."

Colt gritted his teeth. "Do we really—"

"You know Colt," Berry said. "Got another brother named Winchester. We all call him Chester. Got a brother Marlin, and another brother named Browning."

Brenna gave him a confused look. "And . . . those are all guns?"

"All guns," he said proudly.

She couldn't stifle her giggle. "Well, that's—um—interesting."

"You want to see the kind of heat I'm packin'?"

Brenna's face squished up in distaste.

"Berry," Colt barked, standing up. "Get out of here if you're going to harass our employees."

Berry straightened and gave Brenna a wink that made her roll her eyes. "Actually," he said, swaggering over to where Colt sat. "I came to see you. Dad's looking for you."

"He knows where I'm at," Colt said, voice clipped. He picked up the pencil again, trying to look busy. "I have no interest in seeing him."

Berry frowned, adjusting his cap. "It ain't right that you don't want to visit your family, Colt. Dad keeps asking about you. You should go see him."

"If I wanted to see him, I'd go visit," Colt bit out. "I don't need you coming over here to try and shame me into visiting."

"We're your family."

He looked at Berry's dirty clothes and ragged hair. Like he could forget where he'd come from. *White-trash Waggoners.* "I know," he said in a flat voice.

Berry scowled at him. "Asshole. The old man just wants to see you. But I guess you're too good for everyone now." He turned to the door.

Colt said nothing, turning his attention back to the log sheets in front of him until the lodge door slammed shut.

He'd known that moving back to Bluebonnet meant his family trying to get in touch with him. That didn't mean that he had to play along.

"What was that all about?" Brenna asked, her voice full of wonder.

"Just family drama," Dane said easily. "Nothing that Colt wants to talk about."

Damn right he didn't.

"Lucy, sit up straight," Jeanette said for the third time that hour. She smiled out to the others at their table, while poor Lucy fidgeted again. Lucy wore a demure, white-ruffled dress that made her look twelve instead of seventeen, and Jeanette had made Lucy remove all earrings before they'd headed to the country club. As part of her punishment, Beth Ann had to cover all the colorful streaks in Lucy's hair, and she was blond once more.

Today, her father had thrown a fund-raising party for his friend, a local republican senator. The entire family was on display, including Beth Ann. The "save me" looks Lucy kept throwing in her direction were useless, considering that Beth Ann couldn't save herself.

"I cannot believe you are wearing white shoes after Labor Day, Beth Ann," her mother hissed, and then gave a smiling wave to a friend that passed by their table. "What about those pretty shoes Allan gave you? It went perfectly with your pink dress."

Her mother had loved the Louboutins. And she was right, the

pink and yellow Louboutins had matched her light pink sheath with yellow piping perfectly, but she'd given the shoes to Miranda two days ago. She'd paired the dress with white heels and a white shrug instead. "They're white shoes, Jeanette. It's not like I showed up barefoot."

Though Colt would have smiled if she had. She flushed with warmth just thinking about him. She hadn't talked to him in three days—his latest overnight trip. She missed him. He should be coming in soon. Maybe he'd call her and they could get together.

Or maybe he was done with her after that scene with Allan and didn't want to bother anymore? Her heart twinged painfully at the thought. He'd invited her to sleep over tonight, but that invite had gone out days ago. What if he'd had a change of heart after being away from her for a few days? He didn't like drama, and her life seemed to be full of it.

"I'm so disappointed Allan won't make it today," Jeanette murmured to her.

Beth Ann wasn't. It was the only reason she'd agreed to come to the luncheon.

"Do you know anything about that?" her mother asked, turning to her.

Two black eyes, Beth Ann wanted to say. *He won't show his face until he looks handsome again*. She knew Allan all too well.

"I heard that one of the Waggoners trashed his face," Lucy said slyly, and shot a look at her sister.

Beth Ann froze, her hands squeezing her napkin in her lap.

"Oh, those awful Waggoners." Her mother shook her head. "The town would be better off if they all just dropped off the face of the planet."

Beth Ann bit her lip. Great, now she was going to have to endure this for the rest of lunch.

"I haven't heard a thing about this. Beth Ann, do you know what's going on?" Her mother turned her gaze to Beth Ann.

"Yeah, Beth Ann. You know what the deal is?" Lucy's eyes gleamed.

What had her rotten little sister heard? "I haven't heard a thing," she said innocently, and gave Lucy a hard look. If she wanted to play this game, Beth Ann had ammo, too. She raised her water glass deliberately and took a sip. "So, Lucy, honey, how is Colossus? You—"

"I bet it's over a woman," her mother interrupted, and Beth Ann choked on her water. "Allan probably sold her a car that was too expensive. You know those trashy Waggoners don't have two nickels to rub together. One of them likely got mad at all the money spent and went after him with his fists. Disgraceful."

God, this was unendurable.

"Oh, I don't know," Lucy said. "Colt's kind of hot."

Great, now Lucy was baiting both of them.

"Lucinda Janelle Williamson," her mother scolded. "If you show up with one of those Waggoner boys, your father is going to have a heart attack."

Beth Ann stood up. "Gosh, look at the time. I just realized that I have a meeting with a Realtor this afternoon."

"A Realtor?" Her mother's mouth fell open. "Right now?"

"Right now," Beth Ann confirmed. She was going to call the Realtor and insist on seeing a few apartments ASAP, just to get away from this awful mess.

"But, honey," Jeanette said. "You know you can stay with your father and me for as long as you need to. We know you can't afford both an apartment and your cute little business."

Beth Ann's teeth gritted. Cute?

Lucy grinned. "Run while you can, Beth Ann. I'm out of here as soon as I graduate."

Her mother gave Lucy a fierce look. "What did you just say, young lady?"

Oh, thank God for Lucy. A distraction. Beth Ann leaned in and kissed her mother's cheek. "Gotta go. Love you. See you soon." She moved around the table and hugged Lucy's shoulders, too. "Thank you," she whispered in her sister's ear. "I owe you."

"I want pink streaks in my hair," Lucy whispered back.

Beth Ann gave her a thumbs-up and scanned the room for her father. He was deep in conversation with the congressman and wouldn't like to be interrupted. Well, she'd catch him some other time. Pulling her keys from her purse—thank heavens she and Lucy hadn't ridden here with their mother—Beth Ann slipped into the parking lot and pulled out her phone. She dialed the Realtor. "Hey, Georgia? It's Beth Ann. Can we look at some apartments today?"

"This duplex is a little on the high side of your price range, but it's so cute that I just had to show it to you," Georgia gushed with a smile. She waved Beth Ann forward. "Come on."

High end of her price range. Beth Ann stifled a sigh. Georgia was so excited to show her the houses that she couldn't really point out that she desperately needed low end rather than high end. “Of course. Hey, what about that little bungalow Miranda was renting?”

“Snapped up right away,” Georgia said with a grin, twisting the key in the lock. “The good ones always are. Now,” she said, pushing the door open. “There’s new carpet, and brand-new countertops in the kitchen. Isn’t it *cute*?”

Not really. The duplex was small—which was fine with her—but looked hard used. The backyard was overgrown, the fence falling down, and the appliances in the kitchen were from the seventies. The walls were patched over, as if rambunctious prior owners hadn’t been mindful of the drywall at all, and the new carpet was a hideous shade of yellow. The only good thing about the place was the location—five minutes from work. Bluebonnet was low on rentals, though, and she’d prefer to stay in Bluebonnet. She stepped inside, peeking in the rooms. Two small bedrooms, and a rather dim bathroom. The kitchen adjoined to the living room, and the back door was a big, cracked sliding-glass door. Her mother would have wrinkled her nose in horror. Allan would have sneered at it—it was half the size of the house they’d rented together—a pink gingerbread Victorian that was a centerpiece in town. Naturally.

This was small and plain in comparison. But it was clean, and it’d be hers. “How much is it a month?”

Georgia consulted her printout, and then quoted Beth Ann.

She winced at the price. It was tight, but maybe she could up the price on her tanning bed that she’d rented, bring in a little extra. Work an extra day out of the week to bring in some cash. “Okay.”

"And all you have to do is put down a deposit of three months' rent up front," Georgia said cheerfully.

Beth Ann's heart sank. Three months' rent? Up front? She gave Georgia a faint smile. "What if I don't have that?"

Georgia frowned. "Two months' up front might be a tough sell."

"I don't have any to put up front, honey," Beth Ann admitted, glancing around at the duplex so she wouldn't have to look Georgia in the eye. It stung, admitting she didn't have savings. Between the loans for her business start-up and the shop rent, she had only a few hundred in the bank. She refused to ask anyone for the money.

Georgia gave her a soft, understanding look. "I know you're hard up on cash right now, sweetie."

Beth Ann gave her a wavering smile. "That obvious?"

"Well, everyone knows you and Allan are going through a phase," she said.

Oh lord. Here we go again.

"But I'm going to be real honest with you," she said, hugging the printouts to her chest. "This is a tight market for renters. No one has the money to buy right now, so everyone's renting. And I have to tell you that unless you have at least two months' rent to put down in advance, you're going to have a rough time finding a place."

Beth Ann nodded tightly. "Thank you, Georgia."

"I just think—"

Beth Ann's phone rang, cutting them off. She gave Georgia an apologetic look and picked up the phone, heart thrumming. That was the ringtone she'd assigned to Colt. She put a finger to her ear and turned her back as she answered. "Hello?"

"Hey darlin'," he said, his voice sending a thrill through her body. "Where you at?"

"I'm looking at places to rent," she said softly.

"Can I join? Dying to see your pretty face again. Ain't no one on this last trip half as good-looking as you."

She flushed with pleasure. "Missed you, too."

"So?"

"Sure." She gave him the address. "See you soon."

When she hung up and turned around, Georgia was giving her a knowing look. "Was that who I think it was?" She wagged a finger. "I knew it was just a matter of time before you two lovebirds got back together. So you won't be needing my help after all, will you?"

Oh dear. "That was my boyfriend."

You could have knocked Georgia over with a feather. Astonishment flicked over her face, then speculation. "New boyfriend?"

It was going to be all over town this afternoon, if it wasn't already. "I'm dating Colt Waggoner."

Georgia's mouth dropped a little. "One of the Waggoners?"

Beth Ann crossed her arms over her chest. "Colt, yes." The rest of the family was a little rough around the edges, but Colt wasn't like that. "He's a good man."

"Oh, *sweetie*," Georgia said, and moved to Beth Ann. She rubbed her arm. "I know you and Allan are going through a hard time right now, but he's a good man with a great job. He'd marry you if you'd just give him the chance. Don't ruin your pride, tossing yourself at the first man that comes along. You're beautiful. You deserve so much better than a Waggoner boy." She smiled at Beth Ann's frozen face. "Look at you. So young and sweet. You deserve the best man in town. And that man's *not* Colt Waggoner."

Numb with shock at this pep talk, Beth Ann stared at her.

Georgia patted her on the arm. "I realize you're rebounding, and this is a phase, sweetie, so I'm not going to lecture you. Everyone wants the bad boy before they settle down. You'll get it out of your system and then go back to Allan. Here." She pushed the pile of printouts toward Beth Ann, each sheet of paper with a key attached. "I've got another appointment I need to run to. Just return these when you're done and we'll talk about which one you like best, okay?"

"Sure," Beth Ann said in a faint voice. "Thanks."

Georgia gave her a wink and trotted off. Beth Ann heard the Realtor's car start a moment later, and then Beth Ann was all alone.

You'll get it out of your system.

And then go back to Allan.

She looked around the ugly duplex she couldn't afford.

Despair crashed over her. Beth Ann sagged against a wall and slid to the ground, curling her legs close. Hot tears dripped down her face, ruining her careful makeup. She didn't care. She swiped at the tears, but the more she swiped, the faster they fell.

She couldn't afford to move out. Her business was failing. She was failing. Everyone thought she was just having a "moment." That she'd regain her senses any minute now, and run screaming back to Allan because that was the only sane move.

And nobody liked her with Colt. *When are you going to wise up and go back to Allan? You had such a good man,* everyone told her.

But she had a good man *now*. And she should have said it,

should have defended him. But no one listened to what she said anyhow.

Everyone thought they knew what she needed better than she did.

And it was just too much.

A quick knock came at the front door a few moments later, and before she could respond, the door opened and Colt stuck his head in. "Hey darlin'—"

His gaze darkened as he came inside, studied her from where she was crumpled in the entryway of the small, cramped duplex, her face covered in tears. As she watched, his jaw hardened. He very carefully shut the door behind him, then eased down onto the floor next to her, mindful of his knee, and took her hand.

He still smelled of wood smoke and campfires. He'd wanted to see her so badly he hadn't even stopped to shower yet. For some reason, she liked that.

"Was it that cocksucker?" he asked, his voice flat and deadly. "Do I need to go rip his dick off to give him the hint?"

She shook her head, wiping at her cheeks. "I think . . . I think I'm just having a bad day."

He wrapped an arm around her shoulders and pulled her close, kissed her hair. She snuggled up against him and sighed, resting her cheek against his shoulder.

"You want to talk about it?"

She didn't want to talk about all of it, because she knew it'd hurt his feelings. He didn't say much about his family, but she knew that he was sensitive about it. She'd be blind not to know that. "I want to move out from my parents' place," she said in a quavering voice. "As long as I'm there, they're going to drive me crazy with society parties and stupid fund-raisers and trying to push me back toward Allan because he has money."

"I'll help you move out," he said slowly. He leaned in and she felt him rest his cheek against the top of her head, and her heart melted just a little. "You like this place, darlin'?"

"Not really," she said with a hiccup, and then laughed at herself. "I'm being a snob. It's small and the bathroom sucks and I think the neighbor is growing pot in his backyard. But I can't afford it anyhow. I can't afford anything."

"You want to borrow a few grand from me?"

Oh heavens, that would just make her feel worse. She shook her head, her fingers stroking down his arm as she stared at the empty, tiny living room, the brand-new yellow carpet. "When I moved in with Allan, I let him pay for everything. He paid the rental on the house. He bought both of our cars. If I wanted something, he bought it. When we broke up the first time . . . I didn't have anything. My bank account had been joint with Allan's bank account, and we'd long since used up my money to send him through business school. I didn't even go to college. What was I going to do with a degree anyhow? I was only good at looking pretty and fixing hair. So I thought I'd go to beauty school. I'd hidden money over the last year Allan and I were together, and I used that to put myself through beauty school. There was nothing left for opening a salon. I had to borrow money from my parents for a car. I borrowed money from the bank—money that my parents had to cosign for—to start my business. And no one is convinced I can do it on my own." She gave a watery sigh. "No one understands why the mayor's daughter wants to play at having a business and do people's hair. And everyone seems to think I'm going to come to my senses and jump right back into Allan's arms."

"You're not," he said, rubbing her shoulder. "You want to be your own person. I get that. I fought for that for years." He paused for a moment, then stroked her hair. "When I was in high school, I hated everyone and everything in this town."

"You hated me, too?" she asked with a faint smile.

"I did," he admitted.

"That's okay," she said with a sigh. "I was pretty stupid back then."

"You were with Allan back then," he said. "And I was a nobody. One of the Waggoner boys that lived out in a trailer in the junkyard."

She remembered. He'd been there on the fringes of memory—a lean, angry teenage boy in ragged jeans with a permanent scowl on his face.

"When I was in high school," he began slowly, "I wanted so desperately to get away from this place that I couldn't stand it. I'd spend nights running at the school track, doing push-ups and drills, because I couldn't wait to get into basic training. The day after graduation, I enlisted. I shipped out to basic and never looked back. I was so desperate to make something of myself that I wanted to forget everything that I'd been for the last eighteen years. I was going to remake myself into a new man."

Her fingers linked in his. "And did you like the marines?"

"I loved it," he admitted. "I'd still be there if it wasn't for my knee. Two surgeries and I had limited mobility for a few years. Not enough to permanently sideline me, but enough to destroy my career."

She pressed her mouth to his arm. "I'm sorry."

"I spent a lot of time doing survival-training routines when in the marines. When I got out, I decided I didn't want to be around anyone. I bought some land out in the middle of nowhere, Alaska, and built a cabin. I lived off the grid—no running water, no electricity, no nothing—for a year. And when I came into town one day, I called Dane just to find out how he was doing, and his life was a fucked-up mess. I was in the middle of some survival classes. Invited Dane. Didn't realize how much he'd like it. I invited him to come join me. We lived up in the mountains for an entire year. No power, no phones, nothing. But then Dane wanted to come back. And Grant offered the survival business."

"But you would have stayed?" she guessed.

He shrugged. "I didn't care one way or another. But Dane missed people. And I think he was worried about Grant. Grant's wife died five years ago, and the man was still a mess. At ends. Scrambling for projects to fill the day. Dane wanted to help him. So I came."

She'd had no idea. Grant seemed so together. Actually, all three men did. Her hand stroked along the cords of his arm. "Do you regret coming back?"

"Some days," he said lazily, and her heart twanged in response. "But I like you, and I like my friends, and right now that's enough for me. The rest of the town could fall off the map tomorrow and I wouldn't give a shit."

She could understand that. "I shouldn't care so much that they don't see me as my own person," she said softly.

"You care," he said, rubbing her shoulder again. "Because you want to prove to them that you are, and they're not seeing it."

She nodded, and stared at the pile of papers in front of her, the keys carefully tagged to each page. "Look at that," she said with disgust. She leaned out of his embrace and picked up the stack of paperwork and keys. "The Realtor trusted me with all of these people's house keys. Why? Because I'm sweet little Beth Ann Williamson, who would never harm a fly or lie to a stranger. Why not trust me with all these people's houses?" She tossed down the stack with disgust, and the keys jangled on the linoleum.

"You know what I think?" he drawled.

Beth Ann glanced over at him. "What?"

His sharp eyes glinted at her, and she saw a flash of dimple that made her knees weak. "They think you're not the kind of girl to fuck her man in a stranger's house."

The breath caught in her throat, and desire began to pulse through her. "I bet that's exactly what they think."

"Want to prove them wrong?"

"Absolutely," she breathed, a wicked smile curving her face.

He stood up, moved to the front door, and locked it. Colt turned back to her, his eyes gleaming. The front of his pants had tented, his cock already hard. "Shut the blinds, darlin'."

She did, her body quivering with need. Her legs felt curiously weak—one touch from him and she'd collapse like a deck of cards. He did that to her. His touch never failed to make her feel naughty, and sexual, and oh so desirable. As if she were the most beautiful thing in the world and it was all he could do to keep his hands off of her.

She'd never felt like that before. Ever. And she craved it so badly.

As soon as she'd shut the blinds, Colt's hand slid along her ass, cupping it through her dress. "You look stunning today," he said, leaning in to nuzzle her neck. "My cock is hard as a rock just looking at you."

Warmth flooded through her. No comments on whether her clothes were inappropriate or if her shoes were the wrong color. He just liked to look at her. Appreciated her. She tilted her neck so he could continue to kiss it, his hand burying in her thick fall of blond hair.

"More beautiful every time I see you," he whispered against her skin.

She felt the same way. Nothing in Colt's appearance had changed since they'd started to sleep together—she kept his hair cut crisp and short for him. He kept clean shaven. Wore the same kinds of clothes. But every time she saw him, it was like a punch in the gut. The long lashes of his narrow eyes. How had she ever thought them hard? How had she ever thought his beautiful, sensual mouth was turned down in a permanent frown? She lived for those flashes of dimple that told her he was truly amused. That she'd gotten to him.

His arms slid around her waist and pulled her close to him, cradling her, even as he continued to kiss her neck from behind. Not aggressively making love to her this time, then. He'd make love to her soft and sweet. For some reason, that made her eyes prick with new tears. She turned in his arms to face him. "Thank you," she said softly.

He raised an eyebrow at her, inquiring. His hands flexed on her hips, soothing, rubbing. Caressing.

"For knowing what I need," she said softly. "For listening to me. For seeing me."

"Always."

"I'm so glad I have someone like you in my life," she said, laying her hand on his chest. Not over his tattoo this time, but she spread her fingers over his heart, as if she could touch it. "Someone I can lean on and trust when the world around me doesn't seem to make sense any longer."

"Trust," he repeated softly, as if tasting the word.

She nodded, staring down at her hand on his chest. "I can't be in a relationship without trust. Never again. If I don't have trust, I don't have anything." Her head tilted up to look at him and she smiled softly. "And that's why I'm glad I have you."

He leaned in to kiss her, his lips claiming hers in a gentle caress. His tongue stroked lightly against her mouth, then drew back. She continued the kiss, letting her own tongue rub against his even as his hand slid down her thigh, looking for the hem of her dress.

"Pick your poison," he said between low, deep, searing kisses. "Countertop? Living room floor? Dining room? Bathroom? Bedroom?"

"Living room," she said breathlessly.

He grabbed her by the hips and hauled her against him, lifting her a foot off the ground. She wrapped her arms around his neck as he carried her into the living room and gave her another long, sweeping kiss. "This looks like a prime lovemaking area."

She blushed, her heart thrilling at his words.

He set her down, watched her kick off her heels. Colt frowned down at the pale yellow carpet, scuffed a heavy boot along it.

"What's wrong?"

"This shit's cheap as hell."

She gave a little laugh and leaned in to kiss him again. "I can't afford expensive."

He shook his head. "I'm not laying you down on this crap." His eyes gleamed. "I have a better idea."

She *liked* his ideas. Her nipples hardened. "Oh?" Her voice was husky with need.

He glanced over at the window. There were two narrow windows, rounded at the top, equally spaced apart in the small living room. "Let's go over there," he said, and nodded at the first one.

She moved toward it, then gave Colt a questioning look. He took her hand in his own, kissed the palm with a smile, and then placed it on the wall next to the window. Then he moved to her other side and did the same.

Her palms pressed against the wall at shoulder height. If she pushed forward, her face would press through the blinds and she could see out into the street. Sunlight streamed in through the slats in the blinds over her body, leaving stripes of light on her skin.

His hands slid over her hips again, and he tugged her skirt up until it bunched around her waist. The thick raw silk fabric stayed in place, and she felt his hands slide over the soft flesh of her bottom, his fingers sliding her thong down her legs. She daintily stepped out of them and looked over her shoulder at him inquiringly.

"Keep your hands on the wall, darlin'."

"I will," she breathed.

He knelt by her leg, kissed one thigh. "If you wanted to open the blinds . . . that's entirely up to you."

A shocked thrill raced through her. He was going to make

love with her facing this window, then? And if she wanted, she could open it and show the world his body pounding into her? Her breath came in little pants, half aroused, half alarmed. Did she have the courage to do that? Did she even want to? "I . . . I think I want them to stay shut," she said.

He chuckled and kissed her leg again. "That's fine with me. I like having you all to myself."

Her heart fluttered. He'd have shown her off if she'd wanted it, though.

His hand slid up the inside of her thigh. Her lower half was totally exposed, she realized, and he crouched behind her. "Spread your legs for me, Beth Ann."

A tremble flashed through her, and she did, careful to keep her hands pressed on the wall.

"Wider."

She obeyed, her legs now almost as spread as her arms. She stared at the mini blinds, her breath hitching even faster as he brushed his fingers between her legs. "Wet, but not wet enough," he mused. She heard him shift on the ground behind her, felt his hands cup her ass. His thumb slid down the seam of it, sending an erotic thrill through her. She wanted to press her cheek to the wall and lean against it for support, but she couldn't lean into the window. And that was part of the torture—she was exquisitely aware of where and how her body was placed.

His hands parted the cleft of her bottom and for a shocking moment, she thought he was going to touch her there. But instead, she felt his mouth on her core. Her gasp turned into a low moan of need. His tongue stroked inside her, and she felt his nose brush against her bottom. His face was . . . buried there.

Between her legs. From behind. A bolt of pure pleasure shot through her and she moaned, her fingers digging into the wall. Oh God. The mental picture in her mind was so incredibly erotic. His tongue swiped inside her, thrusting as his cock would soon. She rocked her hips gently, moaning at the flutters of need racing through her.

Then he gave her one slow, long lick that seemed to last longer than all the others, so long that her body was shuddering when he finally dragged his tongue away. She whimpered when he dragged his fingers up and down her pussy again. This time she was slick and hot with need, her folds silky from his mouth and her own arousal. "Much better."

She felt his hands on her hips again as he stood and moved behind her. Then they moved off her again and she felt him lean in and press his cock against her, kissing her shoulder, even as she heard him rip a condom open.

"Colt, baby . . . please . . ." Oh heavens, she never called him *baby*. Would he hate that? It had just slipped out.

"I'm here," he said softly. Then she felt him pull away for a moment—putting the condom on. A moment later, she felt his hands grasping her ass again. "Lean forward a little. Push that sweet ass out to me."

She did, stepping backward a bit and gasping when his cock butted up against her heat. When had he gotten undressed? Did she even care? She wiggled backward a little more and felt the head of him sink deep. Was he holding still so she could impale herself on him? His hand tensed on her hip, and the head of his cock stroked inside her, a movement that made her keen with need. He thrust shallowly into her again, a mere tease.

She pushed back against him. Her hands had slid a little and she felt almost bent over in place, her bottom high as she backed up, searching for him.

On her next wiggle backward, she was rewarded with the surge of his hips moving forward, and he sank himself to the hilt. Beth Ann cried out at the intense sensation.

"That what you wanted, darlin'?" he asked huskily, and pumped into her slowly again, pushing until his full length was rubbing inside her.

"Yes," she moaned, her eyes squeezed shut with the onslaught.

"You want me to push into you again? Or was that enough for you?"

God, he loved teasing her. Making her beg for more. "More," she panted. "I need more."

He pushed deep again, the movement slow and excruciating in its exquisiteness. Beth Ann moaned with need. He was making love to her so slowly, so sweetly, but she needed more. When he dragged his cock slowly out of her once more, and then just as unhurriedly sank back in again, she whimpered.

"What do you want, Beth Ann?"

"You," she whimpered. "Harder. Faster. Please, Colt. Take me fast."

She didn't need to repeat it. He surged deep into her again, the force of his thrust rocking her forward on her feet and sending a tidal wave of pure pleasure through her. He thrust again, and again, his hands locked on her hips, and then she was clinging to the wall for support as he thrust into her over and over again, his hard motions rocking the two of them forward with every thrust. His skin smacked against her own, and oh God, she was so close to coming. One hand left the wall and she slipped it between her legs, brushing against her clit as he slammed into her.

"That's my girl," he rasped hoarsely. "Touch yourself."

She did, and immediately cried out as the orgasm blew through her like a tornado. Her body clenched, hard, and she stiffened with a low, guttural moan that she wasn't entirely sure came from her own throat.

He thrust hard twice more, rocking against her body, and then he growled her name. "Beth Ann!" and then he was coming, too, and she felt his body jerk and clench against her own stiff one.

When she came down, she panted, blinking rapidly as her surroundings came back into focus. Delicate pink claw marks marred the edges of the white painted wall where she'd clung to the sides of the window.

Colt's body slid from hers and she felt his hands tug her skirts down, heard his zipper go up and his belt fasten. And then he was pulling her against him from behind, and kissing her neck, now damp with a sheen of sweat. "You are always incredible."

She smiled, wrapping her arms around his and leaning back against him. An "I love you" bubbled up in her throat, and she almost blurted it out.

Then she stopped, shocked. She couldn't be in love with Colt already, could she? Oh lord. Was she crazy? This was supposed to be an easy, casual relationship. He'd think she was rebounding hard if she started declaring love for him after only a month of dating. He needed to declare it first. Then she'd feel safe confessing her own love to him.

"Something wrong?" he asked, squeezing his arms around her

waist and nuzzling his face against her throat. "Nothing," she said lightly, hating that she had to conceal it. All that big talk about truth and here she was lying, too. "Just wondering if I should mention to Georgia that I clawed up the paint job."

"Nah," Colt drawled. He looked at the place, then grinned. "Probably an improvement."

TWELVE

Beth Ann slowly spun around in the barber's chair. She'd painted her own nails, waxed her own brows, dyed a pink streak in her own hair out of sheer boredom.

No customers.

The realization was like a sick, gnawing ache in her stomach.

She'd failed. Her business had failed. Everything she'd worked so hard for. Failed. She rose from the chair and moved to the front door, stepped outside into the autumn breeze. The Bluebonnet town square bustled with people, a few tourists enjoying the quaint shopping, locals getting their chores done. The Halloween Festival banner swayed over Main Street square, and down the street, she could see the utility building. Miranda would be working today—her volunteers never wanted to work on a Saturday. She wished her friend would come over so she could mess with someone's hair other than her own. So it'd look like she had at least one client.

There was nothing sadder than an empty salon.

Almost against her will, she glanced down the street. Still no permanent sign over Cutz, but she could see people sitting in the waiting room, magazines in hand. Were those her clients? How on earth had that woman stolen all her clients?

What had she done that was so wrong? She hadn't changed her prices. She hadn't cut anyone's hair badly or botched a nail job. Beth Ann didn't understand it. And if she didn't understand it, she couldn't fix it. The sick gnawing in her stomach grew worse. The breeze picked up, leaves scattering down the busy street. The Halloween Festival was in two weeks. Soon, she'd be done with that horrible committee, and then hopefully she could avoid Allan for a few weeks.

As if thinking about him had summoned him, Allan's shiny BMW turned down the street. She groaned and quickly headed back inside her shop. *Please don't stop here, please don't stop here—*

The car pulled up into the empty parking space in front of her salon.

"Fuck!" She clenched her fists. Okay, so she'd resorted to cussing. It did feel better than just saying "fiddlesticks" or "fudge." She should cuss more often. It always sounded so sexy when Colt did it.

The doorbell clanged and Allan stepped in, his expensive leather jacket sweeping around him. He grinned over at her, his gaze taking in the empty salon. "Looks like I caught you at just the right time."

"What do you want, Allan?"

He gave her a wounded look, as if surprised by her defensiveness. "I just wanted to talk. Maybe get a haircut."

"I don't really feel like talking right now. We can talk when we get to the committee meeting."

He looked disappointed, his shoulders slumping. "I thought I could walk you over when we were done here."

She sighed. Stared at her empty chair. She was going to learn to live with Allan. If he was going to be polite and nice, she could extend an olive branch as well. With a small smile, she gestured at her chair.

He hung his coat on one of the wall hooks and then bounded over as if she'd given him a prize. "How's business?"

She adjusted the chair, not looking in the mirror to see his eager eyes. "Quiet."

"I don't understand why," he said in a cheerful voice. "Everyone loves you."

That was nice of him. She gave him a faint smile and put the pink cape over him. "I'm sure it's just a temporary thing," she said, though her heart was heavy at the thought. "It's bound to pick up again."

"I'm sure . . . unless. . . ." He paused.

Oh, here we go. She stopped spritzing his hair, comb poised over his head. "What?"

"Unless people are avoiding you because you've taken up with one of the Waggoners."

She groaned. "Allan, don't start this again."

He caught her hand. "Beth Ann, I just worry about you. You're wearing revealing clothing, you're making out with trailer-park trash in public, and you've dyed your hair pink." He shook his head. "I don't understand what's gotten into you."

She pulled her wrist from his grasp and began to comb his hair, avoiding looking in the mirror. "For one thing, I like my clothing. For two, it's one pink streak, not an entire head of pink hair. And three, we weren't making out in public. It's not my fault you were following me." Her hard gaze swept up to the mirror. "Why do you care so much anyway? Remember? I'm a lousy lay."

He flinched, and she was pleased. "I only said that to get at him."

"Mmm-hmm. How long did it take for those two black eyes to heal?"

"He's lucky I didn't press charges," Allan said in a sulky voice.

"No, *you're* lucky he didn't press charges," she said, almost cheerfully. She began to cut his hair, carefully lifting a section and snipping. Petty, passive-aggressive Allan she could deal with. It was expected.

It was when he wept and begged for forgiveness that she couldn't handle it. "I like Colt. And I'm going to keep seeing him."

"You're not just being rebellious to get back at me? Picking the guy I hate the most so you can stab a knife in my back? I saw you with him. His hands under your skirt and touching you . . ." He shuddered. "It turns my stomach every time I think about it."

She rolled her eyes. "Now you're just being dramatic."

"I'm not. Everyone in town can't stop talking about how it's not right that you're with him. They think we should be together."

They thought that because she'd kept her mouth shut about his cheating. She'd told no one—not even her parents—why she'd finally broke up with Allan. And despite it being such a small town, oddly enough, it hadn't gotten out. Allan was careful when he cheated, and Beth Ann was careful to keep his secrets because they embarrassed her.

No one knew why they'd finally broken up, just that they had. Beth Ann hadn't wanted to destroy his character in town—that didn't seem fair to a man she'd spent nine years with. And she didn't hate him, not really. She was just disappointed in him, and in herself most of all for putting up with it for so long.

Allan gave her a solemn look in the mirror. "You know I still love you and I want you back."

Now they were getting back to uncomfortable territory. She shook her comb at him. "Allan, honey, I am allowing you to sit in this chair and let me cut your hair because you weren't declaring love for me. Do it one more time and I'm going to cut you a Mohawk."

He gave her a sulky look in the mirror, and she almost smiled. He looked like a sad little boy now. "I just want what's best for you."

"Trust me to know what's best for me," she said lightly, cutting his hair again. But the seed of doubt had sprouted.

Was she being ostracized by the town because of her relationship with Colt? Did everyone think she was cheating on Allan? That was ridiculous to think about. Still, Colt was convinced everyone in town hated his family. She knew they curled their lips when one of his loud, drunk brothers showed up and caused a scene, but what town didn't have a few odd people? The Waggoners didn't have money and some of them didn't have manners, but they were just people.

And surely this town wasn't small enough that who she dated was going to matter that much . . .

Did it?

Allan behaved long enough for her to finish cutting his hair, and he'd even tried to make small conversation, talking about the Halloween parade and his plans for it. He always did the parade, since his business loaned out the cars for some of the parade members to ride in. His boyish enthusiasm was hard to resist, and she mentioned a few of the plans she had for the Festival—a costume pageant, trophies for the children, a cake walk, and face-painting booths to bring a little cash to the committee. He liked all her ideas, which surprised her.

When his haircut was done, he stood and took a hundred-dollar bill out of his wallet, and pressed it into her hand.

Her throat grew knotted. "I can't break this, Allan."

"I know you can't," he said softly. He leaned in and kissed her forehead. She wanted to pull away, but he didn't press more than that. "I just want to help, is all."

That sour feeling clenched in her stomach again. He was giving her extra because he knew she was failing. And that made her want to scream in frustration—not at him, because he was just being typical, big-gesture Allan.

At herself, for being the one that was failing.

"I can't take this, Allan."

"Nonsense—" he began.

"I can't change it," she repeated, and held it back out to him.

"I know," he said again, and she wondered if he'd brought the big bill in deliberately. Just another quiet, subtle manipulation on his part, or something else?

She nodded at Kurt's Koffee across the street. "Then buy me a coffee and change it out over there."

He did, and they took their coffees over to the committee meeting. To her relief, he didn't sit next to her, and the meeting seemed to go well enough. She noticed a few of the committee members watching her curiously, as if they were trying to figure her out. As if they knew a bit more about her personal life and were trying to peg her back into that easy, understandable slot once more.

And she thought about Allan's words. Were people avoiding her because she was dating Colt? Had Allan told people that he'd caught them making out in the school classroom? Had Georgia said that they'd been house hunting? She felt a small, sick twist in her gut.

The town wasn't going to try and force her to choose between her business and her lover, were they? That was ridiculous.

But she thought about it as she walked back to her salon and got in her car, and checked her phone that she'd turned off during the meeting.

A text from Colt. Her heart gave a small flip of longing as she read it.

You busy tonight? It was from fifteen minutes ago.

I am always wide open for you, she texted back with a grin.

Dirty girl, he replied, and she could almost see his smile. **Come meet me at the ranch. Main office.**

Beth Ann drove out to the Daughtry Ranch and parked her VW. She saw only the usual suspects—Miranda's old jalopy,

Dane's jeep, Colt's truck, and Grant's more sedate Audi at the far end of the parking lot. Not a surprise considering that it was getting pretty late. There was still a light on at the main lodge, though. She headed there.

The front door was unlocked even if the Closed sign was flipped, and so she stepped in with a knock. "Hello?"

"In the back kitchen," Colt drawled.

A surprise dinner? She followed the sound of his voice, smiling, and weaved her way past the large oak desks in the main lobby. The lodge had once been someone's house, though now that it was a business, she guessed the kitchen didn't get used all that often. The lights down the hall were all off, except for one crack of light under a swinging white door, and so she pushed through it.

And stopped in surprise.

The kitchen was a disaster. Flour covered every inch of countertop. Dirty mixing bowls and spoons lay everywhere. There was a puddle of something dark poured down one side of the sink. Just about every dish looked as if it had been pulled out and used.

Brenna and Colt stood in front of this mess, shoulder to shoulder. They both wore aprons, and Brenna had dirty smudges on her cheeks. As Beth Ann watched, Brenna picked up a bowl of flour, grabbed a handful, and tossed it into Colt's face.

Colt's jaw flexed, but his expression remained impassive. He did not look amused at Brenna's mischievousness.

"What's all this?" Beth Ann took a step forward, and then hesitated when her shoe slid on the tile. Flour on the floor, even. Not a surprise if Brenna was throwing it.

Brenna gave a wild, delighted laugh and elbowed Colt. Beth Ann saw Colt's dimple peek out. He glanced over at Brenna.

They both separated and moved to the side. "Happy birthday!"

Behind them, hidden by their shoulders, was an enormous round cake. It was covered in white frosting, with a delicate rose piped along the center. As Beth Ann stepped forward, she saw that *Happy Birthday* had been written across the top.

Beth Ann looked over at Colt in surprise. "It's not my birthday."

He shrugged and tugged on one of her belt loops, pulling her toward him. "Remember what you told me?"

She shook her head, staring at him. Her heart was giving this funny, weird little thump that made her entire body flutter with a mixture of need and . . . something else.

He tugged her close and leaned in to whisper in her ear. "You said you wanted to eat an entire birthday cake one day, just because no one let you. And I was thinking I'd like to see you eat that cake. Put a smile on your face after a bad day."

Her gaze blurred. He knew she'd had a bad day. He'd called her earlier, and though she'd tried to make light of her lack of clients, it had probably come through her voice. And all this—she stared at the mess in the kitchen. This had likely been a few hours of preparation and work.

For her. Because he wanted her to smile. Because he wanted to give her a cake to eat.

She wrapped her arms around his neck and tugged him down for a quick, scorching kiss. Her tongue licked inside his mouth, letting him know just how pleased she was.

He broke the kiss off with a small groan, then leaned in and said in a low voice, “Help me get rid of Brenna. I can’t shake her. As soon as she found out I was making you a cake, she wouldn’t go away.”

Beth Ann looked over at the other woman, who was watching them both with an amused smile. The woman acted childish at times, but Beth Ann suspected it was all very deliberate. “Hey, Brenna?”

“Hey yourself.”

“I’d really like to make love to my boyfriend right now,” she said softly, and brushed her thumb over his lips. He groaned, bit the pad of her thumb, and she gave Brenna a slow smile. “Think you can bail out on us?”

Brenna winked. “Absolutely.” She sauntered to the door, paused by a half-open bag of flour, and grabbed it. “If Grant asks, you two did not see me leave with this.”

And then she left.

Beth Ann turned to Colt, running her fingers down the front of his apron. His was immaculate. Not surprising to learn that the mess was probably 90 percent Brenna. “Are those two sleeping together?”

“Not yet,” he said, his dimple flashing. “They claim to hate each other.”

“Oh, that,” she whispered huskily, and leaned in to suck on his lower lip. When he groaned, she caressed it with her tongue, and leaned back. “I think they’re lying to themselves, then.”

“Kind of like us?”

“Very much like us,” she said softly. Her hands went to his apron and she tugged the strings at his waist undone. She tugged the apron off and tossed it to the side, her hands moving to his belt buckle.

His hands caught hers. "You want to try your cake first, darlin'?"

She shook her head and bit her lip, giving him a naughty look. "I'm kind of hungry for something else."

Need flared in his eyes and his hands went back to brace his body against the counter. "Oh?"

She nodded, finished unbuckling his pants, and knelt before him. She tugged them down to his knees, and then tugged his briefs down. His cock rose, hard and thick already. She continued to tug his pants down, noticing the long white scar that ran along one knee. She leaned in and kissed it, because she knew he hated it. Knew that it was why he'd left the marines. He hadn't had a choice.

But she loved it, because it had brought him here, to her.

"My scar's not half as interesting as my cock," he said in a husky voice.

"Mmm, agreed," she said, lightly brushing her fingertips along the smooth length of him. "I think this would be delicious with frosting." She reached to his side and dug her finger in the corner of the cake, then smeared the glob of frosting on the tip of his cock.

He groaned, his hand moving to the base of his cock to cup it.

"Looks delicious to me," she said, and then reached out to lick it—and him. The frosting was sweet in her mouth, and she twirled her tongue over the head of his cock, making sure to get every bit. Even after the frosting was gone, she continued to lap and smooth her tongue over the crown, enjoying his ragged breathing and the exquisite taste of him. When a salty drop of pre-cum touched her tongue, she looked up at him. "The frosting is delicious."

He reached behind him, and to her surprise, grabbed a bowl of frosting. With one hand on his cock, he tipped the bowl over it, and more frosting, liquid, thick and wet, smeared down the hard length. "Looks like you have a bit more to lick off."

Beth Ann smothered her laugh, looking up at him with a mischievous glint in her eye. "A feast indeed."

And she settled her open mouth against the head of his cock again. His hips thrust lightly, pushing the thick length deeper into her mouth, frosting smearing against her lips. "Oh, fuck me," Colt groaned. His other hand tangled in her hair, and she felt its sticky weight against her head. "That is so damn hot."

She rubbed her tongue against him, lapping at the frosting around his thick length. Beth Ann pulled her mouth off of him and slowly tongued down his length, lapping at the dripping, sweet mess, cleaning his shaft. He groaned in his throat with every new press of her tongue. Decadent vanilla frosting filled her mouth, the taste overpowering and rich, and, accompanying that flavor, the salty, masculine taste of Colt's skin.

Lord have mercy, she loved the taste of him. Loved doing this to him. She moved her mouth back to the crown of his cock, lapping at the droplets of pre-cum there. Again, his hips bucked, as if he wanted her to take him deep in her mouth again. And the thought excited her, so she obeyed, opening her mouth wide.

He surged inside, filling her mouth with more of his sweet, salty flesh. She moaned at his tortured groan, and he pumped into her mouth again. And then again, pushing deeper until he butted against the back of her throat.

"Not going to last, Beth Ann," he rasped, his fingers clenched tight in her hair.

In response, she sucked him harder, and her frosting-covered fingers went to his sac, caressing the globes there.

He exhaled sharply and began to slowly fuck her mouth again, each slow, exaggerated thrust working deep. He watched her, watched his cock disappearing between her frosting-slicked lips, and she knew the sight must have been incredibly erotic for him. She stared up at him, too, knowing that he'd love to see her gaze on him as she took him deep. And as he slid back and forth inside her mouth, faster and faster, she rubbed her tongue along his length.

He came with a burst of saltiness in the back of her throat and a harsh, ragged groan. She swallowed, her mouth suddenly full of his flavor. It cut into the sweetness, the taste sharp and erotic, and she swallowed all of it. She continued to lick at him even as he pulled out of her mouth.

"Fuck," Colt said in a ragged voice. His hands moved to hers, dragging her up to her feet. "I should make you a cake every day."

She stood and smiled at him, licked her lips. They still tasted sugary and delicious, and tinged ever so slightly of him. "It's a shame you used all the frosting on yourself," she said lightly. "I didn't get my turn."

His eyes lit up and he grabbed her by the waist, then turned and set her on the counter, next to the cake.

Beth Ann glanced over at it and smiled. "You're not going to ruin my cake by smearing it all over me, are you?"

He leaned up and kissed her. "Wouldn't dream of it. Stay right here." He leaned down, hitched his briefs and pants back around his waist, then headed to the far side of the kitchen. She craned her neck to see what he was doing, and then began to laugh as he came back into view with a can of frosting. "Really?"

"Really," he said, and handed her the can.

She took it, looking down at it with amusement. Chocolate this time. "I don't get vanilla?"

"You are not vanilla in the slightest, darlin'," he drawled, and as she watched, he carefully took her perfect cake and moved it to the far counter, away from them.

Colt returned to her side and he took the frosting can from her and set it down, then tugged at her sweater. She shucked it off, along with her bra, and when he tugged at her jeans, she helped him slide those off, too. He even took her panties, and a moment later, she was sitting atop the counter, naked except for her shoes, and shivering with anticipation.

"Lay down on the counter for me," he said, taking the frosting in hand again.

She did. Her hair was in flour, and her arm was resting against a sticky spot on the counter, but she didn't care. She watched him with a breathless gaze, watched his big hands on the canister of frosting.

"Now," he said slowly. "I am sure no one in this town thinks you are the type of girl that would lay down and let a man ice her like a cake."

She laughed, and wiggled a little on the counter. "Is that what you're going to do to me?"

"I am," he said, and then pressed a kiss on the closest spot he could find—her knee. "And then I'm going to lick you clean."

Her breath caught at that, her mind filled with images of Colt licking her, his tongue covered in frosting—and her own wetness. She moaned low in her throat.

He tore the seal off the canister and dug a thick finger into the icing. God, it was erotic just watching him with icing on his hands. She wiggled a little on the counter, pulling up her knees. Her pussy already felt slick with need.

He leaned forward and then dabbed a fingertip on the hard tip of one breast. She sucked in a breath, stared down at the chocolate dollop over the peak of one nipple. Her gaze flicked up to his face. He wasn't smiling, his expression intense as he got another finger full of icing and very carefully outlined her breast with it, drawing a circle around it. More icing, and his thumb skimmed over the sensitive flesh of her breast, painting the entire globe with thick chocolate brown. She shivered at his touch.

Then, he turned to the other breast and began to give it the same care, covering her small breast with the chocolate frosting. When he was done, he sat back, licked his finger, and stared down at her.

She licked her lips, waited. "What do you think?"

He smiled at her, a flash of dimple that made her knees weak and her pussy even wetter. "I'm thinking it's a shame we don't have cherries for those little nipples of yours. Guess I'll just make do."

He leaned down and captured the peak of one breast in his mouth, his tongue scraping over it.

She moaned. Oh God. That felt . . . incredibly erotic. He leaned and suckled at the peak, cleaning it with his mouth, his hand holding his dog tags out of the way. His tongue swirled out, grazing over the flesh of her breast, carefully cleaning it off. With every stroke of his tongue, she grew wetter and hotter, her mind ultra-focused on the traveling of his tongue. It slid to the underside of her breast, traced along the valley between her breasts, lapping and rasping. He'd frequently stop back at her nipple, swirling his tongue back over it again.

By the time he moved over to her other breast and began to suck on the sweet peak, she was moaning with need. Her hands gripped at the countertop, and when he licked at the hard nipple, she pushed it farther into his mouth. Needing more. Wanting more. Loving the delicious torture. She needed him to touch her pussy, though, and he wasn't. His fingers were still sticky with frosting. So she thrust her breast into his mouth, and was rewarded with a tiny bite that made her gasp in her throat.

"Stay still," he said with a low chuckle. And his tongue swept over her breast again.

By the time he was done with both breasts, she was whimpering with need. Her sticky hands went to his hair and she tried to pull him in to kiss her. She needed him so badly. But he slipped out of her grasp and grabbed the frosting again. "You taste sweet, but I haven't had all of you yet."

"But—" she bit back her protest. He was going to frost her . . . there?

He dipped another finger into the frosting, looked up at her, and kissed her bent knee. "Spread your legs, darlin'."

With a whimper, she did. "Not in me—"

"'Course not," he said softly. And she felt him slather the top of her pussy, where she kept her mound bare and neat because she knew he liked it. "But I had to give this pretty little thing attention."

And his mouth descended there, ravenously flicking against her mound, then sliding to her clit.

"Colt," she cried out, and then her hands were on his head and she was pushing him there, grinding his face into her pussy. His tongue rasped against her clit and she cried out when he gave it another long, slow, circling lick, then darted away to finish cleaning the frosting off of her mound. He licked his lips as if she tasted delicious, and then his mouth went to her clit again, sucking and lapping as if it was the sweetest treat yet. Her nails dug into his scalp, and a moment later, she felt the orgasm rip through her body. She moaned his name again, and his tongue flicked and flicked, bringing shockwave after shockwave rippling through her bucking hips. When the last ripple of pleasure tore through her, she lowered her hips—she'd been arching them off the counter to push them harder against his mouth, it'd seem—she gave a wobbly sigh.

He pressed a kiss to the inside of her knee. "Never going to be able to eat chocolate again without thinking of you under me, pushing your pussy into my mouth."

She blushed. Like she'd ever be able to think of cake again without thinking of his fist curled around the base of his cock, spilling frosting over the hard length so she could lick it up.

Her hips twitched in response. Down, girl. She turned her head and looked at the cake. "You did that for me?"

"I did," he said, the words a low drawl.

"We didn't even eat a slice." Strange how she wasn't disappointed about that in the slightest.

"Night's young," he said, and ran his teeth over her knee, then caressed it as if he couldn't stop tasting her, touching her. "We could get dressed, shower, and have ourselves a cake party back at my cabin."

She grinned. "That sounds like a plan . . . after we clean the counters here."

His chuckle of response made her heart feel warm.

THIRTEEN

It took an hour to clean up the kitchen, and another half hour before they'd showered and sat back down in his small cabin to eat a piece of cake. Beth Ann had cut a piece of the cake and sat in Colt's lap, naked, her hair pulled up in a towel. He sat under her clad only in his briefs and dog tags, and she occasionally fed him a bite of cake, though he'd insisted that it was all for her. With her hands occupied and her lovely mouth eating his cake, he was free to explore and touch her body. He couldn't get enough of her soft skin.

His hands stroked over every inch of her flesh, his fingers teasing her small nipples as she relaxed against him and ate cake, and told him about her day. As she was telling him about another tedious Halloween committee meeting, her phone buzzed with a text message.

"Leave it," he said automatically, and rolled his fingers over one nipple, eliciting a responsive shiver from her.

"It'll bother me until I see it," she said with a smile. She slid out of his grasp and put her plate next to the small kitchenette sink before heading over to get her phone. "It might be Miranda. She said she was going to send me some pictures of how she wanted to do her hair for Halloween."

"If she's anything other than a sexy librarian, Dane'll be disappointed." He watched her pretty, plump ass sway as she moved to the sink. This was how it'd be if they lived together. Her, naked and wandering around his place, having a conversation about their day.

He'd be down with that.

Beth Ann snorted at his comment, and picked up her phone. She clicked on the phone, and then her mouth tensed.

"What is it?" The protective instinct welled up inside him, and he resisted the urge to take the phone out of her hand and smash it, just so she'd stop frowning so much.

She'd been frowning too much lately.

"It's Allan," she said in a flat voice. "And judging by the amount of typos, he's drunk dialing me." She stared at the small screen, tilted her head and recited, " 'Bethy-babe, I miss you, love you, and want you back. My life is incomplete'—he spelled incomplete wrong, by the way—'without you. You deserve better than that asshole Colt. You don't know him like I do. He's not who you think'—oh, and then it cuts off. Idiot."

Annoyance flared through him. "Why don't you block his number?"

"It's this new phone. I don't know how to do it. Too many

menus." She frowned and flipped through it, skimming a finger over the screen.

"I can do it," he said, and she handed her phone over to him. She went to the sink and began to scrape her plate.

Another message came in. Colt clicked on it before the phone could buzz longer than an instant, and saw it was from Allan again.

> **I talked with the fire chief. Colt kept you in the woods all weekend just so he could fuck you. You want to be with an asshole like that? He thinks you're just a hot pussy to stick his dick in. He thinks—**

"Did you get it?"

Colt quickly deleted the message, anger and guilt flaring through him. So Allan had figured out that Colt had lied about that first weekend they'd spent together, and thought the worst of him? And now he wanted to tell Beth Ann and save her? Unease gnawed in his stomach. She needed to hear it from him, so he could explain.

He finished setting up the block on her phone and handed it back to her, saying nothing about the second message.

Beth Ann tossed the phone aside and crawled back into his lap, pressing her naked breasts against his chest. She tugged the towel off her hair and let the wet locks slither over her skin. "You're frowning," she said, running a thumb over his bottom lip.

"I just hate that asshole," Colt said. It was the truth, even though it was more than that. The dick was trying to ruin what he had with Beth Ann. And he wasn't about to let that happen.

He was going to see that jackass tomorrow and pound his face in if he had to, but the man was going to leave Beth Ann alone.

"Don't worry about him," she said, her voice soft. Her thumb kept brushing against his lower lip, and he wondered if she was imagining his mouth on her mouth, or perhaps lower. "I don't trust a word he says. Being with you is nothing like being with him."

"Good," he said shortly.

That made a smile curve her mouth, and he was struck by how beautiful she was. "I brought you a present," she said breathlessly, and leaned in to kiss the corner of his mouth.

"Oh?" He parted his lips, felt her small tongue flick inside his mouth, felt his cock stir again. Fuck, he was still thinking about frosting. If he closed his eyes, he saw his cock shoved down her throat, frosting rimming her mouth, her gaze up at him as she swallowed his cum. His dick was hard just thinking about it.

She said the word so quietly he almost missed it. "What?" He wasn't sure he'd heard her correctly.

Beth Ann smiled and leaned in to his ear, her tongue flicking against the shell of it. "Lube."

Well damn. He could think of a lot of uses for lube, but one immediately sprang to mind. Fuck all if he was going to suggest that to her, though. He wasn't about to suggest something like that to the woman he cared for. "And what did you have in mind, darlin'?"

Her blue eyes stared up at him, and he felt a tremor race through her body.

"I've never tried anal," she said breathlessly. "I wanted to try it with you."

Because she trusts you. Hot need flared through him. Need . . . and guilt. He took her hand, slipped it between their bodies and placed it on his already rigid cock. "I'm not a small man; Beth Ann. You sure this is something you want to do? It won't bother me if you say no."

He knew his girth intimidated most women. They were fine with it in bed, but only a few kinky ones had ever wanted to even attempt anal with him. And he got that. But still, the thought of burying his cock deep in Beth Ann's ass made him turn hard as a rock.

She leaned in and nibbled at his lip, her hand flexing on his cock. "I'd like to try it. Will it hurt?"

"Not if we go real slow," he admitted. He'd go fucking glacially slow if that's what it took to give her pleasure.

She kissed him sweetly. "Slow and intense sounds good to me."

Good God, but she was an amazing woman. He felt an odd swell of emotion that he clamped down. No sense in gushing emotions like a fucking sissy just because a hot woman told him she wanted his dick in her ass.

So he just said, "Slow and intense," and kissed her. "But first we need to get you soft and ready, darlin'."

She gave a little shiver of delight and smiled at him. Her hand squeezed on his dick again. "Feels like one of us is already ready."

"I'm ready as soon as you walk into the room," he whispered, and liked the blush that pinked her cheeks. His hand moved from his dick to her pussy and touched her. She gasped in response. Wet, but not as soaked as he wanted her to be. He needed her writhing in his lap before he'd attempt anything.

He slid his fingers deep into her, felt her breath catch as he stroked deep into her core. She gasped and clenched her thighs around his hand, her hips rocking against his fingers. He loved the way she responded to his touch. Anything he wanted to do to her body, and she wanted it just as badly as him. He watched her eyes get sleepy with need, her eyes half closed with desire.

She licked her lips, and he watched those little nipples tighten. And all the while, her gaze was on him, watching him, trusting him. Needing him.

Colt leaned in and kissed her again, then murmured, "Feed one of those sweet little breasts to me."

A shiver rocked through her and her hand cupped one of her breasts. She lifted the small mound to his mouth even as he continued to slowly thrust his fingers in and out of her pussy, finger fucking her.

She whimpered softly, as if frustrated that she couldn't raise her breast to his mouth. Beth Ann arched her body, pushing forward against him until he felt her nipple brush against his mouth. Her hips had arched up, so his hand followed her movements, continuing to thrust into her with his fingers even as he bit down on her nipple. She moaned his name, rocking down against him. His free hand cupped her bottom, and he ran his fingers along the seam of her ass, brushing against the tight opening there. Beth Ann inhaled sharply at the sensation, but then she rocked against him again.

He licked her nipple and pressed his finger against the pucker of her ass. When his finger pushed a little deeper, her breath caught in her throat. He bit down on her nipple again, rolling it against his tongue, and she moaned, bucking her hips hard. He could feel her slick and wet under his fingers now, her hips working harder against him. He rubbed his finger inside her ass—she was tight, but she wasn't pushing him away. That was good.

Her hips pushing against his hands became more urgent, and he sucked at her nipple harder, as her moans became more frequent, his name a breathless pant on her lips. His cock was hard as a rock under her gyrating body. Her eyes had closed and she bit her lip, the pleasure intense on her face.

He rolled her nipple against his tongue again, thrust even harder with his fingers. He could feel the quivers moving up her legs, a sign that she was close to the edge.

Very carefully, he slid his fingers out of her lovely body. She gave a whimper of distress, rocking her hips even though there was nothing to buck them against now.

She kissed him then, hard, desperate. He picked her up and took her to the bed across the room, laid her down.

She leaned up and kissed him as he did. "It's in my purse."

"I'll get a condom, too."

She kissed him again. "I'm on the pill."

He stopped. Stared. "You sure?"

"I'm sure."

He kissed her hard, unable to describe what he was feeling. That she trusted him so much. Wanted him so badly that she wanted him bare . . . it did strange things to his insides.

He wasn't going to think about that right now, though. He moved across the room to find her purse, stripping off his briefs. A moment later, he returned with the lube. She'd rolled onto her stomach already, anticipating his return. Her knees rested on the edge of the bed, slightly spread, her cheek pressed to the mattress.

Her beautiful ass was up in the air, her pussy parted and spread wide. He watched her fingers twitch, as if she was dying to touch herself and wouldn't until she had his permission.

"This is beautiful," he said, running a hand up her soft thigh. "Everything about you, so fucking gorgeous."

She gave a small sigh of pleasure, as if utterly content.

He didn't want her content. He wanted her wild with need. He flipped the cap off the lube with one hand, and slid his fingers back to her pussy again. He searched for her clit in the slick wetness, found it, and rubbed.

Instantly, her body tightened and she moaned. Her hands fisted in the sheets. "Colt," she whimpered. "Oh God. I need you. Need your cock deep inside me."

Nothing was hotter than his proper Beth Ann dirty talking back to him. He leaned over the cleft of her ass, and, still stroking her clit as she moaned, dribbled lube down the cleft. When he felt the tremor in her thighs again, he pulled his hand away, hearing her disappointed groan. He put a bit of lube on his hand, and stroked his cock. Fuck, he was hard. Hard and she was going to be incredibly tight. He had to go slow. Make it good for her.

He pulled her hips back against him. The head of his cock, now slick with pre-cum and lube, brushed against her ass. He pushed the head there, getting her used to the feel of him there. When she bucked back against him with a moan, he pulled away and spread her ass cheeks. With a finger, he circled through the slick lube, rubbing against the small opening. She cried out his name again, and butted against his finger, as if trying to take him deep. He pushed it inside her, felt her sharp intake of breath. She stilled on the bed, and then rolled her hips under him again a moment later. “More.”

That softly breathed word was all the encouragement he needed. He stroked his finger deep into her ass once, twice, flexing his fingers as he thrust. She shuddered with every stroke, her fingers flexing and clenching in the sheets. Then, slowly, he added a second lubed finger, and she whimpered, but began to flex her hips up to meet his strokes. He stretched his fingers wide, stretching her slowly. His cock was so hard with need he could feel the pre-cum beading on the head. Any moment now, he was going to throw her down on this bed, ram his cock deep inside her, and fuck her until he came. But he couldn’t do that. Had to make this good for her. Needed to.

With a ragged breath, he added a third finger, and began to stroke deep inside her. She whimpered with every press, her eyes squeezed shut. But when he stopped, she moaned. “More. Please Colt. I need you.”

“You ready, darlin’? It might feel a little intense at first. You tell me if you want to stop.”

She nodded, bit her lip, and her hips flexed under him. He slid his fingers out of her ass, placed the head of his cock at that perfect, tight spot. He was so hard with need.

And he pushed, just a little. Pushed a little more. His hands, slick with lube, pinned her hips in place. He butted his cock against her tight opening, and when she bucked back, he surged forward. Just a little, forcing his way into her tight channel.

The moment he pushed the head of his cock into her ass, he heard her breath suck in sharply.

He froze. Stroked a hand over her ass. Didn't move an inch. "Beth Ann?"

"Tight," she whimpered. "Very tight."

And he'd only shoved the tip in. Need poured through him, and sweat beaded on his brow. Fuck. Fuck. Fuck. He couldn't move until she gave the okay.

She flexed her hips a little. Gasped. "You're so big."

"I know, darlin'," he whispered. "You want me to stop?"

"No," she said, but her breath was ragged, her body tense.

Goddamn it, he was getting all tense. Push deeper, or pull out? He had to make it good for her again. He pushed a little deeper, testing her.

Another sharply inhaled breath, but no indications of pain. Good. He pushed in a little deeper, then a little more, his teeth gritted. God, she was tight as a fist, clenching around him. Her ass was gripping him like a vise, and it felt exquisite. But judging from her silence under him, it wasn't feeling exquisite for her.

He pushed in a little more—more than halfway now—and reached under her hips, searching for her clit. Found it, and rubbed gently.

Her sucked in breath told him that she liked that. He rubbed a little more, patient, even though his cock was throbbing, and he wanted nothing more than to sink deep and start fucking the hell out of her.

But patiently, he rubbed. And felt the slightest little shift of her hips. Felt her inhale, heard her whimper.

A good whimper.

Still rubbing that little bud, he pushed in a bit more, and this time her strangled gasp made him stop. "Bad?"

"Good," she said tightly. "Really good."

He straightened, flexing his fingers on her ass. His dick was almost all the way inside her. "Then can you touch yourself, baby?"

Her hand slid under her body, between her parted legs. A moan immediately rose from her throat.

"That's right," he said softly, pumping just a little. "Touch that little clit of yours."

Her hand flexed, and her face contorted, her mouth stretching into a silent cry. He thrust deep at the sight of that, and was rewarded with her shocked gasp.

"Tight," she moaned. "Oh my God, so tight."

"Bad tight?" he asked, gritting his teeth. Fuck, if it was bad tight, he should pull out. But she was squeezing him so hard, her ass clenched around him like a glove. And without the condom on, he felt every little vibration of her body.

"Good tight," she said breathlessly, then shuddered. "Good tight."

"Good. I'm going to fuck you now, Beth Ann. And I'm going to go slow. Tell me if you want me to stop."

"Go, go," she panted. "Please go."

He pushed. Just a small stroke, enough to feel every clench of her body travel through his cock. Just enough to be sure that he wouldn't hurt her.

"Go," she moaned again. "Oh, go."

He thrust again, withdrawing partially, and stroking back in deep. The lube made her passage slick, but she was still tight around him. The feeling was intense, and when he pushed in deep a third time, his eyes nearly rolled back in his head at the pleasure.

Under him, she moaned softly. Yes. That was good. He thrust again. Beth Ann moaned once more, and he watched her hand move in little circles against her clit.

"You touching yourself, baby?"

"Yes," she moaned, and the sound was tense with desire. "Oh, Colt, you're so full inside me."

"I know, baby," he gritted. His hips jerked and he thrust deep, hard, unable to help himself. She whimpered, and he froze, but then he saw that hand working against her clit, felt her body flutter under him.

She was going to come. Fuck yes. He thrust hard, slamming into her, and she cried out his name. Fucking slammed into her all over again, and again, and then she was screaming his name under him, and he felt her body jerk, felt it spasm underneath him. Knew she was coming. Over and over, he thrust into that tight, sweet ass. "Keep touching yourself, Beth Ann. Don't stop."

"Go," she sobbed. "Go."

He was going to go. He thrust and thrust, and then his balls tightened and he came deep inside her, all the breath escaping his body. He rocked into her, filling her with his cum, and she sobbed underneath him as he thrust slowly, one more time, and then pulled out.

Breath was still shuddering through her. He rolled her over and touched her cheek. "Beth Ann?"

She smiled at him, and slid her hand from her pussy—damn. She'd been touching herself the entire time she'd come, and the entire time he'd come. The responding smile she gave him was sleepy, boneless. "Good lord," she said softly. "That was . . . intense."

He kissed her, because he wanted it to have pleased her, so much. "In a good way?"

"Very, very good," she said with a soft sigh.

He grinned. Good. He got a towel, cleaned her, then himself, and pulled her close to him.

Her breath was still shuddering through her. As he pulled her close into his arms, she cuddled up against him. "I love you, Colt."

And there came that sissy knot in his throat. He kissed her forehead and held her close.

Beth Ann stayed with him all day Sunday. They ate so much cake they were both sick of it, made love all weekend, and when he slept, she lay with her arms wrapped around him, as if she couldn't get enough of him, even in her dreams.

Which made him feel even more guilty.

He had to tell her about that stupid first weekend together. That he'd lied and deliberately detained her in the woods. But as she left his place to go in to work on Monday, he couldn't tell her just yet. Her face was pale and strained, though she tried to smile. Monday was normally her day off, he knew, but she was going in to try and get a few walk-ins in the hopes of getting some extra money. Six days a week she was going to keep her salon open, and he knew if this didn't work, she'd be open every day, determined to make it successful.

"Is there anything I can do?" he asked as he kissed her on the doorstep. "You want me to drag all my clients for impromptu haircuts?"

She smiled, though it was forced. "It's all on me. I'll succeed or fail on my own merit."

He knew that. And right now she was failing and there wasn't a damn thing he could do, and that was going to drive him bug-fuck insane. So today, when she went off to work, he was going to go take care of something he could control.

Colt gave her a hard, fierce kiss when she left, and waited in his cabin until he was sure she was down the highway heading back to Bluebonnet. Then he got in his Jeep and pulled onto the highway, but headed in the opposite direction of town.

Allan Sunquist's dealership was a good drive down the highway, and impossible to miss. Sunny Motors was halfway between Bluebonnet and the next biggest city. One of the largest dealerships in the area, and Allan ran the damn thing.

He could have lived out *there*, Colt thought with irritation. Instead, he made the long drive back and forth between Bluebonnet and the dealership because he was the big man around town. In a bigger city, he'd just be nobody, and Allan Sunquist couldn't stand to be a nobody.

Colt pulled in next to a row of shiny trucks, all decked out and sparkling clean. His own Jeep was clean, but it was also older. He didn't see the need for a big expensive vehicle. Most of his money went to savings anyhow. He wasn't going to be like his father—living in a broken-down trailer, selling scrap metal for money. He saved, and he invested in CDs. He had several he'd bought back when he was in the military that were about to mature and it'd be a nice chunk in his savings account. Beth Ann could use the money. He'd give it to her if she asked. He'd clean out the entire damn account to bring a smile to her face.

But she wouldn't ask. And that made him feel helpless.

This, at least, he could do.

He strolled into the enormous building. Glass double doors opened and slid back as he stepped inside, and Colt glanced around. There were several offices behind glass partitions, but he also knew Sunquist made a lot of money. He'd have an office somewhere.

"Welcome to Sunny Motors. Can I help you?"

Colt turned to see a man with a fake smile and too-perfect hair grinning at him. Salesmen. He hated 'em. Colt turned and looked around the showroom again. There was another BMW a bit like Allan's, but not quite the same. "Looking for Sunquist."

"Do you have an appointment?" the man asked politely.

Colt turned and gave him a scowl. "No. But I'm not leaving until I talk to him."

"Gotcha," the man said with a too-friendly wink. "Follow me, friend. I'll let you talk to his secretary."

So he was getting pawned off on someone else? That was just fine. Colt followed a few steps behind, and the man led him past the suite of glass offices to a back room. The room had a reception desk and boasted a fake plant in each corner. Award after award dotted the wall, along with pictures of salesmen. Allan's image was in several of the photos—salesman of the month, salesman of the year. He certainly was good at selling people a story.

"Can I help you?" the woman seated at the desk said sweetly. Her voice was young, and when he turned his gaze back to her, she smiled. She was pretty—thick, curly brown hair streaked with red highlights. She wore a little too much lipstick, and her blouse was low cut. He could practically see her damn navel when he stood over her.

"I'm here to see Allan."

She smiled up at him and smacked her gum. "Your name?"

"Tell him Colt Waggoner needs to have a talk."

She scribbled down a note and gave him a coy smile. "Be right back." She slid from her desk and crossed the room, disappearing out a door behind her desk that was marked PRIVATE.

Not before he caught a flash of red sole, though, and his attention was drawn to her shoes. Pink. High-heeled with a red sole. Beth Ann had been wearing the exact same shoes when he'd rescued her from the mud. She'd laughed when he'd snapped the heel off.

"I always got a pair of these when Allan cheated on me," she'd told him. And it seemed that Allan had given the exact same pair to his mistress. Fucking asshole. Colt clenched his hands, feeling the need to smash his fist through the man's face.

The secretary returned a moment later, all smiles. "Mr. Sunquist will see you now."

Good. He nodded at the woman, and then pushed through the door.

When he entered the room, Allan was standing, frowning at Colt. He was dressed in an impeccable dark gray suit, a red collared shirt underneath, slightly open. And he was frowning intensely at Colt.

"What are you doing here, Waggoner?"

Colt stood in front of the desk, crossed his arms. "You and I need to have a talk. I want you to leave Beth Ann alone."

Allan snorted and sat back down at his desk. It had stacks of paperwork neatly piled in one corner of the desk, and the other had trophies crammed together. Behind him, on a shelf, he saw even more trophies—car sales mixed with football trophies from high school and college—and a picture of Beth Ann and Allan smiling, their cheeks pressed together. They both wore formalwear, Allan in a tuxedo, and Beth Ann in a sedate black dress, her hair pulled back in a tight updo. She looked young in that picture, but even in the photo, Allan's face seemed to take up most of the picture, as if she were just a charming accessory and he the star.

"I'm not leaving her alone. Not when I think she's making a mistake." Allan sneered at him. "You do realize this is all a phase, right? She's mad at me. She's going to pout and insist on her independence for a few months, and then she's going to miss me. And when I apologize again, she's going to take me back, and we're going to get married." He gave Colt a dismissive look. "You're just a speed bump in the road."

"Really."

"Yes, really."

"You're full of shit," Colt said, suddenly furious. "You treated her like garbage. You cheated on *her*. She's done with you." He glanced back at the door. "I saw your secretary's shoes. Beth Ann had a pair just like that. You give everyone you fuck expensive shoes so they don't ask questions?"

Allan's face flushed red with anger. "You need to mind your own goddamn business—"

"I am," Colt said flatly. "Beth Ann is my business. And you don't need to text her and try to get her back because you miss her. You had her. You lost her."

Allan's face grew sly and he tilted his head back, staring up at Colt's looming form on the far side of the desk. "I see what this is. You're mad because I found out the truth."

"What truth?"

Allan waved a hand. "About your little weekend rendezvous. About how you lied to her so she'd have to spend all weekend with you in the woods. She was probably desperate and lonely and you probably nailed her as soon you could get her alone. What was it—she needed to cuddle up against you for warmth? And you just had to slip your hand in her panties and diddle her?"

Colt's hands twitched, images of pounding the man's face in flashing behind his eyes. "You don't know shit."

"I know plenty, you piece of trash," Allan bit out. "I talked with Rob over at the fire department. He said you called him and said there was no one else out there that weekend and you were heading in. But to hear Beth Ann tell the story, you two were stranded and had to stay out there all weekend. Sounds like a hookup to me."

Colt's jaw clenched. "That's not what it was."

"No? Then what was it?"

Colt said nothing. The weekend had started out to teach her a lesson. To make a spoiled, prissy woman get knocked down a few pegs. To get subtle revenge on a town that hated him and thought he was garbage because of his last name.

But that sounded just as bad. Worse, maybe. So he said nothing.

Allan's smirk was knowing. "I thought so. Let me tell you

something, buddy. Beth Ann is always crying about trust and how much she values it. And as soon as she finds out your ass lied to her, you're out the door and I'm back in it."

Rage burned through his mind. He wanted to grab the man's face and slam it into the front of his desk. Deck him with one of those stupid trophies. "You're not going to say a thing," he bit out.

"No? And why wouldn't I?"

Colt clenched his hands. Forced himself to breathe. This shithead was baiting him.

Allan just smiled, the look smug. As if he'd won. "Why wouldn't I?" he repeated.

"Because I know your secrets, Allan Sunquist," Colt said with a drawl, pretending a casualness that he didn't feel. "Big man of Bluebonnet. Everyone's favorite town councilman. A veritable saint. No one can figure out *why* Beth Ann left you. They just can't understand it. I guess they don't know that you cheated on her, do they?"

Behind the desk, Allan stiffened.

"But I know the truth," Colt continued. "She won't tell anyone that you cheated on her, will she? She doesn't want to hurt you like that. She's not mean like that." He leaned over Allan's desk. "But . . . I am. And I'm not afraid to tell everyone how you cheated on her—repeatedly."

Allan gave him a cold stare.

"It sure would make everyone in town look at you differently wouldn't it? To know that you had a beautiful, smart, funny girl like Beth Ann and you couldn't keep your dick in your pants?

That you had to fuck anything moving just because you needed to feel like the big hero?" He glanced around the office, then back at Allan. "I'm sure reputation's very important in a job like yours. How many cars you sell to the good folks of Bluebonnet?"

Allan's face had turned a dull red again. He said nothing for a long, long moment. Then, slowly, he gave Colt a narrow-eyed gaze. "So is this all a master plan?"

"Plan?"

"Take my fiancée. Destroy my job. My reputation. This some big revenge plan because of who I am and who you are?"

Colt barked a laugh. "Fuck you. It has nothing to do with me."

Allan tilted his head. "Liar. That's what it is, isn't it? You want everything that I have—everything you didn't—and you want to destroy it because you're jealous. Because you've never had what I had."

Now the man was just talking nonsense. "All I want is for you to leave Beth Ann alone."

"That's what this *is*," Allan repeated again, his eyes angry slits in his handsome face. "Well, I'm not going to sit here and let you walk all over me, *Waggoner*." He emphasized Colt's last name with a sneer. "You cross me and I'm going to make your family so fucking miserable they won't be able to see straight. Your father has some outstanding warrants, you know. Needs to clean up his property or they're going to haul his ass to jail. He can't run a junkyard on private property. The neighbors are complaining. I'd hate for such an old man to be carted off to jail, but what can you do?"

Colt stared at Allan's evil smile, hate seething through him.

Allan stared back, not moving.

"You leave Beth Ann alone," Colt said slowly. "Or the next time I pound your face in, I'm going to do more than give you a few black eyes."

"Is that a threat?"

"It's a promise." And he stalked out of the dealership.

FOURTEEN

Colt slammed into his Jeep and punched the steering wheel. Fuck. Fuck. Fuck. Any leverage he might have had over that smarmy asshole was gone. His father had fucking *warrants* out for his arrest? The Waggoner property had always been a disaster. Had someone finally complained? The old man was going to get tossed into jail. And Colt was going to have to be the one to bail him out. Berry didn't have the money. Marlin worked as a truck driver. He wouldn't have the money, either. Goddamn it.

He tore onto the highway, driving back toward Bluebonnet. Marlin didn't answer his phone. Browning was working out at an oil rig in Louisiana for the next six months. Chester was probably still in prison out in Huntsville. Two more years. Berry, then. He called his brother's job.

"Big Burgers," Berry said with a familiar drawl. "Can I take your order?"

Fuck his goddamn family. "What's the deal with Dad and warrants out for his arrest?"

"So you found out about that?"

Colt gritted his teeth in frustration. "Just tell me."

"Needs to clean up the property. I told him I'd help, but I've been working double shifts here at work, you know. He's waiting for Chester to get out."

"Chester doesn't get out for another two years," Colt growled.

"That's about right," Berry agreed.

"I'll take care of it," Colt gritted, and hung up the phone. He tossed it into the passenger seat, wishing he could smash it down on the road.

Damn his family. They'd been a thorn in his side his entire life. He'd known that if he came back to Bluebonnet, they'd crawl back into his life again. Lazy, poor, trashy Waggoners. His mother hadn't been able to stand it—she'd left when he was twelve, unable to handle looking after four Waggoner boys and his father on a supermarket salary. She was tired of working so hard, she'd told his dad. Tired, and she was going to go find herself a nice sugar daddy that would take care of her. That was the last time Colt had seen her. He hadn't wanted to be part of that family after she'd left. He'd been unable to escape being one of the Waggoner boys. The clothes that were handed down from his dad. The food stamps. The name calling from the other kids in town. The day after he graduated from high school, he'd left to join the marines. He'd never looked back.

And now, he was back and he was going to have to clean up their messes again.

Before they ruined his new life, and his relationship with Beth Ann.

He'd just have to tell her the truth, as soon as he got his father squared away.

Even when Colt was growing up, Henry Waggoner's home had been a shithole. Colt hadn't seen it in almost nine years, and wondered if his memories had made it worse than he'd thought.

Nope. It was just as bad as he recalled. The road was little more than potholes—the city wouldn't maintain this far out. It was up to the residents to have gravel poured every couple of years, but anyone that lived out here couldn't afford something like that. His Jeep bounced down the rutted dirt road. His father's old mailbox popped into view down the road, and Colt pulled up next to it and stared out at the yard, his lip curling in disgust.

When Colt and his brothers had been boys, they'd played among the broken-down cars on cinderblocks. They'd collected aluminum cans to bring in a few extra nickels. They'd chased one another through the high weeds and made forts out of scrap metal and old, discarded tires.

Now, when Colt looked across the yard, all he saw was trash. His father owned three acres and had set his trailer back at the edge of the property, away from the junk. But the junk butted up to the trailer now. Colt parked and picked his way toward the trailer. Busted cars, bikes missing wheels, piles of piping lay scattered amid thigh-high weeds. There was a stack of tires that was easily thirty deep. An old tractor that looked as if it should have been torn apart for scraps balanced precariously on two wheels, the other side half buried in dirt and grass. Every inch of his father's yard was covered in garbage.

A dog barked in the distance. That must be Roscoe. He'd been little more than a puppy when Colt had left, and he'd been furious—once again—that his dad had spent several hundred dollars on a hunting dog rather than fixing the leaking roof on the single wide. "He can help us catch dinner," his father had proclaimed proudly.

Colt hadn't understood it then. Hell, he didn't understand it now. No one in his family seemed to take responsibility for their poor living situation. The money for the dog could have bought T-shirts for his little brothers. But they weren't mad, either. They'd been thrilled that they had a dog. And that was just one memory out of dozens.

His father had made a living when he was younger selling scrap metal and fixing junkers, or if they couldn't be fixed, tearing out the useful parts and selling them. People had always dropped their broken shit at Henry's trailer, and eventually it'd be cobbled and used up and taken away. But it looked as if Henry had let things pile up. Colt was revolted. He pushed to the front steps and noticed several bags of trash sitting next to the stoop. Fucking disgusting.

He banged on the door.

No answer.

Colt knocked again, harder. He could hear the radio on. He glanced back at the road—his dad's junker truck was there, so he had to be home. He banged on the door one more time, and the dog began to bark loudly.

Colt sighed and pushed at the door knob. It wasn't locked. He took a step in, then squatted as Roscoe came up to him, dancing with excitement. The dog's muzzle was gray with age, and he looked a little worn out. Had it really been so long? Roscoe barked a warning, then licked Colt's outstretched hand.

He smiled, petting the dog on the head. He'd hated the animal when he'd left, resenting the meals and clothing Roscoe had represented. Stupid to hate a dog.

"You need to answer your door, Dad," Colt warned, then stood. The interior of the small single wide was a mess, too. Ramen noodle cups littered the counter, along with empty beer cans. The fridge was yellow with age, and the lone chair that sat in the living room was covered in masking tape on one corner, the upholstery destroyed.

Colt felt a twinge of guilt. Had his father been living in this heap with no help because Marlin was out driving his truck?

"Dad?"

No response. He thought he heard a thump in the back bedroom, but hell, that could have been trash falling over. Still, he took a step forward and frowned when the entire kitchen seemed to creak under his foot. Damn. The trailer was falling apart. He took another step forward, toward the door shut at the end of the single wide, where the lone bedroom was. He and his brothers had piled into that one room while his dad had slept on the couch. Colt glanced back at the living room. Back when he'd had a couch, anyway. "Dad?"

"Colt?" The sound was wheezing, faint, and made Colt's heart clench in fear. He pushed forward, wincing when he stepped on a rotten patch and his foot nearly sank through the floor of the trailer. He pushed open the thin door and stared at the mess. The small room had a bed pushed to the corner. His dad was on the floor, covered in blood and bruises. His long, white hair lay stringy across his face, and several days' growth of beard covered his worn face.

"Colt?" His dad struggled to get up. "I—I'm stuck."

Underneath him, the floor of the trailer had collapsed in one section, rotted away. His dad had fallen through, his leg trapped somewhere under the trailer. His father winced, in obvious pain, and there was blood on the floor next to him.

Colt moved in carefully, his heart pounding. He knelt beside his dad, gripped his hand. "It's okay, Dad," he said softly, guilt and fear crashing over him. "We're going to get you out of here and take care of you, okay?"

And he pulled out his cell phone and called 911.

The next few hours were a nightmare for Colt. The emergency vehicle couldn't get close enough to the trailer, so Colt and a few of the paramedics had to haul his father out of the trailer and carry him across the junk-strewn field. From there, he'd followed the ambulance to the closest hospital, thirty miles away. His dad had been taken to emergency, leaving Colt in the waiting room, sick at heart. Berry was working a double shift and would be by when he was done, and Marlin was currently en route to Vegas, and wouldn't be back for days. Browning was on the rig and couldn't be contacted.

That left Colt.

Colt, who was racked with guilt. He'd deliberately ignored his father's requests to see him. He'd been furious at the old man, holding grudges for his upbringing. It had taken a pissing match with Allan to get him to go see his father. What if it had been a few more days?

His father could have starved to death, a prisoner in his own damn trash heap of a trailer.

Colt didn't like to think about that. He didn't know what to do, either. He'd called Beth Ann and she'd promised to be on her way as soon as she finished with her customer.

They'd wheeled his dad into a room a bit later. He'd simply been dehydrated from being stuck in the floor. His leg was bruised and the enormous scrapes covering his leg infected, but they'd given him antibiotics and set him up on IV fluids. He could go home in the morning, the nurse had assured him, and then they'd discussed payment. His father had no insurance, naturally. Colt gave them his address to send the bill.

The nurse had pulled him aside and talked to him for a bit longer, concerned about his father. He showed poor nutrition for a man his age, and was suffering from several vitamin deficiencies. She asked what he'd been eating—Colt couldn't tell her. She also cited concerns about his living conditions, and again, Colt had no answers.

All he knew was that he couldn't let his dad go back to the trailer. It was not fit to live in, and if he went back, Colt'd just be fishing him out of it within weeks. He couldn't let the thing fall down around the old man's ears. They discussed options—the nursing consultant suggested a home, but Colt shook his head. His dad was stubborn. He'd never stay in a home.

It had been one of the longest hours of his life—the nurse

grilling him about his father's care, and Colt having no answers. He felt . . . ashamed.

Like a bad son.

When he returned to his father's room, Beth Ann was already there. She sat next to his father's bed, filing his nails with a pink buffing file. She chatted gaily as Henry looked on with a baffled smile. She'd cut the old man's hair, too, Colt noticed, and the gray locks had been carefully smoothed down over his head.

"He's very good at what he does," she was murmuring to his father. "The entire time we were in the woods, he was never lost at all."

"He was a smart boy," his father commented, his voice raspy.

"Oh, honey," Beth Ann said with a laugh. She called everyone honey. Everyone but him, he realized. "He is sharp like a whip. And never worried a lick about us getting lost, either. He just took care of the situation. We didn't know which way was north at one point, so he made a compass—"

The door creaked as he pushed it open a bit farther, and both of them turned to look at him. Beth Ann's gentle smile made his heart stutter with love.

His father's gaze was wary. "Son."

"Hi, Colt," Beth Ann said, and waved her nail buff at him. "I was just helping your dad get cleaned up."

He nodded, moved to his dad's side. His throat went dry; he didn't know what to say. After a moment, he brushed a stray hair off of his dad's shoulder. "Just don't let her put a pink streak in your hair."

The old man chuckled. "She mentioned a bow."

"A ponytail," Beth Ann said in a mock huff. "And that was only if he wanted to keep his hair long. Which he didn't. And he looks very handsome now. Just like his son."

Beth Ann smiled, and Colt smiled back at her. His dad, however, wasn't smiling any longer. He was watching Beth Ann thoughtfully.

Colt couldn't take his eyes off her, either. He was so proud of her. Here was his redneck father, the town's biggest joke, and she was helping him fix his hair and bragging to him about Colt. He got that damn knot in his throat again. God, he loved her so much. He wanted to pull her into his arms and bury his face in her hair. She was at his side. Whatever he had to do to take care of this, she was at his side and would support him.

He suddenly felt like the luckiest fucking man on earth.

He moved to his dad's side, took his hand, clasped it. "I had Dane swing by and get Roscoe, Dad. He's going to stay out at the ranch for a few days."

His dad nodded, looking over him. "You look good, son. Like a man."

He nodded. Because hell, what could he say to that?

The older man's eyes brimmed suddenly. "You look like your mother."

Beth Ann cast Colt an anxious look and she hopped to her feet. "I'm heading down to the cafeteria to get some snacks. I'll pick up some stuff and be back shortly." She leaned in and kissed Colt on the cheek before slipping out of the room.

Colt said nothing, simply gripped his father's hand as he composed himself. He wiped his eyes with shaking hands, then nodded at the door. "Isn't that Allan Sunquist's girl?"

He gritted his teeth. "They broke up last year, Dad. She's with me." *I love her.*

But his father looked concerned. "Allan must be furious. He's never liked you."

"I don't care what he thinks, Dad."

He shook his head. "He hates you because of your mother. You just be careful of him, Colt. Those Sunquist men can be ruthless bastards. They don't care who they hurt as long as they get their way."

Odd that they were talking about this. "Beth Ann is done with him, Dad. I've got it taken care of."

"She's never going to be done with him as long as you're with her, son." He shook his head. "Find yourself a different girl. A girl that Sunquist boy don't have his sights on."

Irritation flashed through him. A girl that wasn't out of reach of a Waggoner boy, did he mean? "*I'm* with Beth Ann. She's the one that *I* want, and I'm not changing my mind just because Allan is obsessed with her."

"It's not just her," his father said. "It's you. You and your mother."

"What the fuck does Mom have to do with anything?" he exploded, then bit his lip. Christ. He was yelling at a sick man in a hospital bed.

But his father seemed to accept his outburst. He patted Colt's hand. "Because of your mother," he repeated. "And who you are."

"And who am I?" he asked in a dry voice.

"Not my son," Henry said quietly.

Colt stiffened. He hadn't heard that right. "Come again?"

Henry gave him a guilty look, ran a hand down his haggard

face. "It's true. I'm not your real father, Colt. Andrew Sunquist is. Your mother slept with him, got pregnant, and when he wouldn't marry her, she married me."

Colt stared down at him in shock. "You're delirious. The meds—"

"Allan knows, son," he said softly. "He's known since you were teenagers."

"And you never told me?"

"You hated me enough. I didn't want you to hate me even more." He shook his head. "I couldn't give you what the Sunquists had, and I knew he wouldn't acknowledge you publicly. Your mother wasn't around to confirm it, either. You resented us enough—you would have hated us even more if I told you."

He stared down at his father, at the wide nose, the bushy eyebrows. He'd always looked like his mother, he assumed. He remembered her—pretty but sad. But then he thought of Allan. Of his narrow, blade-like eyes. Just like Colt's. And his father had been a smiley lawyer who had moved to Houston years ago. Died early, too. He remembered the picture of the man in the newspaper, of him smiling and laughing with a senator. He'd had a dimple in his cheek. The same one Colt did.

Nausea flooded through him.

He recalled Allan's words. *"You want her because she's with me. Because you want what I have. This is some sick revenge game, right?"*

Oh, hell.

"I'm sorry, son," Henry said. "I wish you were mine. I've always been proud of you."

And all his life, he'd resented a man who had no money, but

had still married a woman pregnant with another man's child and raised him as if he were his own. Even after his mother had left Texas, leaving Henry with four small boys to look after.

Emotion burned in the back of his throat and he clasped his father's hand harder. "Beth Ann doesn't know. I don't want to tell her until the time is right."

His father looked at him sadly. "I don't know how she'll take it."

Not well, Colt knew. Not because it was his fault, but because of what he represented to her. Would she still love him if she knew he was just the poorer, paler version of Allan?

Or would she be sick at the thought of touching him?

FIFTEEN

When Colt's father went to sleep, Beth Ann insisted on dragging Colt back to his cabin with her. "He's just going to sleep all night," she soothed, concerned about the stark look on his face. He'd held his father's hand all afternoon, and even though the man was going to be fine, she knew Colt was concerned. In a private moment while his father was napping, Colt had admitted the state of his father's home and the warrants for his arrest if he didn't get it cleaned up. Henry couldn't move back there.

But the problem with the property and the warrants couldn't be solved that night. At her fussing and Henry's insistence, they drove from Huntsville back to Bluebonnet, then out to the ranch. Colt hadn't protested when she'd offered to drive.

Nor had he protested when she'd checked his fridge, found nothing in it, and insisted on going to the main lodge to make him a few sandwiches. When she'd returned, he still wore that stark look on his face, and she'd had to coax him to eat. He'd wolfed the sandwich down without a thought, and when it was gone, he tugged her into his lap and just hugged her close.

She felt tears prick her eyes, and ran her fingers along his scalp lovingly. What a terrible, tough day for him. "I'm sure we can figure out a solution for your father."

He nodded, then tilted his face up. She kissed his lips automatically, smoothing her fingers over his cheeks, caressing him.

"How was work?" he asked. "Business picking up?"

"Not yet, but I'm hopeful," she said. She'd always be hopeful. If it didn't pick up, well, she didn't like to think about that.

It's because of who you're dating, that awful voice whispered, and it sounded a lot like Allan in her head. She ignored it and slid from Colt's lap, tugging on his hand. "Come to bed."

He rubbed his face and nodded, rolling into bed, fully dressed.

She laughed and tugged at his boots. "You can't sleep like that."

"I've slept in mud," he said, and she could almost hear the amusement in his voice. "Sleeping in my clothes ain't nothing."

Well, she wasn't going to wake up with a hiking boot in her back. She plucked at his laces until they were undone, then wrapped her hands around his boot and tugged. It fell to the ground, and she quickly removed the other, just as his hand began to languidly trail up her leg. When she turned to unbuckle his belt, he was watching her with avid, hot eyes. Her fingers stroked over the crotch of his jeans, finding him hard already. His hand smoothed up and down her leg, caressing her. She rubbed her hand along his shaft, then loosened his belt. When she undid his zipper, she slipped her hand inside, cupped his hot length through his briefs. He groaned in need.

"You're the best thing that has ever happened to me, Beth Ann."

She gave him a saucy smile. "You always say the sweetest things when I have my hand on your cock, Colt Waggoner."

Tonight, he wasn't in a teasing mood, though. The look he gave her was solemn. "It's true."

She laughed lightly.

He wasn't laughing. He continued to stare up at her. His hand moved to her cheek, brushed his thumb over her lip. "I love you."

Her breath caught in her throat. He . . . She hadn't expected that. Colt was someone who scowled whenever he saw a sappy commercial on TV. She knew he cared about her, had assumed in time that he might confess how he felt. And she didn't mind waiting. But this. This felt like . . . a gift, with him staring up at her so intensely, need in his eyes.

Unexpected emotion pricked at her throat. She slid onto the bed, straddled him, and leaned over his body to kiss his mouth. "I love you, too," she whispered, and then flexed her hips down over his.

Colt groaned, his hands moving to her breasts and pinching the nipples through her shirt. Desire crashed through her and she gasped against his mouth. He thrust against her, grinding his cock against her core.

"Get undressed," he said, his voice a harsh rasp. "I want to see your breasts bouncing while you ride my cock."

His words made her inhale sharply at the mental image, and she tugged her top off, casting it to the floor. She'd worn a camisole instead of a bra today, and it was quickly discarded as well.

His fingers went to her nipples, brushing over them, his movements gentle and teasing. As she rolled off him to remove her pants, he removed his own. Moments later, she straddled him again, feeling the hard length of him resting against her pussy. She rocked against his heat, sliding her hips up and down on him. She wasn't wet enough—not yet. So she placed his hands back on her breasts and sat up, gazing down at his intense face, while he gently teased and rolled her nipples against his thumbs. His hips flexed slowly under her, making her body rise, and her pulse began to beat slow and steady through her body, thrumming with building need. Her own hands moved to his nipples, playing with them, feeling the hard nubs against her own fingers, flicking them to watch his response.

His eyes were gleaming slits as he watched her, his hips bucking underneath her again, rolling gently. "You wet enough to take me, Beth Ann?"

"Hmm," she said softly, and reached down between her legs, sliding two fingers into her pussy. She pulled her hand away again and brushed her fingers against his mouth. "What do you think?"

She could tell from the look on his face that her small movement had pleased him. But her own breath gasped in her throat when he caught her hand in his and held her fingers against his mouth. He sucked one deep into his mouth, his tongue rasping as he licked it clean. "Delicious."

Her pussy clenched as his tongue moved over her other finger. Her own hips rocked, her breath hitching.

"Slide over me, Beth Ann," he said softly. "Ride me."

She braced one hand on the bed, raising her hips. Her other hand reached for his cock and she braced it at the core of her body, then began to push back, seating him in her body. His fingers had moved back to her breasts, tugging at the peaks as she gasped and worked herself down his hard length. And when she had seated herself fully, she sat back and moved her hips, just a little. He was so full inside her, and this way she got to look down at his delicious body. Her hands ran over his chest—so gorgeous. All hers.

His hands slid to her hips, and when she raised them, he pushed her back down, the thrust hard and unyielding. She moaned, immediately raising her hips again to repeat the motion. Again, and again, she rode him, lifting her hips to meet the upward thrust of his. He felt so good slamming into her body—and without the condom on, she felt even more. His fingers squeezed her nipples, the hard tips tightening, and her body jerked in response to that jolt.

He groaned, no doubt feeling it all the way down to his body. His thrusts became harder, and though she had initially started out in control, he'd quickly taken back over again—that was fine with her—she loved his control in bed, his mastery of her. When his hands slid back down to her hips to slam her down on his cock, her hands moved to her nipples, tugging at them as he rocked into her over and over again.

She came a moment later, tensing and crying out his name. He gave a fierce jerk underneath her, and then she felt the wash of his cum inside her. She leaned over him, tracing her fingers over his face, his mouth.

He pulled her close and gave her a hard, fierce kiss. "Thank you for being there for me today."

"Always," she whispered, and meant it.

Colt couldn't tell her.

He'd wanted to while she'd slept next to him last night. He'd fucked her hard that morning, too, but he'd been unable to make the words come out of his mouth. She wouldn't understand. Hell, he didn't understand it himself.

That douche bag Allan was his brother. It made his skin crawl at the thought. And if he told her that and mentioned that he'd lied to her about that first weekend? She wouldn't understand.

He'd tell her. She needed to know. Just . . . not yet. Not while he was raw with it himself.

He was quiet as she'd driven him back to the hospital. He knew she was concerned, but she'd simply kissed him and told him to call if he needed her.

"Hey, Dad," he said as he entered his father's room. "How are you feeling this morning?"

"Much better," Henry said with a smile. "I'm surprised you came back after what I told you yesterday."

Guilt flashed through him. "Nah," he said. "You've always been my father. Always will be."

Henry squeezed Colt's hand. "I'm glad. I've missed you."

He'd missed his father, too. Seeing him had made him realize that even though he didn't agree with the way Henry Waggoner had lived his life, he still loved the man. Colt cleared his throat. "How you feeling this morning?"

"Just fine. Nurses say they're going to keep me one more day just for observation. I can go home tomorrow."

Colt shook his head. "You're not going back to that dump. It's not safe. The entire thing should be condemned and the yard cleaned out."

His father began to protest. "There's lots of money in that scrap metal—"

"And you owe even more in fines to the city than it's worth. I'm going to have to clean it up."

His father set his jaw, mulishly. "It's my stuff."

"You can't clean it up. You're sick, and your leg is messed up. Let me take care of it." He was sure Dane—and maybe even Grant—would help with the cleanup. And if they wouldn't, he could always hire someone to haul trash. Either way, he was cleaning out that property. "I already talked to Grant. We have an extra cabin next to Brenna's and I'm moving you in there."

Henry's jaw set stubbornly. "I won't be a parasite on your finances."

"You won't be," Colt lied. "Just the other day, Grant was talking about how he needed someone to maintain the lawns around the houses and tune up the ATVs and handle the paintball guns. I'm hiring you for the job if you want it."

Of course, he'd have to run it past Grant, but Grant wouldn't care. The only reason the man was so invested in their damn business was because he'd go crazy with nothing to do. They could bleed money for years and Grant wouldn't give a shit—he was loaded.

His father gave him a skeptical look. "How much does this job pay?"

"Minimum wage," Colt drawled. "Take it or leave it."

"I'll take it," his father said. "If you think I'm needed."

He'd have Brenna break the equipment every week just to give his dad something to do. He clapped a hand on his dad's shoulder. "Absolutely. Leave the rest to me."

She had no customers. Beth Ann stared at her empty salon chair, trying not to feel depressed and like a failure.

She couldn't even run her own business. She *was* a failure. She was a very broke failure. Her savings was tapped out. She had just enough to pay her rent that was due in two weeks, but that was it.

Colt would loan her the money, if she asked. She didn't want to ask, though. She didn't want to depend on anyone. If she couldn't do it on her own, then what was the point? Her phone rang, and she leapt to answer it. "California Dreamin'!"

"Hey, girl, it's me." Miranda's voice was cheerful. "What are you up to?"

"Nothing." She sighed, fighting back depression as she stared at her empty salon. "Just working."

"Oh." Miranda sounded sad. She knew Beth Ann was struggling. "I could use a trim on my bangs. Can I come by?"

"Of course, honey," she said, her mouth twisting in a wry smile. "But I cut your bangs last week."

"Oh. Well. Maybe a new manicure? I thought I might go for something in red."

She smiled. "You can't single-handedly save my business, Mir. It's sweet, but you should probably save your money for your wedding."

Miranda groaned into the phone. "Don't remind me. I think

Dane's mom is going to be a bridezillla. Momzilla. Whatever. I got a package from her the other day and it was a box full of bridal magazines. God. Dane took one look at it and ran out of the house."

Beth Ann laughed, moving to the window and peeking at the shop across the street. Still full of people. She didn't understand it. How could the other salon be so much better than hers? She'd never had complaints before.

Something wasn't adding up.

"So anyhow," Miranda said. "I got Dane to volunteer for the dunking booth. We'll set up in town square, and he promised to wear a hockey helmet and a jersey. It's for a good cause, right?"

"That's great," she said, watching another customer stroll down the street toward the other salon. Her teeth clenched. "You still going to give all the proceeds to the library?"

"Yup. I think it'll be a great fund-raiser. Much better than another charity drive."

"Much," she said absently, then frowned. "Hey, Mir, let me let you go. I need to check something out."

"Sure, catch you later. Call me."

Beth Ann ended the call and tossed her phone down on the counter. She flipped the sign on her door, and then headed down the street, curious to find out what the other woman had that she didn't. Because darn it, she was tired of wondering. And now she wanted answers.

Beth Ann entered the other salon hesitantly. Her bravado had disappeared somewhere during the walk across the street, and now all she felt was anxious.

She glanced down at the row of customers. All four seats in the waiting area were full. In the salon section, a woman stood behind a barber chair, curling Mrs. Potter—her old client, she noticed—into a ragged-looking updo. Hmph. At the back of the room, another woman sat, painting nails. Twins. She hadn't realized there were two women. They were pretty, too, though the one curling hair needed to wear less makeup. She wore tight capris and a leopard sweater, her black hair pulled back into a sleek ponytail. She gave Beth Ann a quick glance as she entered, and Beth Ann noticed she was wearing false eyelashes. Good lord.

"We can't take walk-ins today," the woman announced, a thick drawl to her voice. "Too busy. Earliest I can get you in is Tuesday. You have a coupon?"

"She's not a walk-in," Mrs. Potter said in an unpleasant voice. "She's the competition."

Hateful woman. Beth Ann frowned. "I'm not here for a haircut." Oh heavens. What was she going to say now that Mrs. Potter had pretty much sold her out? *I came to snoop and see why you're selling so much better than I am*? The decorations on the walls were generic, the equipment the same as hers. She didn't get it. "I came over to say hi and see how business was going."

The hairstylist gave her an uncertain smile. "Business couldn't be better. Thanks for asking."

On a nearby seat, a woman held up a purple slip of paper. "Here. I have an extra coupon if you need it. You could get your nails done. Probably be nice to have someone do yours for a change."

Numbly, Beth Ann took the coupon, too polite to point out that she could do her own nails for free . . . and then froze.

Bluebonnet special—80 percent off of her regular prices? Beth Ann glanced over at the sign on the window, and did some mental calculation. Even with the woman's astronomical fees, with this coupon, she was still much cheaper than Beth Ann's prices.

Coupons. Of course. How stupid she'd been. People were attracted to a sale, and this woman was undercutting the hell out of her and making it seem like a bargain. Annoyed, she flipped over the coupon.

Her heart stopped. The coupon postcards had a small, cheerful sun in the top left-hand corner, along with a return address. They'd been sent out from Sunny Motors. She'd recognize that logo anywhere. Fury slammed through her, and she sucked in a deep breath, then marched over to the woman with the false eyelashes.

"Excuse me," Beth Ann said, and shoved the coupon at her. "Who's behind this?"

The woman—Jordan, judging from her nametag—smiled at Beth Ann. "New business incentive." She winked. "I almost thought it was too good to be true, but Allan assured me it's on the up-and-up."

"Oh, he did, did he?" She studied the woman a bit longer, the fake eyelashes, the enormous rack. "Did he ever buy you shoes?"

Jordan grinned over at Beth Ann. "You know Allan, too?"

"Not for much longer," she muttered, tucking the coupon into her pocket. "Because I'm going to kill him."

SIXTEEN

Another mistress. Beth Ann was furious. Worse. She was beyond furious. She was seething with rage. How *dare* he. How dare he try to push her business out of town and set up one of his mistresses? Had he been bankrolling Cutz's coupons just to try to force her to quietly shut her doors?

She was utterly, utterly livid. To think that he would do something so low, so controlling. Beth Ann slammed into the first parking space at Sunny Motors and tore inside, the coupon clutched in her hand. She held her keys like a weapon and marched to the back office, and stared down Sammi, his secretary. Another mistress. Who hadn't Allan slept with? God, why had she ever taken him back?

"I need to talk to Allan," she said tightly. "It's an emergency."

Sammi gave her an insolent look. "He's busy."

Beth Ann felt her entire body quiver with rage. She grabbed

the stack of paperwork off the girl's desk and threw it at the opposite wall, enjoying the rain of papers falling all over the room almost as much as the shocked O on Sammi's face. The girl got up from her desk and moved to pick up the first piece.

Beth Ann pushed her way into Allan's office.

He was in there. Alone. And he looked thrilled to see her, standing up immediately and moving forward to give her a hug.

She pushed him away. Shoved the coupon at his chest. "What. The. Fuck. Allan."

He flinched. "Language, Bethy-babe."

"What the *fuck*?" she cried again. "What the fuck are you trying to do to me?"

"I'm not sure what you're talking about—"

"Don't lie to me," she said, clenching her fists or she'd slam them into his face. "Quit lying to me and just tell me the truth for once in your life. What are you doing? Why is that new salon sending out *80 percent off* coupons with *your* logo on them? Why does 'Jordan' think that it's some sort of Bluebonnet business incentive? How much are you spending just to try and run me out of business?"

Allan got quiet. He stared down at the coupon, and then back up at her. "You weren't supposed to know, Bethy-babe—"

"That you were trying to run me out of business?" Her heart pounded painfully in her chest. "Why are you doing that to me? How could you be so cruel?"

He grasped her shoulders. "Because I want you back," he said desperately. "And as long as you think you're independent and on your own, you won't come back to me. I want you to need me again. I want you to love me again." Tears filled his eyes. "Beth

Ann, I can't live without you in my life. At my side. Please. I wasn't trying to hurt you. I just wanted to make you need me again."

She slapped him.

He recoiled, touching his cheek in surprise. Then, he shook his head, the look on his face determined. "I deserve that, but I won't change what I've done. Please. Please, Bethy-babe. I love you so much—"

"I don't love you," she said furiously. "How could you destroy me for your own selfish needs? That's not love. That's possession. Learn the difference."

"I will," he said quickly. "If you'll show me."

"Show you?" She laughed bitterly. "You're lucky I don't sue you."

Allan looked truly astonished at her words. "I just wanted you to come back to me. I wasn't trying to hurt you."

Once again, she didn't really exist to him, didn't matter. He honestly did not understand why she was so furious. "You have spent thousands and thousands of dollars trying to sink me!"

"It's worth it if I get you back," he said quietly.

She shook her head. "You've tried to undermine the thing that I'm proudest of. I can't ever trust you again. *Won't* ever trust you again. I want you to stay the hell away from me. If you don't, I'm going to tell everyone in town just why we broke up so they stop giving me those concerned looks because they just don't understand."

"Beth Ann, listen—"

"No," she said violently. "You listen to me. I'm tired of being the bad guy to save your reputation. No longer! I did that to help you, to protect you because I still cared about you and we had nine years together. But if you can't respect me even this little bit," she said, snatching the coupon from him and ripping it in half. "Then all bets are off."

He stared at her, aghast. "This isn't like you."

"I know," she said, furious. "Ain't it fucking great."

His lip curled in an ugly sneer. "You even sound like that asshole now."

"That asshole is the best thing that's ever happened to me. I love him. He supports me."

Allan's smile got even uglier. "You love him? Is it because he's the Sunquist you can control? You had to go for the second-rate version?"

The conversation had just taken a bizarre turn. "Sunquist? What are you talking about?"

Allan laughed mirthlessly. "Did your little boyfriend lie to you about that, too? Bad enough he made you go through that whole bullshit weekend of being stranded just so he could nail your ass. And you fell for it."

"What are you talking about?" she repeated.

"Your little weekend 'stranded,'" he said, and made finger quotes in the air, mocking her. "Everyone's been talking about it. You weren't stranded that weekend. Ask anyone. He deliberately kept you out in the woods so he could seduce you."

Her heart pounded in her chest, blood roaring in her ears. "You are lying. The river was flooded."

"Am I? Did he show you this flooded river? Did anyone else get stranded out there?" At her silence, his mouth twisted in a hurt smirk. "No? Just you? And you don't find that to be a coincidence?"

Beth Ann said nothing. An ache started in her chest, and her fingernails dug into her palms. He was lying. Had to be. Had to. Colt wouldn't do that to her. He knew how much she valued trust.

Didn't he?

Allan shook his head. "You fell for it. All of it. That brother of mine is a sneaky bastard." He sneered. "No pun intended."

"Brother?"

His mouth twisted. "Guess you didn't know that, either. You're fucking my brother. And I'm pretty sure he only wants you to get back at me."

She didn't know what to do. Beth Ann thought about going back to her salon, but she knew there would be no customers waiting there. She didn't want to go back to her parents, or to Colt's cabin. God, Colt. Allan had to be wrong. Had to be.

So she drove around the lake, trying to calm down. Trying to stop her heart from hurting so badly. She didn't want to ask. Oh sweet heaven, she didn't want to ask Colt, to find out her heart had been broken so easily again. She didn't want to know that he'd used her. She loved him—more intensely, more deeply than she'd ever cared for Allan. His betrayal would devastate her.

But she had to know. She had trusted him.

Had she been betrayed all over again?

Beth Ann drove to the Daughtry Ranch. Sat in her car for a

few minutes, trying to feel something, anything. All she felt was numb. Cold and sick to her stomach. She locked her car and entered the main cabin.

Brenna perked up at the sight of her. "Hey, girlfriend! You enjoy all that birthday cake?"

Her stomach roiled. Beth Ann was going to be sick if she thought about the birthday cake. But she gave Brenna a polite smile. "Have you seen Colt today?"

She could have called him, but this . . . she needed to see his face.

"Yup! He's over in the spare cabin, fixing it up for his dad. Mr. Waggoner gets out of the hospital tomorrow."

She nodded. Paused. "Hey . . . Brenna . . ."

"Yup?"

"You know that weekend I got stranded with Colt?"

Brenna suddenly looked uneasy. "Maybe."

Her discomfort told Beth Ann everything, but she still needed to hear the words aloud. There was an enormous knot in her throat as she asked. "Colt told me that when we were stuck out there, it was because the evacuation team had already left, and the river was too high to cross. He told me we were stranded. Is that true?"

Brenna suddenly began typing, as if she'd just had a flurry of inspiration.

"Brenna?"

The assistant bit her lip. "You know, Beth Ann . . . I think you'd better talk to Colt."

She was definitely going to throw up. "Thanks, Brenna."

Beth Ann walked out of the main cabin, shut the door behind

her. Moved to the small cabin. The door was open, and she could hear someone cussing inside. Heard a thump. Beth Ann moved into the doorway. Colt was setting up a single bed, neatly tucking the corners in. Military flat, just like he did their bed every morning. She flicked the light to get his attention.

He turned and the flicker of emotion that crossed his face was one of pleasure. "Hey, darlin'."

She didn't smile. "I need you to tell me if you've lied to me, Colt. About anything."

She waited for him to be confused. For him to quirk an eyebrow and ask what she was talking about.

But his eyes got hard. He sat down on the edge of the bed and patted it. "Sit down and let's talk."

Tears started in her eyes. It was all true. It was all true and she was going to be sick. She'd fallen for a man who had lied to her about everything. Who he was. What he wanted from her. Did he even love her? Or was that just part of his game?

"I don't want to sit down," she said in a wobbly voice. "So Allan's your brother?"

"He is," Colt replied in a flat voice.

"And are you with me because you're trying to get back at him?" Her voice quavered, breath catching on the words.

Colt's handsome face grew hard. "No. Never."

"How can I believe you?" she cried. "You know how important trust is to me."

"I know," he said in a ragged voice. "I was going to tell you."

"When?" she cried. "When you felt like it? When the mood struck you? When it suited *your* purposes? What about me? Doesn't what I think count?"

He said nothing, simply watched her with slitted eyes.

She laughed bitterly, throwing her hands up. "And if that wasn't awful enough, now I find out that you lied to me that first weekend. Was that just so you could fuck me, too? You made me go through all that mud and camping and being stranded in the rain just so you could *fuck* me? How about you ask a girl out on a damn date?"

"It wasn't like that," he said quietly.

"Then how was it? Tell me."

To her surprise, he looked uneasy. "When I saw you, you were nasty to me. I was bored. Irritated at you." He shook his head. "Thought I'd teach you a lesson."

"Teach me a lesson?" she cried out. "Are you serious? You hated me so much that you were going to drag me through the mud for an entire weekend? Are you sick in the head?"

"It was only supposed to be for one night," he said softly.

"Oh? And after that, I suppose we were really stranded?"

He said nothing.

Hurt rolled through her, wave after wave of hurt. "Oh. I see. So first you were pissed at me. Then you wanted to fuck me." She shook her head. "And I fell for it. God, I must be really, really stupid."

He stood up. Moved toward her. "You're not stupid, Beth Ann. I'm a fucking dumbass. I shouldn't have done it. And I should have said something."

"Yes," she said flatly. "You should have."

"I love you," he said, his gaze intent on her. He reached out a hand.

She flinched away. "How can I even trust you? How can I ever trust you again?"

"You can judge me by my actions," he said solemnly. "I know what I did looks really bad. I can't make it look better. But I have never treated you badly. I love you and I don't want to lose you. You can hate me for a month. You can slap me across the face. Whatever it takes to make this better. Just tell me we're okay."

"We're not okay," she said, tears streaking down her face. She slapped his hand away. "We're *so* not okay. I don't know if we will ever be okay again. I can't trust you, Colt. That's the only thing I've ever wanted from you is trust. To know that you have my back."

"I do—"

"You don't," she said, and pressed a hand to her forehead. It was either that or start screaming. This was Allan, all over again. Once again, she'd been lied to and betrayed. The hurt was so deep this time that she felt cold. Just cold all over. "I don't even know what to think right now, except that you betrayed me when I needed someone that I could trust the most."

There was anguish in his eyes. She didn't care. "Beth Ann," he said softly. "I didn't plan on falling in love with you, but I did. And I never meant to hurt you, but I did, and I'm sorry."

Her mouth twisted into a bitter smile. "You know who says 'sorry'? Someone that lied." She shook her head, dropped his hand. "I've heard enough apologies to last a lifetime."

And she walked away.

Beth Ann half expected him to come after her. To follow her back out into the parking lot, stop her at her car. Tell her he'd never meant to hurt her. That he'd never do it again. That's what Allan would have done.

But Colt wasn't Allan. He didn't chase her out. He wouldn't chase her, she knew that. He'd never chase her. He'd always let the decision be hers.

And somehow, that hurt worse than anything. She returned to her salon—her empty, empty salon—that she'd closed during the middle of the day. She'd been gone for hours. She remembered that first weekend, when she'd come back to a voicemail box full of unhappy clients that she'd missed out on. How she'd taken that for granted. She'd kill for a voicemail from just one unhappy client now.

But her voicemail was empty. And she couldn't even call Colt to complain. She kept the CLOSED sign flipped, turned the lights off, and went to the back room. Her air mattress was there, and she lay on it, suddenly bone weary and exhausted. Beth Ann grabbed her pillow, clutched it to her chest, and cried.

She'd never felt more alone or more unloved in her entire life.

SEVENTEEN

One week later

Colt flung a thick section of pipe into the Dumpster. He grabbed a nearby tire and hauled it to the Dumpster as well. Sweat poured down his shirtless, lean body. He'd been out in the sun, working since dawn to clean his father's property. He'd paid the fines but an inspector was coming by next week. He'd hired a day crew to come by and help, and Marlin would be by as soon as he finished his truck run. That was fine with Colt—this was something he wanted to do himself.

Next to him, Dane leaned against the Dumpster, chugging at a bottle of water. "Slow down, man. You're making me tired just watching you."

Colt didn't want to slow down, though. He adjusted his work

gloves and grabbed at the item under the tire he'd moved—chicken wire. A whole roll of it. "Needs to get done, Dane. I can rest later."

"You've been working since sunup without a break, Colt. This isn't going to get finished in one day." Dane swiped at his forehead. "And punishing yourself isn't going to bring her back."

Colt glared at his friend. His jaw tightened and he swung the chicken wire into the garbage. "This isn't about her."

"Bullshit," Dane said easily. "You think I haven't been where you are? You hurt her. It's eating you up inside that you hurt her, and so you're punishing yourself, because you can't stand the fact that you're such a dick." Dane swigged more water, then tilted his head. "Am I right?"

Colt said nothing. Merely clenched his jaw and went back to work.

Grant appeared a moment later. He wore an old T-shirt and jeans, and a surgeon's mask over his nose. "You're not going to believe what they found back behind the trailer."

"Is it Jimmy Hoffa?" Dane joked. "Because I'd believe just about anything else."

"Worse. A dead skunk." He grinned at Dane. "I came to get you because I figured your stink could cover the smell of it."

Dane threw his water bottle at Grant, who caught it and threw it back.

"You two fuck off," Colt snapped. "We're trying to clean this shit up, not play games."

Grant glanced over at Dane. "Still mad at himself?"

"Yup," Dane said lazily.

Christ. He wanted to punch them both in the face at the

moment. Colt clenched his gloved hands and grabbed another tire from the enormous stack. "Either you two help out or get out of here. I'll do it myself if I have to."

"More punishment," he heard Dane whisper to Grant. "I told him he needs to make it up to her—"

"I can't," Colt ground out, turning to face his friends. "I can't make it up to her. I fucking hurt her and humiliated her. And she doesn't want to speak to me, and I don't blame her. In her eyes, I'm no better than that piece of shit Allan. What do you want me to do, Dane? Buy her something to make her happy again? Because that worked so well for Allan?"

Dane said nothing. He adjusted his cap lower on his forehead and shrugged.

"You lied to her," Grant said slowly. "You can't change that fact."

"What about a big gesture?" Dane said. "I showed my dick to half the damn town to make Miranda happy."

Colt leaned against the Dumpster, warring with emotion. Rage that he was still so fucking furious with himself. Annoyance. And gratitude that his friends were ignoring his shitty mood and helping him try to set his life back together.

Because it had turned into a big pile of shit ever since Beth Ann had left him.

"Not a big gesture," Grant said thoughtfully. "Beth Ann doesn't want a big gesture, if what you're telling me is true."

Colt looked at his friend. "Then what does she want?"

Grant spread his hands. "She wants to trust you again. Whether or not that'll happen, she has to decide. You can't beg her to come back to you."

No, he couldn't. He thought of Allan's relentless begging. It had only hardened Beth Ann's heart against him.

"The only thing you can do," Grant continued, "is wait patiently for her to come around, and grovel when she does."

"Groveling," said Dane. "Sage advice from the only one of us ever married."

A dark current of emotion swept over Grant's face, and was just as quickly gone. He punched Dane in the arm. "Come on. That skunk's not going to take care of itself. Let's give Colt a moment's peace here."

He watched the two men leave, suddenly weary to his bones. He wanted Beth Ann back. Wanted to kiss her smiling face. Touch her hair. And it wasn't just because his body missed hers. He missed her. Her funny, brave little smiles. Her determination to succeed. Her fearlessness.

And he'd fucked it all up. He should have told her the truth. But he'd been afraid that he'd lose her. And in the end, he still had—he'd just prolonged it.

Worst of all, he couldn't beg her to come back. He couldn't—wouldn't—buy her things to sweeten her to him again.

All he could do was sit and watch the woman he loved and ached for with every fiber of his being walk away from him.

And Bluebonnet was small. They were bound to run into each other, over and over again. And he wouldn't be able to do it. He wouldn't be able to watch her turn away from him with disgust. Watch her smile fade into icy politeness. That wasn't fair to her, and it'd destroy him.

He couldn't stay in Bluebonnet and see that happen.

"Hey," he called out to Dane and Grant. When both men

turned, he asked, "If I need to head back to Alaska for a while, will you two watch over my dad? Keep him occupied at the ranch?"

"You're leaving?" Grant asked, his eyebrows raising in surprise.

"I might need to get away for a while," Colt said, squinting up at the October sun. "Clear out my head, live off the grid for a bit. Lose myself in some mindless tasks for a while."

Maybe a year or two. Until the ache went away.

Grant put his hands on his hips. "Well, I guess so. We can hire another instructor. But you don't have to leave, you know. We're all adults. If she can stay in the same town as Allan, you can, too."

But he knew how much Allan's constant presence hurt her. And he knew that if he saw her with someone else, laughing and smiling at another man—or worse, going back to Allan, oh fuck—he was going to lose his shit.

"Just kind of need to get away, I think. From everything."

Grant nodded at him, and then glanced at Dane. "I'll start asking around for another instructor, then. You take the time you need. Your job'll be here when you get back."

That fucking sissy knot of emotion was back in his throat. He gave a crisp nod to his friends, then reached down and grabbed another tire.

Someone banged on the salon door. Beth Ann pulled the pillow over her head and ignored it. When the banging came again a few moments later she groaned. "Go away!"

"It's me, Miranda," a voice called. "Open up already. It's a hair emergency."

Dang it. Beth Ann dragged herself into the front of the salon. Through the glass door, she saw Miranda hold up a bottle of wine, and behind her, Brenna held up a pizza, all smiles.

She unlocked the door and let them in, a reluctant smile tugging at her mouth. "Hair emergency, huh?"

"Seeing as how I figured you'd been here all week without a shower, I thought the hair emergency was appropriate," Miranda said, giving Beth Ann's rumpled pajamas a distasteful look. "I just didn't say it was *my* hair emergency."

Beth Ann touched her tangled hair. "Thanks. I think."

Brenna shut the door behind her and locked it again. "We're having an official girls' night in, we decided. Since the boys are all bonding over garbage, we thought we could bond over nail polish and pedicures." Brenna fluttered her lashes at Beth Ann. "If you're willing to give us pedicures, of course."

She laughed at that. "Don't tell me you two mooches just came by for free nail polish."

"Not free," Miranda said, and waggled the bottle of wine at her. "We're paying with booze."

"And gossip," Brenna added. She set the pizza down on an empty chair and dragged Beth Ann toward the barber's chair. "Sit. We'll tell you everything we know."

She wanted to ask about Colt. No, scratch that, she didn't. Finding out more about him would just hurt even more. "I don't care about town gossip."

Miranda got out paper cups and began to pour the wine as Brenna grabbed a hair brush and began to tackle Beth Ann's tangled hair. It made her mouth quirk into a smile—half the time, Brenna's own hair was so ridiculously wild that it was funny to see her fussing over Beth Ann's hair.

"Oh come on," Miranda said slyly, passing her a paper cup of wine. "You don't want to hear about the big coupon fiasco over at Cutz?"

Her stomach clenched painfully. "I know enough about it already."

"Well, someone called in an anonymous tip to the mayor, it seems," Miranda said sweetly, handing a cup of wine to Brenna.

"Just call me anonymous," Brenna said with a grin.

"And," Miranda continued. "It turns out that our beloved Mayor Williamson was furious that someone was trying to underhandedly run a business out of town, much less his daughter's business. He's very proud of his daughter, you see."

Beth Ann choked on her sip of wine. She stared up at the women, incredulous and delighted. Her father supported her business? "What? Really?"

"It's true," Miranda said. "I heard he's been trying to call you all week."

She glanced over at her machine. She hadn't been checking it. She'd closed the salon, and didn't want to hear from the occasional stray customer. That'd just make things worse. The red light was on, but she'd thought it'd been a jillion calls from Allan. Or Colt, begging her to take him back.

Her gut clenched, sick at the thought. Sick, because she missed him and hated that she was so weak.

"Soooo," Brenna sang, "this Jordan chick had to stop honoring the coupons, immediately. And when her clients found out that they had to pay two hundred dollars for a haircut instead of forty bucks? The shit hit the fan. Her place has been deserted for days."

Beth Ann swigged her wine, shaking her head in surprise. She hadn't noticed. "Wow."

"If you'd open your doors," Miranda said encouragingly, "I'd bet some of your clients would come back."

"Oh, oh," Brenna said, hopping. "And I got six hundred dollars back from your landlord for you." She pulled a wad of cash out of her bra and shoved it in Beth Ann's hand. "Guess who was putting the heat on your landlord to raise your rent?"

"Allan?" she said in a flat voice.

"Biggest asshole ever," Brenna singsonged. "Anyhow, your dad went and had a long talk with him and apparently Allan has vowed to leave you alone for a while. I heard he's dating his secretary."

Huh. She was suddenly filled with love and affection for her father. Beth Ann leaned in to get a piece of pizza. How sweet of her dad to step in for her when no one else would, not even Colt.

She stopped, holding the slice of pizza in her hand and staring at it. She hadn't told Colt about Allan's manipulations. She knew what he would have done if he'd have known—and she smiled, picturing Allan with a busted nose and two more black eyes. Strange how Beth Ann could feel such a vicious twist of glee in her stomach at the thought.

Then again, Colt had protected her before, in the past. He was always very protective of her. He glared at anyone that he thought might be making her uncomfortable.

An uneasy feeling shivered over her skin. She bit into the

pizza, trying not to think about it. She was just trying to paint a sunny picture of Colt, because that was what she always did. Right?

"Well?" Miranda asked.

"That *is* good gossip."

"It is," Brenna agreed, twisting Beth Ann's long hair into a braid. "What else do you want to hear about?"

Beth Ann grinned as Miranda grabbed her foot and pulled it into her lap. She pulled out a toe spacer and pushed it between Beth Ann's toes. So the makeover was going to be her own, was it? Her friends were the best. "What have you got?"

Miranda thought for a moment. "I could tell you all about who checked out *The Joy of Sex* from the library. Hint. It's a man, and he's eighty."

Beth Ann giggled and took another swig of wine.

"That's boring," Brenna proclaimed.

"Well, do you have anything better?" Miranda said, giving Beth Ann a long-suffering look, and then refilled her paper cup with more wine when Beth Ann held it out.

"No," Brenna said. "I've been busy following Pop around."

"Pop?" Beth Ann asked between sips of wine.

"Colt's dad. We call him Pop. Colt set him up in a cabin at the ranch, and now I keep breaking stuff so he has things to do."

Beth Ann smiled at that, her heart hurting a little. "That's sweet."

Brenna shrugged, then grinned. "It drives Grant crazy, so I look at it as a personal challenge."

She would.

"Pop's an old sweetheart, though," Brenna said with a smile, grabbing the pink strand of Beth Ann's hair and braiding it separately. "It's just going to be a challenge keeping him at the ranch when Colt leaves."

Her heart stuttered, thudded painfully. "Colt's leaving?" Her voice was a thready whisper.

Miranda reached over and poured more wine into Beth Ann's cup. "Drink up, girl."

She looked at Miranda. "Is he really leaving?"

Her best friend's eyes were sympathetic. "Dane says he's having a rough time right now. He's really upset."

He wasn't the only one, she thought with an ache in her chest.

"Dane says he's going back to the cabin in Alaska in a few days. Wants to live off the grid again and all that crap." Miranda shook her head. "It drives me crazy enough that Dane's cabin doesn't have electricity. I can't imagine living completely out in the middle of nowhere by yourself for months on end."

He'd been out there alone before recruiting Dane, licking his wounds after being discharged from the marines. And when Dane had showed up, they'd lived off the grid for a year. She remembered his joke about the mountain man beard.

Hurt and longing swirled through her. If he left this time, how long would he be gone? Would he miss her? The ache building in her chest told her that she'd miss him intensely. "Oh."

Brenna just shrugged. "They love that survival shit. Happy as pigs in mud if you mention you need a fire built. They don't seem to realize that it's not fun for anyone else to think they're stranded." Her gaze went over to Beth Ann and she grimaced. "Sorry."

"It's okay. I'm not mad at you. I just don't understand why

you didn't say something to me earlier." She'd seen Beth Ann and Colt together. She'd participated in making Beth Ann's birthday cake, for crying out loud. And she'd never thought to hint that Colt might be with her for shady reasons?

Brenna shrugged her shoulders. "Because Colt's my friend, too. And it was so obvious how totally in love he was with you. If I'd have known it'd hurt you like that, I'd have said something, though."

It was so obvious how totally in love he was with you. The words echoed in her head, and Beth Ann stared at her cup.

Miranda took that as a cue to refill it. "It doesn't change the fact that he lied to her about it," Miranda said defensively.

"No, it doesn't," Brenna replied. "I thought it was kind of a dick move, but then he seemed so happy about all of it that what could I say? You were happy, too," she said with a nudge to Beth Ann's shoulder. "Almost as happy as when he made you that cake."

"Cake?" Miranda asked.

Beth Ann stared at her cup, now full. *Judge me by my actions*, he'd begged her. *I love you and I never meant to hurt you.*

His actions. She thought of the time they'd spent together—his protectiveness of her, his slow, easy smile. The cake he'd made her. Him punching Allan for daring to insult her. The way he cuddled her close after sex. The way he devoured her with his eyes, as if he'd never seen anything half as tempting as her.

The way he'd looked so uncertain and defensive after he'd dropped her off at her salon after that first weekend. Asking her out, as if certain she was going to turn him down.

And she'd come on to him while drunk, too. He'd very gently pried her off of his body and held her instead.

Judge me by my actions.

A knot formed in her throat. She didn't know what to think. Her mind and her heart were trying to steer her in different directions. Beth Ann tossed back the remainder of her wine and grimaced at the taste.

Miranda held out the bottle. "You sure you want more? You never drink much."

She took the bottle from Miranda's hands and swigged directly from it as Brenna laughed. Her skin was prickling with awareness of the alcohol. Good. More and she'd maybe drown out the confusion in her heart. "I've turned over a new leaf in the last year," Beth Ann said. "Not going to be used by men anymore. Not going to let anyone support me but me. Not going to care what others think. And right now, I want to get drunk with my friends."

"Hear, hear," Miranda said, and lifted her cup.

The next morning, Beth Ann woke up in her salon with a raging hangover. Dane had picked up Miranda and Brenna late last night, and while a drunken Miranda had showered kisses on Dane, he'd had to endure Brenna's railing about how men were evil and should all go back to Alaska. And last night, that had suited drunk Beth Ann just fine.

But this morning, she felt regret. She drank a glass of water, took some aspirin, and laid back down on her air mattress, trying not to think about Colt leaving.

They'd broken up. He could leave if he wanted—she had no

pull on him anymore. But the thought of him leaving stabbed her with pain.

Did he miss her? Did he think about her when he was lying in bed at night? Did he miss her, too? Or was he just annoyed that he'd been found out?

He was Allan's brother, and he'd kept that from her. Did he think she'd be okay with it when he finally revealed it? Have a nice laugh with him? It wasn't funny. It hurt. And she was vaguely uneasy about sleeping with the brother of her ex-fiancé. Was there a motive? Had he decided to sleep with her simply because she'd been Allan's and thus a challenge? It was no secret to anyone in town that Colt Waggoner and Allan Sunquist would always hate each other. What better way to get back at your rival than to nail the woman he still wanted?

It was just entirely too coincidental, and she'd been betrayed too many times in the past to turn a blind eye.

All she knew was that he'd hurt her. She'd told him trust was so important to her, and he'd never told her his secrets, even when he knew they'd hurt her. Especially then.

She suddenly wanted to talk to him. Beth Ann leapt out of bed, then groaned as her stomach lurched. Light crashed into her eyes. She fumbled for a pair of sunglasses in her bag that she kept tucked under the cot, and slid them on. Better. A quick glance in the mirror showed her hair still stuck in the random, crazy braids Brenna had made. Oh well. She threw on some jeans, changed her shirt, and then locked the salon, getting into her car. Well, after she got a coffee for her aching head. They'd looked at her funny in the coffee shop, no doubt thinking she'd gone mad, what with her business problems and now her man problems.

She didn't care. She didn't care what a single person in town thought. And so she gave them all a cheerful smile as she grabbed her coffee and headed back to her car.

When she got to the ranch, though, her stomach turned at the sight of Colt's Jeep, parked in the corner of the half-full parking lot. She pulled in and entered the main cabin. Brenna was the only one there, head cradled in her hands, her bangs bright purple. Oh. She only vaguely remembered suggesting it to Brenna last night. It had seemed like such a good idea after an entire bottle of wine. "Hey," she said softly.

Brenna groaned and lay her cheek on her desk. "Go away. My head hates you."

"Is Colt here?"

She shook her head and stared blearily at Beth Ann. Circles ringed her eyes. "He's out with a class for the next five days. Hardcore group."

She frowned. "It wasn't on his calendar."

Brenna yawned, then laid her head back on the desk. "He switched with Dane. They got all of Pop's land cleaned up and he owed him a favor."

"Oh." Disappointment flared through her. She'd wanted to see him. "I think I left something in his cabin," she lied. "Can I go—"

Brenna waved her away.

Beth Ann slipped out and headed over to Colt's cabin. The overgrown grass around the cabins had been cut, the flagstones removed. It looked like a real lawn. She crept up the steps and knocked on the door. No answer, of course. She tried the knob—

it opened. Of course it did. No one would come out to his cabin but Colt. She paused for a moment, then stepped inside.

It was a mess. Surprise rocked through her. Colt was always so neat, so ordered. Dishes piled in the sink, and clothes lay strewn on the ground. She idly picked up one of his shirts and smelled it. It smelled like sweat, and like Colt. Her eyes pricked with tears. Why had he lied to her? She glanced over at the bed—it was unmade as well. Her hand moved to the edge of the mattress, and she ran her hand along it, then sat down on the edge.

She'd loved sleeping here in his arms. He'd kiss her ear, her temple, and then pull her in close and cuddle her before they went to sleep. As if he couldn't get enough of touching her. That was nothing like Allan, who hadn't even been interested in sex with her anymore.

Colt had loved her. Loved touching her. She sighed, lay down and put her head on his pillow. Her hand touched something underneath it, and she pulled it out.

One of her shirts. It was a pink one she often slept in. Why was it under his pillow? Warmth flushed through her as she pulled it to her chest. Did he hold it and think of her?

She set it down gently again and got up. Wishing for this wasn't helping. She wanted Colt back in her life, but her need for him warred with her need to not always be the one to say "I forgive you."

And she was going to drive herself crazy with all this speculation. She just needed to talk to him. Rationally. Calmly, now that she'd gotten all her hurt and anger out, and all that was left was this aching numbness that didn't feel better being apart from him. It felt worse.

When she emerged from the cabin, Mr. Waggoner rode past on the riding lawnmower. She waved at him, her cheeks pinking a little as he turned the mower off and glanced at her, then back at his son's cabin.

"How are you feeling?"

The man smiled. "Better than my boy is right now."

Her smile faltered.

Mr. Waggoner looked chagrined. "Didn't mean it like that, Beth Ann. He did a real bad thing, lying to you, and he's paying for it now, I imagine."

Beth Ann nodded slowly, crossing her arms over her chest. "I told him that I needed trust in a relationship, and he still lied to me."

Pop nodded. "Been a hard month for that boy. First me going in the hospital, then the thing about his mom, and now losing you. I imagine that's why he wants to run back to Alaska."

She ignored the old man's speculative look. "What stuff about his mom?"

Pop scratched his head. "'Bout his daddy not being me."

Her breath caught. "What do you mean, 'this month' ? How long has he known?"

Allan had told her that Colt had known for a while. That Colt had deliberately chased a relationship with her because he'd wanted to prove something. That he'd chased her as a subtle revenge on Allan. He'd implied that the only reason that Colt had wanted her was just to drive Allan insane.

Oh, why the hell did she *ever* listen to Allan?

"Told him two weeks ago, when I was in the hospital," Pop admitted. "I didn't want anything to happen to me without him knowing. He was real devastated, too. I thought he'd never talk to me again. But he turned to me and said I was his only father. The only one that ever mattered. And then he got me this job and cleaned up my land so they wouldn't throw me in jail."

Her heart hammered as Pop rambled. Colt hadn't known until then? He'd only found out days ago? It hadn't been a factor when they'd started to date? It hadn't been the reason he'd chased her?

Hope shot through Beth Ann, made her entire body tremble. "But why didn't he say anything to me?"

"Well," Pop said slowly. "He knew Allan hurt you real bad. I suspect he didn't want to hurt you more. He loves you, you know."

She was beginning to think she did know. Tears pricked her eyes behind the sunglasses. He'd struggled with his family, frustrated by their reputation and their poverty. And yet when he found out he wasn't a Waggoner at all, it hadn't mattered to him. He hadn't abandoned his father. He loved him, even though he could have walked away. He just quietly took care of things to show them that he loved them.

And he loved her.

Judge me by my actions.

He was going to Alaska *because* he loved her, she knew. Because he thought that was the right thing to do to give her space. Because he didn't want to harass her like Allan did, and he was courteous and thoughtful, and he loved her.

And she realized, suddenly, that there was nothing to forgive.

She didn't care about being stranded that weekend. He'd lied to her about it, true, but his actions every step of the way afterward were not those of a man that was just stringing along a woman he didn't care about. Nor did it matter that he was Allan's brother. Because Colt was *Colt*, and he wasn't like Allan in the slightest.

Beth Ann moved to the mower, leaned in and kissed Pop's cheek. "I'm glad we had this talk. Thank you."

"You're a good girl," he said, patting her hand.

Five days without being able to talk to Colt felt like eternity. She reopened her salon and threw herself back into the Halloween Festival preparations, since they were only days away. Colt was returning from his trip on the thirty-first, the same day as the festival.

Her customers had started to trickle back in now that the coupon extravaganza was over. It'd take a bit for them all to return, and if they didn't, well, that was okay, too.

Allan had sent her flowers and an apology card. She'd refused them at the door. When he'd come by for a haircut, she'd thrown him out of her salon. She was well and truly done with him. No more being nice. Nice only got her shoes, with Allan. He could go to hell, and take those shoes with him.

And now, Colt was due back tomorrow and she was getting antsy. It was her day off, so she'd driven all the way in to Houston with Miranda, digging through a local costume shop and getting supplies for the festival. Miranda had to buy a jersey for Dane since he hadn't kept one, and a hockey helmet. For her costume, Miranda had decided to be a fifties librarian, and they'd gotten her adorable cat's-eye-shaped glasses, a poodle skirt, and matching sweater, and Beth Ann had practiced old-fashioned hair styles on Miranda's long hair until they'd found one that looked suitably sexy.

They were in a costume shop even now, flipping through costume books.

"I can't believe Brenna wants to be Bettie Page," Miranda was grumbling for the tenth time that hour. "Wasn't Bettie Page naked in all those photos?"

"We'll just get her a leopard bikini and she'll be fine, honey," Beth Ann soothed. "All the other women in town will hate her for it, though."

"Maybe we'd better buy her a nice leopard cover up, too," Miranda added. "What are you going to be?"

Beth Ann flipped through books of costumes, then shrugged. "I don't know. I haven't been able to concentrate on it. I keep thinking about Colt."

"How about matching costumes?" Miranda said, her eyes gleaming with fun. She knew all about Beth Ann's waffling about the breakup, and was convinced that if her friend would let Colt grovel correctly, they would be back together and happy again.

Beth Ann was kind of hoping the same.

"Matching costumes?" Beth Ann said dubiously. "I don't know if he'll want to dress up. He might be mad at me. He might not want to show up for the festival at all once he knows I'm there."

"I'll get Dane or Grant to bully him," Miranda said stubbornly. "I'm sure he wants to at least talk to you."

Beth Ann wasn't so sure. But her hand rested on one particular costume, and she paused. And smiled.

Perhaps she knew the perfect costume after all.

When they returned to the ranch, Beth Ann steeled up her courage and left the box in his cabin, along with a note. What if he didn't come back in time for the festival? She headed into the main lodge to chat with Brenna.

"He's leaving tomorrow, actually," Brenna said with a sad face.

"Leaving? What do you mean he's leaving?"

"For Alaska," Brenna said. "Grant's driving him to get to his flight tomorrow right after he comes back. His tickets are all ready and everything."

"But he hasn't even packed," Beth Ann protested, her heart thudding with panic.

"He doesn't need much," Brenna said. "Just a couple changes of clothes and a picture of you to jerk off to. Everything else, nature provides." She rolled her eyes. "Or so everyone keeps telling me."

"Can you make him stay?"

She looked thoughtful. "I guess I could misplace his ticket."

"Please do," Beth Ann said. She raced back to his cabin and took the note off of the box, and wrote another one.

She'd leave him the message in his cabin, and leave a message on his phone. And if he still left without talking to her, well . . .

Then she'd have her answer.

EIGHTEEN

The next day

Beth Ann sprayed pink glitter into a fairy's hair. The pigtails sparkled bright pink, and the mother seemed almost as excited as her daughter.

"She looks so cute," the mother squealed. "I love what you did with her curls."

They'd been carefully stiffened with styling wax and pomaded into bouncy spirals that made others stop, stare, and then pay five dollars to have their child's hair fixed as well. Next to her, Brenna painted faces on squirming children, her cave-girl costume and Bettie Page hair surprisingly adorable. She'd cut her purple bangs in a thick, straight fringe across her forehead, just like Bettie Page, and the result made her impish face even more charming.

"Do you do birthday parties?" the fairy's mother asked her. "She has a birthday in two months and I'd love to have a makeover party for the little girls. It'd be so cute."

"I haven't in the past, but I can," Beth Ann said easily, slipping a now-glitter-covered card out of her costume's bodice and handing it over. "Just give me a call."

"I will," the woman said, collecting her daughter with a smile. The little girl waved, her hair full of sparkles and curls and the plastic tiara that Beth Ann had fitted into the curls. She did look cute, Beth Ann thought proudly. The Halloween Festival was full of little girls with sprayed hair from her booth—it had been a bigger success than she'd imagined. That was the fourth birthday party invite that she'd gotten—she'd turned none of them down.

She looked over at Brenna, who was helping a child down from her chair. "I'm going to go check on Miranda and see how she's doing," she said, wiping her hands with a towel.

"Got it, boss," Brenna sang out. "I'll hold down the fort."

Beth Ann slipped away, crossing the bustling festival in the town square. The costume contest would be in a few hours, and judging from the people dressed up, it'd be just as much of a success as the fund-raising booths were. The crowd today was massive, easily double the size of normal Bluebonnet shindigs. The Halloween festival was a big deal in the area, though, and she wouldn't have been surprised to find out that people from nearby small towns had stopped in to join in the fun. People in costumes crowded the town square, both adults and children. She passed by a pumpkin pie booth, smiling at the person seated there, and a booth where they served cider. At the far end of a row, Lucy was taking tickets for the cake walk, and Beth Ann raised an eyebrow at the sight of Lucy's helper. It was a tall, skinny man in a fur loincloth and cape. His goatee was so long that it had been rubber-banded. The infamous Lord Colossus? Heavens, what did Lucy see in that man? She made a mental note to drop by and ask Lucy if Colossus had brought a shirt.

On the far end of the square, past a long row of booths, Beth Ann heard a splash. She headed there, pushing past the long line of people with camera phones held up. Over in front of the dunking booth, Miranda held up a beanbag and shook it. "Who's the next person that wants to give Casanova Croft a dunk?"

"You can't dunk me," Dane yelled from inside the booth to the next person that stepped up—a young boy of no more than eight. He wiped water from his eyes, his white hockey helmet streaming water down his face. Clearly he'd been dunked recently. He pointed at the first person in line. "Hey, you. Your aim sucks. Why don't you try to slap shot—"

The beanbag hit the target. There was a cranking whoosh, and then Dane slid into the water, to the cheers of the crowd. He emerged a moment later, his hockey helmet askew, rivulets of water cascading down his cheeks. He grinned and mock shook a fist at Miranda.

His fiancée laughed and turned back to the line of waiting people, her poodle skirt flaring. "Who's next?"

As Miranda took money and handed off the next set of beanbags, Beth Ann moved forward to chat with her friend.

"How's it going, Wonder Woman?" Miranda drawled with a smile at the sight of Beth Ann. "Your ass is doing admirable things to those star-spangled panties."

"You look pretty cute yourself," Beth Ann said with a grin, adjusting her costume. She wore a red Wonder Woman bodice and the blue panties that were covered in stars. A bit chilly for October, but the day was warm and sunny, and she didn't mind it. To complete her costume, she wore a pair of plastic red boots that pinched her feet and a gold headband. She didn't dye her hair black, however. Instead, she simply curled it until it was big and bounced around her shoulders in a mass like Lynda Carter's hair from the TV show. Close enough. "I don't suppose you've seen Colt today, have you?"

Miranda shook her head, taking money from another person that stepped up, and handing them beanbags to throw. "Not a sign. He might not be back from his campout yet."

Or he might not be coming at all, Beth Ann worried, but said nothing. She smiled tightly, trying not to think about it. "Well, just let me know if you see him, honey."

"Will do," Miranda said with a salute, and turned back to her line. "Okay, who's the next person that wants to teach Casanova Croft a lesson? One dollar gets you three beanbags, and all donations go to the Bluebonnet Public Library!"

Colt finished shaking hands with the last member of his class and sent them on their way. Once every picture was taken, paperwork filed, and every car out of the Daughtry Ranch parking lot, he sat down on the lodge couch, rubbing his face. His knee sent up a flare of pain in protest, reminding him that he needed to be more careful with it.

Fuck, it had been a long week. He wanted nothing more than

to crawl into bed, kiss his woman, and sleep for days with her curled against his side.

That familiar ache settled in his chest again. He no longer had Beth Ann. He'd never see that sweet smile curving her mouth as she looked at him. He'd never hold her again. Hear that sexy whimper when he sank deep inside her. He'd lost everything he cared about, all over again. And this time, the scar wasn't on his knee. It couldn't be worked out with physical therapy and dedication. It was on his fucking heart, and it wasn't ever going to mend.

The thought just made him even wearier.

Grant came into the room, set the camera down on his desk, and grinned at Colt. "You about ready to go to the airport, then?"

"Need to say good-bye to my dad," he said slowly, not wanting to move from the couch. If he got up, he was really going to do it. Leave Bluebonnet behind again.

Leave Beth Ann behind.

Give up on her. On him with her. But wasn't that what he deserved for being such a dick to her? Strange that he didn't want to leave Bluebonnet—once, he'd never wanted to come back. But Beth Ann had changed all that. Now he didn't want to go . . . but he had to. For her.

"Your dad's at the Halloween Festival," Grant said. "Everyone is. I just stuck around to give you a ride out to Houston."

"Damn it," Colt said slowly, and rubbed his hand down his face again. "I guess I'll call the old man when I get to the airport." Strange how that bothered him. He'd wanted to see his dad again before he left. "Where'd Brenna put my tickets?"

Grant shrugged, heading into the kitchen. Colt hauled himself off of the couch and moved to Brenna's desk. He saw an envelope with his name on it and opened it.

Out fluttered an IOU and a note. I LOST YOUR TICKET, Brenna had written in block letters. GUESS YOU CAN'T GO.

Well wasn't she fucking hilarious. Still, his mouth quirked at her obvious attempt to get him to stay. "She's a shitty assistant."

"Yes she is," Grant called from the kitchen.

Well, he'd just have to buy a ticket at the airport.

Grant appeared in the doorway of the kitchen again, sandwich in hand. "You bout ready to go, then? I want to stop by the Halloween Festival after I drop you off, so we need to go soon."

He was. "Just about."

"You need to check your cabin for anything else?"

He did want to get the shirt Beth Ann had left there. He missed the sweet smell of her, and it still lingered on the shirt she'd left at his place the last time she'd been there. "Just gonna check the cabin one more time."

"Okay," Grant said, and grinned as he bit into his sandwich. "I'll be right here."

He headed out to his cabin and opened the door, staring inside. It was a mess, but he didn't care. That was how he felt inside—all torn up and hopeless. He needed time away from all of this. The mess could wait until he got back—or he'd just ask Brenna to clean it up. He moved to the bed, searching for that pink shirt.

And stopped. There was a box on the bed, and a note. With one finger, he flipped open the folded piece of paper. His heart thudded at the sight of Beth Ann's loopy, girly handwriting.

We need to talk, the note read. *Come be my hero?*

When he opened the lid, a faint smile tugged at his mouth. And he felt a sliver of hope.

He wasn't coming. Beth Ann struggled to breathe through the crushing disappointment even as she conducted the costume contest. She smiled, announced the names of each contestant, waited for the crowd to applaud, and every moment she was dying inside a little more.

He wasn't here. He wasn't here.

Why was she here? She should be at the airport in Houston, begging him to stay. Asking him to talk to her so they could work this out. That she wasn't mad anymore. That she didn't want to lose him over one stupid lie that had turned out to be the best thing that had ever happened to her.

But she stood up on the stage, numb, and announced the costume contest winner. The man, dressed in a soup pot with the legs cut out and a mishmash of stuffed animals sticking out from under the lid—she wasn't even paying attention to what he was supposed to be—took the trophy from a cheery Brenna. They were done. Beth Ann almost stumbled in her haste to get off the stage, rushing down the steps of the platform. Panic flared through her—she needed to get to him. Talk to him before he left. Explain how she felt—

Miranda stopped her at the bottom, seeing the look on her face. "You okay? What's wrong?"

"I need to stop Colt," she said, her breath catching in her throat. "I should be in Houston begging him to stay. I can't let him go. I need to go to the ranch, see if Grant's left with him yet—"

Her words died in her throat as she saw a black swish of cape that quickly disappeared as someone stepped in front of her. She pushed ahead, and . . .

There he was. Batman. Colt. A giddy, nervous laugh bubbled in her throat—a laugh of relief, of hope. He hadn't gone yet.

He'd put on the costume she'd left for him. Oh. Her heart thudded at the sight of him. Of the broad shoulders in the costume, the plastic bodysuit, the long sweeping cape. The cowl Batman mask that nearly covered his entire face, but not his scowl. And she couldn't stop smiling.

Beth Ann approached him slowly, noticing that the fake muscles of the costume were not nearly as impressive as the tight sweep of his abdomen. His hands clenched in the black gloves as she walked toward him. A good sign? Or bad? She couldn't tell, but she hoped it was good.

"Hi, Batman," she said breathlessly.

"I always knew you'd make a great Wonder Woman," he greeted in a cautious voice, eyeing her costume.

"Can we talk?" she asked. "Somewhere private?"

He held his hand out to her. She raised her hand in response and then realized he was holding something out to her.

An apple.

She took it from him, staring at it in wonder, her chest aching with the sweetness of the gesture.

He nodded at it. "I hear you give that to a girl if you're interested in her."

Beth Ann looked at the apple, then back at him. "That's right."

This time, when he offered her his hand, she took it, and he led her through the boisterous, noisy crowd, back to the far side of the town square. To her shop. Looked at the door, then back to her.

Trembling, she pulled the key out of her red bodice, remembering the time they'd made love in her salon. Her fingers fumbled as she pushed the door open, then gestured for him to enter.

He did. She followed him in, then shut the door, turned back to him.

His hands went to her cheeks and then he was kissing her, his mouth pressing against hers, tongue flicking against the back of her mouth. The apple fell from her hand and onto the floor.

At her sharp intake of breath, he pulled away again. "You can slap me for that if you want to."

She shook her head, noticing how his body was still pressed up against hers. Her nipples had grown hard under her bodice. She wished he wasn't wearing the big cowl mask—oh heavens, the costume had seemed like such a clever idea at the time. Now she just wanted to see his face. "I'm not going to slap you."

"I wouldn't blame you if you did." His thumb brushed over her cheek, caressing her. "I've missed you," he said huskily, then abruptly pulled away. "I'm sorry. You don't want this shit. Here I am forcing what I want on you—"

"No, it's okay," she said quickly. Her hands went to the rubber front of his costume, traced the bat symbol there. "But I think we should talk."

He stiffened. "Talk, then."

She took in a ragged breath. "That was a total dick move, lying to me about being stranded."

Silence. She peeked up at him.

"I'm not going to apologize," he said in a low, husky voice. "If it got me you, even for a short period of time, I'm not going to be sorry about it."

Warmth flushed through her body, her pulse starting a slow, languid beat between her thighs. "I . . . I don't like that you lied to me, but I'm glad about the outcome," she said, lightly tracing that bat symbol because she was terrified of looking at his face, watching that expressive mouth firm into disapproval or irritation that she was changing her mind. "That day, when I got angry, I . . . I didn't realize that you hadn't known that you were Allan's brother. When I saw Allan that day—"

"I told that asshole to leave you alone," Colt murmured. As she watched, his mouth thinned into an unhappy line.

"I know," she said quickly, her fingers tracing the symbol even more rapidly. She looked down at it, unable to meet his gaze. "But the coupon thing had me furious, and then—"

His hand caught hers, stopped her fingers from their dance on his chest. "Coupon?"

She glanced up at him. She quickly explained the situation with the salon across the street—the coupons, the fact that Allan was trying to run her out of business so she'd have no choice but to go back to him. And she'd found it all out the same day, just before discovering that Colt had lied to her.

His jaw clenched with fury. He turned toward the door. "I'm going to fucking kill him—"

"It's okay," she said, grabbing his arm and tugging him back toward her. Her hand went to his cheek and she forced him to look at her. "It's been taken care of. My father put the fear of God in him."

"Good," Colt seethed. "I'm still going to break his jaw the next time I see him."

"That's beside the point," she said in a rush. "I found out everything that day. Here I'd been betrayed by Allan all over again in the worst possible way, and then I found out that you had lied to me, too." She grimaced. "I overreacted."

His mouth parted a little. "You never overreacted—"

"I did," she soothed. "I know that now. I was so upset and furious that day that I just didn't think. All I knew was that I was hurt, and angry, and betrayed. All I could see was that you'd lied to me the entire time we were together, and I was being made a fool again."

"I wanted to tell you the truth about the camping trip," he murmured, taking a step back toward her.

"I don't care about the camping trip, Colt. I wanted you to tell me about Allan. How he's your brother. If you would have come to me instead of keeping me in the dark, I'd never even considered the fact that you might have been sleeping with me to get revenge on him."

"I'm not." He clenched his jaw, hard. "That has never been a factor in why we were together."

"I know that. Now."

He shook his head. "It's not something I'm proud to know. I hated being a Waggoner all my life, but . . . I kinda think I hate being a Sunquist more. I kept waiting for the right moment, but then—"

"I know," she said softly as his body pressed against her own. He'd pushed forward against her and instead of backing up, she'd held her ground. Her breasts pressed against his costume, and she felt his gloved hand slide to her hip.

"Your business?" he asked, staring down at her through the mask.

"Recovering," she said. "I'm going to be just fine."

"I'm not," he said in a ragged voice. "I need you."

Her heart thumped wildly in her chest. "I need you, too."

"I don't want to go to Alaska," he rasped, his hand grasping her ass tightly. "I was going just to get away from you. So you wouldn't have to have me in your face all the time like Allan."

"I don't want you to go," she said softly, and to her horror, her eyes brimmed with tears. "I still love you."

"I fucking worship you," he said in a gruff voice. "I'm not worth your time of day, but I love you, and I want to make you happy."

"You do," she said with a tearful smile. "You do."

His mouth captured hers, the thrust of his tongue hard, needy. His kiss was the only response she needed.

Beth Ann moaned, her arms twining around his neck. "Colt," she whimpered. "I need you."

"God," he whispered in a ragged breath. He pushed her forward, until they slammed into the counter of her hairdressing station. Her legs wrapped around him and his hands supported her, wedged between his hard body and the counter.

"Can I take this shit off?" he rasped.

A happy laugh bubbled in her throat. "But I've always wanted to make love to Batman."

"Fuck Batman," he said with a growl. "I want you to fuck *me*."

Her breath caught in her throat. “Let’s go to my air mattress in the back,” she said softly, and scraped her nails over the chest of the costume.

His arms wrapped around her and he carried her back to the small private area. Her small bed was there, and he gently set her down. Her hands immediately went to his belt, and she began to undo the costume.

“I don’t know how Batman fights crime in this shit,” he grumbled, tugging at the rubber cowl on his head. “I feel like a giant, sweaty condom.”

She laughed. “But you look so sexy.”

“Then it’s worth everything,” he said, his voice muffled as he tugged the mask from his head. Then it was Colt looking down at her, Colt with his beautiful, predatory gaze that raked over her. His short hair clung to his scalp in sweaty spikes, and she saw a smear of dirt on his forehead. As he shucked the rest of the costume off, she caught the faint scent of him—wood smoke. Her pussy clenched with need. “You just came from the woods?”

“I did.” He paused. “I should have showered. I didn’t think—”

“I don’t care,” she said, tugging his now-naked body down to her. “I just want you.”

His fingers slid to her star-covered panties, moved between her legs and rubbed just as he gave her another deep kiss. She moaned as he continued to rub her, and she felt wet and aching even through the costume. “So beautiful,” Colt murmured, then stood up and took her foot in his hands. He tugged her boot off and gently kissed the arch of her foot. It shot a bolt of lust straight to her pussy and she gasped at the sensation. He grinned at her response, and quickly removed her other boot. His hands slid to her panties, and he pressed his mouth to her clit through them, burying his face there.

She cried out.

"Missed you," he said, kissing her through the satin. "Missed you so much."

She had, too. It felt glorious to touch him again, to feel his hard muscles, damp with sweat, under her fingers. To feel his mouth on her. He tugged her panties down a moment later, then smiled at her bare pussy. "Stayed waxed?"

She gave a soft little laugh. "Hope springs eternal."

"Mmm," he said, leaning to press a kiss there. "Hope tastes delicious, too."

She shivered, then shimmied into a sitting position. "Help me get this corset off."

He did, and a moment later, she tossed it aside, and they were both naked together. He fell over her, and she felt his bare chest press against her breasts, felt his dog tags flutter against her skin.

Tears pricked her eyes as he bent over her to gently, reverently kiss her breasts.

"Beth Ann?" He looked up at her watery sniff. "Baby?"

She locked her legs around him, digging her heels against his hips to try and pull him down. "I just want you inside me, Colt. Now. Please."

He kissed her breast, hard, in response, and then lifted up. His fingers slid between her legs, brushing against her clit, sliding through the moisture there. "Wet and ready for me."

"Always ready," she said softly. "I need you."

His hand went to his thick cock and she watched his hand

grasp it, move it to her waiting hips, nudge the head of it at the core of her. She cried out softly when he pushed inside her, slowly, carefully, exquisitely. Her name was a soft, wondering breath as he pumped into her body, his thrust hard and claiming. Her nails dug into his shoulders as he began to immediately rock into her, hard. Yes, oh God yes, she needed this so badly. Needed him. And this was the most exquisite kind of torture. Her hips rose to meet his, her movements jerky with the need and tension through her body. "Please," she whispered. Heat throbbed through her with every stroke. "Please, Colt."

"I'm here, baby," he said softly, and she felt his fingers reach between them, felt his thumb go to her clit. Felt it rock against her flesh when his cock surged inside her again. Her moans of pleasure became cries of ecstasy, and moments later, she was falling, the orgasm splintering through her body. He continued to rub her clit as he stroked into her body, and she gasped and moaned with every motion, feeling another orgasm speeding through her, feeling it build through her body. Then he stiffened. His thumb twitched against her clit as he came, his body jerking with release, her name a mere breath on his lips.

She grasped his fingers and held them to her clit, using his hand to rub until she came a second time as well, her pussy clenching around him.

When breath returned a few moments later, he leaned over her and began to kiss her face tenderly. "We're going to need a better bed than this."

She smiled sleepily, lazily dragging her fingers over his shoulders. So broad and tight. "Maybe in a few months, when I can afford it again."

He kissed her neck. "I think you should move in with me."

"Only if I pay half the rent."

"Deal," he said instantly. "I'm sure no one would think you're the kind of girl to move in with a guy like me," he said, sliding onto the narrow bed with her and tugging her close.

She turned toward him and wrapped her arms around his neck, her face so close to his that their noses were almost touching. "I've decided I don't care what anyone in town thinks."

He raised an eyebrow. "Really?"

"Well, maybe," she said, a thought coming to her that she liked very much. "You know what I think, though? I think that no one would expect you and I to stay together."

"They wouldn't," he drawled, and pressed another firm kiss to her mouth.

"They wouldn't think we're the type to run off to Vegas and get married, either," she ventured.

He stilled on the bed next to her. Stared at her.

She bit her lip. "Too soon?"

He slowly shook his head, then leaned in and kissed her hard, again, and then again, as if he couldn't believe she was in his arms and he needed to keep kissing her to remind himself. "I was just wondering," he drawled, "how you're going to pay for your half of the airfare."

She laughed.

He kissed her even more fiercely. "You want to get married?" he asked. "Really?"

She nodded. "But only if you want to."

"Fuck yes, I do," he said, his hands tight on her body. "But are you sure? You and Allan—"

"We're done."

"No, I mean . . . you never married Allan? You were together nine years . . ."

She shook her head. "And you want to know what's different now?" She ran a finger down his chest, then moved back up to tug on his dog tags. "He never asked. I was too stupid to figure out that he was just dangling the carrot. We only got engaged after he cheated on me the first time." She shrugged. "So I guess I never married him because I felt that we couldn't get to that point in our relationship."

"And you're there with me?" he asked, his voice thick.

She nodded. "What we have is totally different than what I had with Allan. I know the difference now. And I know that I love you and want to spend the rest of my life with you." She ran her hands down his slippery back, and gave a light shrug. "But if you're not sure—"

"I'm sure," he said, and kissed her hard again. "But I must insist on making the cake."

"Deal," she said, and smiled into his eyes.